Books By
Misha McKenzie

The Magic of the Heart Series
Magic Found
Magic Hidden
Magic Lost
Magic Revealed

Single Titles
RavenStorm Witches

Aria's Law

Burke Witches Series

Misha McKenzie

ICASM PRESS
SAVANNAH

Published by Icasm Publishing LLC
5710 Ogeechee Rd. Suite 200 #278, Savannah, GA 31405
www.icasmpress.com

Library of Congress Cataloging-in-Publication Data

McKenzie, Misha
Aria's Law / Misha McKenzie
    p. cm.

ISBN-13:978-1-942318-34-7 (Trade Print)
ISBN-13:978-1-942318-35-4 (Mas Market Print)
ISBN-13:978-1-942318-33-0 (eBook)
I. Title

Printed and bound in the United States of America

10 9 8 7 6 5 4 3 2 1

This book is dedicated to everyone who has stuck with me into this new series. I lived with the characters in the first set of books for over twenty years. We knew each other better and longer than I knew some of my friends, lol. When I started this new series I didn't know if I'd be able to let the old family go. They were as much a part of me as my actual loved ones. But through creating and writing about these new characters, I found I still treasured the Marquands but I could love the Burkes just as much. I look forward to seeing them grow and come into their own and I hope you do too.

Thank you for all of your support. You'll never understand how much it means to me.

PROLOGUE

"We've done all we can." Iris, the eldest of the Burke coven, looked at the group of people seated around her. Each wore an expression of weariness. In all of her ninety-three years, Iris had never before seen the likes of what they'd just faced. It had taken thirteen of the most powerful witches in their line just to imprison him.

He'd been a man once, but no longer. Now he was an unstoppable force. A monster with unimaginable power, bent on exacting vengeance on them all.

"And we're sure this will hold him?" asked Marcus, another elder.

"As sure as we can be," Iris answered gravely. "This magic he now wields is strong and dark. It allowed him to withstand our greatest efforts to defeat him. This was our only other option."

"Maybe this will be the last of him." The hope in Hester's voice was undeniable. "Maybe he'll be locked away forever, and we'll be safe."

Iris felt a familiar energy beckoning. As seer of the coven, it was her privilege to allow the powers that be to use her as their vessel. As she rose to her feet, twelve pairs of eyes turned to her expectantly.

Words filled her mind and flowed, unheeded, past her lips.

"Witches born—two light, two dark
Each possessing an element's mark
Air and Water by the brightness of day
Earth and Fire by the moon's subtle ray
These signs will one day come to bear
And evil kept caged will wake and prepare
As every year passes the bindings grow weak
While the force within strengthens and seeks
Four babies born as foretold by this seer
They'll have until their twenty-fifth year
To mature, to learn, to find their right path
For it's up to them to end its wrath
Their destined arrival is the key
Personal sacrifice will set them free
On the anniversary of their birth
Four into one defeats the devil unearthed."

Iris slumped back into her chair as stunned silence reigned.
"He'll return." Iris felt the fear ripple through the room.
"And our fate will rest on the shoulders of a new generation of
Burke witches."

1

It was three o'clock in the morning, and Aria Burke was into hour seven of a twelve-hour drive. This desolate stretch of highway, which wound through the mountains of North Carolina, was treacherous on a good day. But add in extreme exhaustion and pitch-black conditions, and she knew she was courting disaster.

But what other choice did she have? Her visions wouldn't give her any respite. For the last several days, since the very first minute of her twenty-fourth birthday, they'd taken a dark and deadly turn. She'd seen, over and over and in great detail, the deaths of her sister and brothers.

Only a week ago, Aria remembered vividly crying out in anguish and heartache after awakening from the first horrific scene. She jerked upright and pulled her legs up and into her chest, wrapping her arms tightly around them. She sat, huddled against the headboard, trying to convince herself the images weren't real as her head pounded from pain her visions had never caused before.

At some point she dozed off. When she woke again, her body was stiff and sore from being curled up for so long. As she carefully stretched out her cramped muscles, she glanced at the clock. The bright green numbers told her it was still very early, but after what she'd just witnessed, sleep was no longer an option.

Gingerly, she rose and hobbled to the bathroom for a long, hot shower.

Aria stood and let the steaming spray soothe her aching body. She was nearing her mid-twenties, but at the moment she felt much, much older. As her limbs slowly came back to life, she thought about what she'd seen in that shocking vision.

Her siblings lying dead. Covered in blood. Each scene more gruesome than the last. They hadn't died together; they'd all been alone—separated from the others. Anna crumpled to the ground, her silver-blonde hair stained red. Evan with a huge, gaping wound, his shirt soaked in blood. And Ethan, the youngest of the four, lay charred, his body still smoldering from the fire which had engulfed him.

She knew in her heart that her family really hadn't been killed while she'd slept, but there was no way her mind would ease until she spoke to them. She took her time showering and getting ready, giving the clock a chance to move forward to a more appropriate time to call and assure herself they were, indeed, okay.

She made sure not to mention anything of what she'd seen. Doing so would mean admitting to what was really going on. And she wasn't nearly ready for that yet.

But the days and nights wore on, and the relentless onslaught continued. Aria could no longer ignore the fact that everything her parents had told her was true.

The prophecy was real. And so was the evil it had foretold.

When she and her siblings had been old enough to understand, their mother and father had sat them down and explained what it all meant, and what would need to be done.

As a result, she'd spent the vast majority of her youth in training to defeat this...whatever it was. None of them even had a clue exactly what they'd be facing, let alone where it had come from, *or* how to vanquish it. They knew only that it would destroy them if it were allowed to rise.

To that end, they'd been taught to hone their abilities to a fine edge. They'd learned everything there was to know about spells, potions, and magic. Anything that could aid their fight was included in their preparations. The broad education was necessary, because the stupid prediction had given no hint of what was actually coming. Only that they'd have until they were twenty-five to figure it out.

By the time she graduated from high school, doubts clouded Aria's mind. She questioned if anything were even out there. It had been hundreds of years, for God's sake. If someone…or something…truly wanted to kill them, wouldn't it have shown itself already? Made its presence known somehow? Why not strike while they were young and unable to defend themselves?

Those thoughts, along with the heavy burden placed on her adolescent shoulders, as well as the disciplines she'd lived with all her life, had become too much. At eighteen, Aria had fled, not stopping until she'd landed in a small town in Ohio. There, she could be what she'd never been.

Normal.

And for the last six years, that's exactly what she'd been. As time had passed, Aria felt more secure in her belief that it was all just a myth. Crazy words written by an even crazier old lady. A story told through the ages to children at bedtime. She'd finally been able to forget and enjoy the creations she made with her own two hands.

Her wind sculptures were starting to draw attention from serious collectors, and the few she'd sold had brought more money than she'd ever imagined. She loved working with the materials she scavenged and repurposed. Shaping the metal, affixing the fabrics, glass, or whatever else called to her, and forming it into designs meant to catch the slightest breeze. Once in motion, the entire concept would come alive. Many times she'd stood in the middle of her studio and had sent the air swirling, just to watch them spin and dance.

And now, all that joy and freedom and *normal* had been ripped away. She hadn't wanted to believe it, but she knew if she continued to ignore the warnings, those visions of death and destruction would come to fruition. And she couldn't allow that to happen.

So now here she was, on the road, in the middle of the night, headed back home to Florida. Aria remembered that, according to the prophecy, in a year's time, she, her twin sister Anna, and their twin brothers, Evan and Ethan, would have to step up and do what no one else had been destined to do. Put an evil back into the ground, and save the future of their line.

What Aria didn't understand though, was if D-day were still twelve months away, why was she seeing this stuff now?

Unless...

They didn't actually have that long.

Were her visions trying to warn her that something had set the wheels in motion? That they were already being hunted?

There were no answers to her many questions. At least, not while she was on her own. Discouraged, Aria cranked up the radio to drown out her thoughts and continued down the road.

As she neared the eighth hour of her journey, fatigue was starting to take hold and she yawned. Reaching down, she adjusted the vent blowing cool air on her in an effort to stay awake. Her eyes felt gritty and they burned. She was sure the ice-blue would be surrounded by brilliant red. All she wanted to do right now was close them to find some relief.

She rubbed one, and then the other, trying to keep at least one eye on the twisting and winding mountain road. Maybe at the next rest stop, she'd pull off. Even if she didn't sleep, she could at least relax her tired eyes. Aria briefly lifted her long silvery-blonde hair off her neck, letting the cool air bathe her skin. Returning both hands back to the wheel, she drove on.

The next thing she knew, the sound of a blaring horn was ringing in her ears. She jerked back to wakefulness and swerved when she saw that her car had drifted into the other lane.

"Oh, shit." Aria's attempt to correct her trajectory came just seconds too late. She'd already veered into the motorcycle traveling alongside her and driven it off the road. The last view she had was of it careening over the shoulder and into tall grass.

She slammed on the brakes, came to a screeching stop, and threw it into park. As she ran on shaking legs to the last place she'd seen the rider, she thanked whoever happened to be listening that they hadn't gone over the opposite side. That way led straight over the side of the mountain. And to certain death.

Aria searched the ditch where she thought the bike had gone down. She watched for signs of movement but couldn't detect anything in the darkness. It was so deep and shadowed she couldn't see anything.

She grabbed her cell phone out of her pocket with trembling hands and used the flashlight app to look for the unfortunate driver, praying they were all right.

The dim light did next to nothing, but she ended up stumbling across the big bike. She searched in all directions, but the biker was still unaccounted for. Panicked, she continued to make her way along the ditch until, about sixty feet past where the motorcycle rested, she finally saw him. He was lying face down in the dirt.

She ran to him and got her first look at who she'd hit. He was clad in black leather from neck to toe and had a black, full-faced helmet covering his head.

"Sir?" Aria called to him as she knelt, her denim-clad knees sinking into the soft ground. "Sir, can you hear me?"

No response.

Aria couldn't believe she had been so careless. She'd lived her entire life by the one hard and fast law of all witches: An' it harm none. And now, because of her own negligence, she'd put this man's life at risk.

Please, please don't be dead. Her natural gifts didn't lean toward healing, but she had enough in her to find out if he were hurt badly. Aria calmed her mind and focused.

She sighed. It was taking too long. She'd neglected her magic, and now she was paying the price. She pushed harder and then…there! His heart. Beating, strong and true. He must just be knocked out. Relieved, Aria gently rolled him onto his back and aimed the light over his face.

The tinted visor shielded his face, but she could just see his closed eyes and the full dark brows over them. Setting her phone aside, she unfastened the chin strap and gently pushed the helmet off of his head.

In the shadows of the trench, she didn't know if the unruly hair that sprang free was brown or black. But it did look wet. Another jolt of panic hit. Aria snatched up her phone, directed it at his head, and ran her free hand around and through his hair, checking for cuts or lacerations.

Doubts assailed her. Had she missed something? Had moving him caused further injury? She frantically inspected his head but found nothing. She sat back on her heels and breathed a sigh of relief. It wasn't blood. It was sweat.

Now that she knew he was okay, she couldn't help but marvel at how soft his hair had been. Fascinated, Aria studied the dark locks and was surprised to see that where her hands had lifted it away from his scalp, it curled, just a little.

Those silky waves were in complete opposition to the harsh and rugged features of his face. Even unconscious, he looked rough and hardened. Not anyone she'd want to meet on the side of a dark, lonely highway.

Tearing her attention away from his face, Aria shut off the light and slid it into her pocket. Hands now free, she pulled the zipper on his leather jacket down a few inches and again tried to rouse him.

"Sir?" she called. "Can you hear me?"

She took a deep breath and slapped his cheek a couple of times, hoping he didn't wake up swinging.

Aria kept calling to him until finally, he started to respond. Before he was fully awake, she backed away several steps to give him some room. It also gave her a head start, in case he decided to come after her for wrecking his bike.

"Are you all right?" Aria asked from where she stood.

"What happened?" He sat up and eyed her warily.

"I, uh, must have fallen asleep and swerved into your lane. I ran you off the road," she admitted. "I'm so very sorry."

The stranger gradually got to his feet, and Aria saw what she hadn't noticed while he'd been lying prone on the ground. He was huge. Not as tall as her brothers who were six-four, but it wasn't his height that caught her attention. Where he surpassed Evan and Ethan was in the breadth of his chest and shoulders.

Holy crap.

Aria took an involuntary step back. This guy outsized her by at least double. She and Anna were both a solid foot shorter than their fellow quads. She and her twin had topped out at five foot four, and with her petite build this bruiser outweighed her by at least a hundred pounds. There was no way she could fight him off if things got physical.

"Are you okay?" she asked him again.

"I'm just fucking *great*." He looked over and pinned her with an angry glare. "Why wouldn't I be, after getting thrown off my bike at sixty miles an hour, just because *you* don't have enough goddamned sense to stop for the night?"

"I'm sorry." Aria held her temper in check since it *had* been her fault. "I'm glad you're not hurt, and I hope your motorcycle isn't damaged too badly."

"You'd better hope it's not," he warned, "or I'll take it out of your little pixie hide." He took a step towards her, and then stopped when his foot connected with something in the dark. He reached down and came back up with his helmet. With it clutched in his hand, he stomped around her and went to inspect his bike.

Aria turned and followed a few paces behind him. "There's no need for threats. I fully intend to pay for the repairs."

He ignored her as he stowed the helmet and then hefted the big machine up onto its wheels. When he bent to look it over, she heard him mutter, "Can't see shit." The stranger glanced up to where her car was parked and made some sort of decision. He grasped the hand grips and started to push it up the incline. About halfway up it stopped, and no matter how hard he heaved, it wouldn't go any farther.

She jumped when he snapped out, "Hey! Get your ass over here and help me push."

Aria just stared at him. There was no way in hell she was going anywhere near him. And besides, she wasn't strong enough to move that behemoth.

"It's got to weigh five hundred pounds," she sputtered out. "I can't push that."

"It's seven hundred and ninety-five."

"Oh, okay, no problem then." Sarcasm dripped from her tone.

If it were possible, he got even grumpier. "Look, Pixie. You got me into this mess, so you can damned well help to get me out. Grab the ass-end and help me push this bitch up the hill."

Aria threw him a dirty look but slowly moved to stand behind the motorcycle. She placed her hands on the small rear seat. "Stop calling me that," she snapped.

He looked at her over his right shoulder, but it was too dark to make out his expression. "On three," he ordered.

"One."

"Two."

When he shouted three, she strained with all her might as

he shoved against the front. They moved it about a foot before it stopped and rolled back.

"Again," he ordered.

This wasn't going to work. Aria knew the slope was too steep, and she just wasn't strong enough. She needed some help.

When he said one, she called to the power that was hers through the mark on her shoulder. On two, she gathered the air around her. And when he reached three, she directed it to the rear of the bike where it swirled up and under the fender, giving them the push they needed. With his added brawn, they were able to get it up the hill.

Once it was on level ground, she pulled back the wind while he maneuvered it to the front of her car.

"Turn your lights on."

His commanding orders were starting to grate on her nerves. "Not much for asking, are you?" she pointed out as she passed him, not caring what his reaction was.

When she reached her car, she got in and flipped on the headlights. Some little jab of defiance made her hit the switch for the high beams, hoping it would blind him.

That proved to be a mistake though, because it gave her the first clear view of the burly biker. He'd stripped out of his riding gear, leaving him in a tight gray t-shirt that hugged every inch of his ripped upper body. He had some kind of ink work done on both strong arms, starting a few inches above his wrists and disappearing under the sleeves of his shirt. Aria wondered idly how far the tattoos went and what they depicted.

When he bent to check for damage, her gaze was pulled lower. The leather chaps that covered his legs from his ankles to the top of his thighs framed his denim-covered ass to perfection. She decided his physique was much more appealing than his attitude.

Aria sat mesmerized by the view until he straightened and walked around to the other side. She gasped when she saw just what those chaps called attention to in the front. She knew that even if he looked, he wouldn't know she was staring at him, but she still needed to get control of herself.

He was hot, yeah, but he was *so* not her type. She didn't do Neanderthal. And besides, she'd never see him again after this night from hell was over.

She took a breath and got out of the car. "How does it look?"

"Some road rash, but the highway bars and saddle bags saved most of it." He threw his leg over the seat and, after a few adjustments, hit a button that had it roaring to life.

He left it running and dismounted. She watched as he removed his helmet from one of the bags. Once he had that back on, he slid back into his jacket and zipped it up.

Aria was a little surprised when he again straddled the motorcycle. *Was he leaving?* She stepped closer so he could hear her.

"I said I'd pay for the damages," she shouted over the loud exhaust.

He leaned close to her. His voice was muffled inside his helmet, but she still heard him. "Next time, Pixie. Got places to be."

The stranger slapped the visor down, stepped on the shifter, and with a rev of the engine, sped off down the road.

Aria was shocked at his abrupt departure. "Okay, I guess he's not worried about it." Just as well. The less interaction she had with him, the better. He was kind of a dick.

With a shrug, Aria returned to her car and continued on her way.

When lights up ahead indicated a more populated area, Aria prepared to stop. But after her harrowing encounter on the highway, she wasn't feeling tired anymore, so she just filled up her car, grabbed some snacks, and got an energy drink for later.

2

Aria hit the Daytona Beach city limits at nine in the morning, and shortly after that was pulling into the driveway of her family home.

She got out and stretched, taking a moment to let the sound of the waves lapping against the sandy beach on the back side of the house soothe her. A soft breeze caressed her face as if welcoming her home. Aria closed her eyes and returned the greeting.

The loving reception continued when she turned and saw her parents standing on the porch.

Paul Daniels was still a handsome man at fifty-six. Aria noticed there was a little gray sprinkled through the light brown that their video chats hadn't revealed. She thought it over and decided she liked it; it gave him more character.

He stood tall at five-eleven, a height his sons never stopped ribbing him about as they'd passed him at the age of fourteen. His body remained strong and solid. When he smiled at her, there was a sparkle in his dark blue eyes.

As usual, he had his arm wrapped around his wife's waist. For as long as Aria could remember, they had always touched in some way. A light brush as they passed. A hand resting on a thigh as they snuggled on the couch. Or a soft caress for no reason at all. Aria had always secretly hoped that she'd find someone who would adore and love her in that way.

Those intimate moments she'd seen between her parents had always reassured her that, at least for the moment, all was right in a world that could, and would, bite her in the ass. She looked at her mom now, and in the time it took to take a breath, her whole world shifted, righted itself, and became clear.

Mary Burke had always had a calming effect on those around her. And being the mother of headstrong quadruplets, especially those destined to fulfill the prophecy, she'd needed that in spades.

Aria couldn't imagine the burden her mother had carried, knowing that it would be *her* children who would one day face off against the evil that had threatened the Burkes for centuries. There were faint lines showing in Mary's face, a sure sign that as Aria and her siblings grew nearer their twenty-fifth birthdays, their mother was feeling the strain and worry.

But even with that, at fifty-one, she was a beautiful woman. Soft features, hazel-green eyes, smiling mouth, and at least this month, dark auburn hair.

Aria felt her heart squeeze and tears burn in her eyes. As her mom started towards her, Aria walked into her arms.

"My baby," her mother whispered into her hair. It didn't matter that she'd been born first of the four. "I'm so glad you're home." Mary clung to her for a moment and then released her, keeping hold of her hands. "Why didn't you call and let us know you were coming?"

"It was a last-minute decision," Aria admitted. "I'll explain everything. But I had to come back. Something is happening."

She saw fear cloud her mother's eyes. Always attuned to his wife, her father joined them. "What is it?" he asked her, concern clear in his voice. Though not a witch, her father would do anything to protect his children from the evil coming for them.

"I need the others here first," she told her parents.

After giving her daughter a reassuring hug, they went inside, and Mary put out the call. Half an hour later, her siblings started arriving. Anna was first. She lived the closest out of the three who'd remained behind.

"Aria," Anna said as she threw her arms around her sister. "Missed you."

She and Anna were carbon copies of each other, as were the two boys who made up their quad set. When their mother had become pregnant, her first ultrasound had shown triplets. One set of identical twins and a single baby. It wasn't until the next scan that the fourth and final baby was detected. The doctors were excited to tell her that she was carrying two sets of identical twins. But Mary knew the truth of what that fourth baby could mean.

And her fears were confirmed when they'd been born bearing the marks, triggering the events that would come to a head when they turned twenty-five.

Aria looked at the other half of herself and felt whole again. "Missed you too," Aria said as she pulled her in for another hug. Talking on the phone and video chats just hadn't been enough.

The boys arrived at the same time about ten minutes later. They were the exact opposites of her and Anna. Where the girls were petite and had light hair and eyes, Evan and Ethan were exceedingly tall, and had black-as-night hair and eyes.

Two light, two dark.

Seeing them now, she realized how much she'd missed them. Duplicates, other than the shadow of stubble Ethan wore. Both still wore their thick hair a little shaggy. The Florida sea breezes always had it tousled and mussed. And if the number of girls who'd always noticed were any indication, the guys must be considered attractive. To Aria, they were just her dorky brothers.

Evan crossed to where she was standing, wrapped his long

arms around her waist and picked her right up off her feet. He gave her a big bear hug and a kiss before passing her, still dangling off the floor, to Ethan, where she got the same treatment. They'd done this to her and Anna for as long as she could remember—lifting them and throwing them around like their own personal toys.

She and her sister had gotten some serious air time at the beach when they'd all go swimming. The guys loved to see how far they could throw them out into the water.

Aria smiled and thumped Ethan on the side of the head. "Put me down, you ape."

"Hey," Ethan complained, rubbing his head. "What ever happened to doing no harm?"

"That only applies to other people—not pain-in-the-butt brothers like you." Aria gave him a stern look as the rest of her family looked on and laughed.

These moments of levity and unity were like a soothing balm to Aria's soul. Her mind had been so full of death and torment lately, she didn't think she'd ever feel like this again.

"So what made you haul ass home?" Evan asked her as they each took seats around the living room.

She got right to the point since it involved them all. "I think whatever it is the prophecy warned us about is strong enough now to start making its presence known."

"I thought you didn't believe in any of that stuff?" Ethan asked.

"I didn't, but I was wrong." And she owed her parents an apology. "Mom, Dad. I'm sorry I didn't trust in what you tried to teach us growing up. I thought getting away from all of this would make it disappear."

Taking a deep breath, she addressed the entire room. "But I can't ignore the obvious anymore."

Aria fidgeted with her hands. "Ever since our birthdays a week ago, my visions have taken a dark and twisted turn.

Whenever I try to sleep, I'm bombarded with scenes of your deaths. In vivid detail."

Her mother drew in a sharp breath and clutched her father's hand in hers.

Aria studied the faces of her siblings, but they didn't seem to register the surprise she'd expected. And then she knew.

"Something's happened with all of you, hasn't it?" Her eyes darted to each one of them in turn. "It's shown itself to you too."

Anna nodded. "I can feel it. I keep getting the sense that it's a man—or at least, it used to be—but whoever he is, he absolutely hates us to his core. I've never felt so much hostility. But just like you said, it started that morning."

All eyes went to Anna in concern. "Are you okay?" their mother asked.

Her sister was a very sensitive empath, whose power allowed her to feel every emotion of everyone around her, and it had always taken its toll. Especially when they'd been young, and she hadn't yet learned to shield herself. As they'd grown, their magic and control had strengthened, and those barriers had solidified to block out the worst. But they all remembered how much she'd been tormented, and even now they continued to worry.

"I'm *fine*," Anna answered, exasperated. Aria knew her sister considered the rest of them overbearing and unnecessarily protective. But old habits were hard to break.

Evan stepped in, drawing everyone's attention away from Anna. "I can sense him shifting and growing underground. The earth is taking the brunt of his anger right now. I can feel the tremors."

Ethan was the last to speak and said only one word. "Dreams."

Six people sat in silence as they accepted that each of the four had connected with this monster in some way. A year earlier than expected.

"Is he purposely taunting us?" Aria rubbed her tired eyes. Exhaustion was creeping back in. "Or do you think, because we were the ones chosen to fight him, that we have some kind of direct link to him?"

"If we do," Evan, ever the warrior, added, "then we'll use it to our advantage. We'll need any insight we can get."

They'd never say it, but Aria knew she was their biggest liability right now. She'd chosen to leave. She'd been arrogant and ignored what her parents had tried to tell her. While her siblings had continued to train and practice, she'd purposely neglected her gifts. The most she'd used them for in the last six years was to check the movement of her sculptures and push a motorcycle.

If she hoped to be of any use to her family in this fight, she'd have to work her ass off to get her mind and body back in shape.

Aria hadn't realized she was almost dozing in her chair until her mother's voice roused her.

"I think the first thing that needs to happen is for Aria to get some rest." She turned to the rest of her children. "You all clear out, but I expect you back for dinner. We have a lot to focus on right now, the most important being Aria's visions. We need to go over them with a fine-toothed comb."

Evan stood up. "I've got to get into work anyway. I'm already forty-five minutes late, and with Bike Week coming up, it's all hands on deck." He came over and gave Aria another hug. "I'm glad you're home, sis."

She watched her brother leave and shook her head. She still couldn't believe he'd become a cop. He was the kid who'd always insisted on being the bad guy when they'd played as children.

Law enforcement was the last place she'd expected him to end up. Yet, it had been shortly after she'd left home that he'd joined the police academy. After graduating, he'd steadily moved up the ranks. He was now a detective on the Daytona Beach police force.

"That works for me too." Anna rose from her seat. "I have an appointment I have to get to before my class."

"Is everything all right?" Aria asked her.

Anna worked at the elementary school and was the teacher of a very special class. She had five students ranging in age from five to nine years old. Each of them had some type of learning disability. Anna's empathic power allowed her to connect with and help them in ways that no other teacher could.

"Yup. It's all good," Anna nodded. "Just something I can't miss."

Aria sensed there was more to that appointment but didn't push in front of their parents. She'd pin Anna down later and find out what was up.

Then Ethan left and Aria was alone with her parents again. "I don't think I'll be able to sleep, Mom." The resignation was clear in her voice. "Every time I let my guard down, the visions are there, haunting me."

Mary pulled her to her feet and moved her in the direction of the room she'd shared with Anna. "You let me worry about that."

Aria was so tired, she didn't argue. She knew this would be a futile effort. As long as she was awake, her shields were up and strong. But when she slept, they weakened and made her mind vulnerable.

She lay down anyway at the urging of her mother. "Now just be still."

Mary cupped each side of her head in her hands and massaged her temples gently. Aria was soon floating in that half-wake, half-sleep state when the words she hadn't heard since her childhood flowed from her mother's mouth.

"A mind tormented with unease.
Calm and quiet now is my plea.
Sleep deep and dreamless, protected from harm.

This mother's love is always the charm."

~~~

Many hours later, Aria awoke feeling more rested than she'd been in over a week. She smiled as she thought of what her mother had done for her.

Although she'd forgotten it until the moment her mother had begun to speak the words, it was the same spell Mary had used on her and Anna as small children—when the outside world had become too much for them to handle, and the barriers they'd needed were still being built. Several nights, as the twins had struggled to rest, her mother had aided their slumber by reciting those exact words.

Feeling better now, Aria sat up and looked at the clock. Six fifteen. Her brothers and sister were probably back by now. After a quick stop in the bathroom to freshen up, Aria made her way to the dining room.

As she'd guessed, her parents and siblings were all just sitting down to dinner.

"Good," Mary greeted with a sunny smile as she set a platter on the table. "You're just in time."

Her mom took a moment to come over to her, place her hands on her cheeks, and look steadily into her silver-blue eyes.

She must have been satisfied with what she'd seen, because she gave a quick nod. "Sit down. Eat."

Aria took the seat she'd occupied until the day she'd left. Anna was on her right, the boys across the table, and her parents on either end. She hadn't realized how much she'd yearned for these family dinners until this very moment.

As everyone started to pass dishes, Mary spoke up. "I know there's a lot we need to discuss, but this is the first time in years that I have all my children at the same table. So for the next hour or so, I'm going to enjoy it before the dark has to
~~~

intrude again."

She looked at Aria. "Tell us about some of the pieces you've created recently. I can't wait to see some of them in person. I'm sure the pictures don't do them justice."

That set the tone for dinner. There was easy talk and abundant laughter, and Aria enjoyed the nostalgia, almost like no time had passed. Even amidst the danger hanging over them, it was a much-needed reprieve to still have these carefree moments.

Once the dishes were clear and the kitchen set to rights, they returned to their chairs around the table. Mary brought out a pad of paper and pens. "I guess it's time to delve back in."

She flipped to the first clean page as she sat. "Walk us through what you saw, Aria. Every detail you can remember— the time of day, what everyone was wearing, what they were doing, where they were, how it…happened." She paused before continuing. "Anything you can think of. The more information we have, the better prepared we'll be."

Over the next hour, the six of them examined her visions from all possible angles. They each asked questions and went over the specifics with her multiple times. The predictions, in their entirety, were recorded for further study.

If there were any sort of clues as to when this would happen or the events leading up to it, they needed to know. Her parents were nothing if not thorough. They'd had to be. With the threat of death hanging over their heads since the day their children were born, they'd learned not to overlook the small stuff.

When her mother deemed they had all they were going to get, she and Aria's father retreated to the library. They took these new pieces of the puzzle and added them to what they'd collected over the last twenty-four years.

Once the extended family had confirmed that the birth of the quads had triggered the prophecy, everyone who had journals or records of the family history had sent them on to Mary, hoping that they would one day help.

Her mother had picked up where generations of Burke witches had left off and now meticulously kept the chronicles current.

Aria knew, very soon, she'd have to read through it all again. Reacquaint herself with the old stories and learn anything new that her family had been able to uncover in the last six years.

But not right now. At this moment, she needed something else. "I'll be back in a few minutes," she said to her siblings as she excused herself.

Aria got to her feet, walked out the rear of the house, and onto the back patio. She took a second to kick off her shoes and then stepped, barefoot, into the soft grass.

It was ten steps before her toes landed in the warm white sand. Aria went right to the water's edge, knowing that as it ebbed and flowed, it would bathe her feet in its velvety waves. She wrapped her arms around her middle and breathed. In the soft light of dusk, the fresh ocean air brushed over her skin and played with her long hair.

Aria had forgotten, or more likely blocked out, how much she loved it here. The gentle breeze that surrounded her now had been her loving companion since the day she'd first drawn breath.

The three swirls within a circle on her right shoulder blade tied her to this particular element. No matter where she was, she'd always been able to pull it close and ask anything of it. But there was something special about the air here at home. There was a tighter bond, a more profound connection, an effortless communication. Though she hadn't let herself acknowledge it, being away had left a hole in her.

Aria inhaled deeply, welcoming back her dear friend. She let it fill her up as it breathed life into her once again. It cleansed her soul and healed the chasm she'd lived with during her absence from this place. Aria felt more at peace than she had in years as she stood quietly in the sand and surf.

She sensed her mother's presence behind her. "I really missed this," she admitted without turning around.

Mary walked up to stand next to her. They both gazed out over the water. "You could have come home at any time."

Aria looked down at where her toes were digging into the wet sand. "I was so sure that none of this would ever happen." She stopped, took a breath, and then turned to face her mom, prepared to confess a terrible truth.

"That's not true. I *made* myself believe it wouldn't. I thought if I didn't acknowledge it, didn't think about it, then it wouldn't be real. It was easier to stay away. Here, the prophecy is everywhere. There, I could forget it even existed. I didn't understand, and I didn't want the weight of this mess to fall on me. On any of us."

"Oh, honey." Mary laid her hand flat on her chest. "When the four of you were born, I knew what those birthmarks would mean for you, and my heart wept. I have been soul-deep scared from that moment to this one." Tears gathered in her hazel-green eyes. "If I'd thought, for one second, that it could have saved you, I would've sent you all away long ago. But I knew what was coming, and that there was no escaping it."

Her mom took a shuddering breath. "So I buried that panic and that constant worry, and did what I had to do. Your father and I have lain awake *so many* nights, hoping that what we've taught you four is enough to ensure that you survive this and take that bastard down. For good."

Aria smiled weakly, met her mother's eyes, and shared the real source of her unease. "I'm not ready, Mom. Things are already starting to happen and my gifts are rusty, because I've barely used them at all in the six years that I've been gone."

Aria looked down at her hands, embarrassed to admit the next part. "I didn't just leave home...I left that part of myself behind too." She looked up, shamefaced. "And now I'm worried that there isn't enough time left to catch up."

Mary's eyes softened before she spoke in a determined voice. "I have no doubt that you will defeat this evil. Your gifts are a part of you, Aria. Even neglected, they are still there, ready to be put to use. We will work together until you are certain again of your abilities. Each of you is strong on your own, but together—*together* you'll have everything you need."

"To what end, though?" Aria asked in a defeated tone. She had always feared one particular line of the prophecy more than any other. She recited it now. "'Their sacrifice will set them free.'"

Mary's fierce gaze held hers. "*All* of you will get through this, do you hear me? I know my children, and I know the magic that courses through your veins. You are Burke witches, with a long line of power behind you. You remember that, and hold on to it."

A grin lifted the corners of Mary's mouth. "You'll kick its ass right back to hell, where it belongs."

The complete confidence she heard in her mother's voice went a long way to calming Aria's fears. She reached out and wrapped her mother in a hug. "Thank you, Momma. I love you, and I really am sorry."

Mary's arms tightened. "I love you too, baby, and you have nothing to apologize for." She pulled back enough to see her daughter's face. She reached up and tucked Aria's hair behind her ear. "You know that all things happen for a reason. As much as I hated it," Mary smiled tenderly, love shining in her eyes, "I believe that your leaving was meant to be. It was something you needed to do. And you're just as much a Burke witch today as you were the day you left."

3

The next few days had Aria hitting the books and exercising her magic. She'd get up early, make coffee, and take a cup with her into the library where her family kept all the historical documents and everything pertaining to the entity that would come for them. She wanted to look at it all with fresh eyes. Ones that truly, and fully, believed.

In the afternoons and evenings, she worked with her mother to hone her gifts and recondition her mind. She worked hard, and it came back to her with ease.

By lunchtime of the third day, her eyes were crossing as she read the original prophecy for what seemed like the hundredth time. She'd studied it and Iris's account of the final battle so much, it was almost like she'd been there. She kept thinking there was something in those lines she was missing. Some clue or hidden meaning that would make it all become clear.

But no matter how many times she looked at the spindly handwriting on those pages, it was always the same. He'd become too strong. Everything they'd thrown at him had no effect. They couldn't completely defeat him, and their only option had been to lock him away.

There was nothing that gave her any clue as to what was coming or how to fight it.

Aria was rubbing her eyes when Anna came in. "Mom said you've been at it for too long. She told me to get you out of here.

Let's go."

"Shouldn't you be at work?"

"It's Saturday, genius."

"Oh." It didn't really matter what day it was; she still needed answers. "I can't," Aria told her sister through a yawn. "I need to—"

"No, you don't," Anna interrupted, and then reached out and pulled her from the chair. "If you haven't found anything in all that mess yet, you're not going to. Come on. We're leaving to get some food."

Aria grinned at her sister's forceful tone. "We are, are we?"

"Yes." Anna scowled at her. "So don't fight me."

"Really." She couldn't help but ask, "And what will you do if I try?"

"You'd be surprised." Anna gave her a sly look, as if she knew something her sister didn't.

Aria went willingly, more out of curiosity than anything else. Evidently, it was time for a long-overdue twin-to-twin chat. There were obviously a few things Anna had neglected to share during their almost-daily phone conversations.

Anna drove straight to one of their favorite seafood restaurants. The whole place was based on a popular movie, with memorabilia up everywhere. Everything on the menu was amazing, but what Aria and Anna invariably went back for was the seasoned peel-and-eat shrimp and loaves of garlic bread.

Once they were seated and their orders taken, Aria leaned forward on the table. "All right, give it up. What's going on with you?"

"Nothing," Anna denied. "I don't know what you mean."

"Don't play dumb. I know you as well as I know myself. You're hiding something."

Aria held off on her interrogation when the waiter came back with their drinks.

Her thoughts were derailed though, when Anna extended

her arm to bring her sweet-tea closer. The sleeve of her shirt pulled up, and Aria caught sight of a dark purple bruise the size of a baseball on her sister's upper arm.

"What the hell happened to your arm?" Aria demanded.

"Oh." Anna twisted it around and looked at it as best she could. "It's nothing. I didn't dodge fast enough."

Aria's temper instantly flared at the thought of someone hurting her sister. "Is someone hitting you?" Aria's voice held a sharp edge. "Who is it? Tell me."

"No," Anna stated calmly and sipped her drink.

Aria was taken aback. "What the hell do you mean, *no*? You can't expect me to just let that go." Her gaze dropped to the injury.

"But I do," Anna countered, not giving an inch. "And you'll say nothing about it to anyone else."

Aria was at a loss for words. There was no way she was going to sit back and knowingly let someone abuse her sister. Whoever this asshole was would have a rude awakening if they thought this would continue.

"Oh, all right!" Anna burst out, frustrated. "God, I can just about see the smoke rolling out of your ears. I'll tell you where I got the bruise, but you have to promise to keep quiet about it."

Anna crossed her arms over her chest with a stubborn, expectant look until Aria finally caved. "Fine. Now explain."

"I've been taking self-defense classes."

Just the thought of Anna doing something like that brought Aria's protective instincts to the surface. She was about to list out the reasons why it was dangerous for her to be in that type of environment when Anna spoke.

"And that," Anna pointed a finger at Aria's face, "is exactly why I didn't tell you in the first place. You all think I'm some delicate piece of china that will break with the slightest pressure. I'm sick of it." Exasperation colored her tone. "My shields are strong—stronger than they've ever been. I've worked my ass off at making my mind a fortress. Nothing gets through that I don't let in. And I don't need anyone to bundle me up in bubble-wrap anymore."

"But Anna—"

"No, Ari." Anna sat back and pushed her long silver-blonde hair back away from her face, her icy-blue eyes determined.

"I finally met someone who treats me like a normal person. Not some fragile flower that can't survive without protection. He's kicked my ass on a regular basis for the last eight months. So, *yes*, I have marks on me. But nowhere near as many as I started with." Pride shone in her face. "I love it, Ari, and I won't give it up. I finally feel alive and free."

Anna's shoulders sagged a little. "You ran away and left me, to find that very thing. Well, this is *my* Ohio, and I need this." Anna tilted her head slightly. "I'd think you of all people would understand that."

Aria did recognize that need. And no matter how she felt about it, there was no way she would deny Anna her escape. *Whatever* that happened to be. But she would make damned sure that whoever this person was, he knew that if anything happened to her sister, there would be hell to pay.

"Okay." Aria gave in with a resigned smile just as the server brought their pots of steaming shrimp. Once he'd left, Aria dug in and tried to pry a little more information out of her. "So, who's the guy?"

Her twin laughed and shook her head. "Oh, no, you don't. We are *so* not going there. I don't need you checking up on me and giving him the third degree."

And she obviously meant it, refusing to answer any of Aria's more probing questions about the secret identity of her trainer.

Even with Anna's evasions, they had a wonderful lunch. Being together again was as essential as the air Aria had taken into her body on the beach.

They were still laughing and chatting on the drive home

when a vision blindsided Aria. Normally, they washed over her with no lasting effects. But not this time. As before, it felt as if a knife were being thrust into her skull.

At Aria's gasp, Anna swung to the shoulder of the road. "What's wrong? Tell me what's happening."

Aria couldn't answer. Spikes were driving into her brain.

She was helpless as she watched Evan being stalked. Aria could do nothing as his assailant rushed him from behind and sank a lethal-looking blade deep into his side.

Oh, God, this was her vision. Evan was going to die, and she was watching as it happened. Aria screamed as the burning torment of the knife cutting through skin and muscle and tissue echoed in her own body. The searing pain was almost more than she could bear.

At the exact same moment, Anna cried out.

Through the haze of agony, Aria turned to look at her sister, noting that she was also clutching her side. Anna had felt it too.

As suddenly as the vision began, it stopped. The pain slowly receded, and a quick glance told her that Anna was recovering as well.

"Who was it, Ari?" Anna asked. "Who was hurt?"

"Evan." Aria ran a shaking hand over her aching forehead. "My vision is happening right now. We have to find him before it's too late." In her mind she let it replay, taking note of elements she'd not seen before. "I know where he is. It's over on Beach Street, where the vendors set up."

Anna took a deep, steadying breath and, with a quick look behind her, pulled back onto the road and sped off.

"Explain this to me," Anna commanded as she made the turn that would take them over one of the bridges connecting the peninsula to the mainland. "Your visions have never caused you pain before. Why did you feel Evan's injury? Empathy's my gig."

"I don't know," Aria told her honestly, rubbing away the lingering throbbing in her head. "Maybe it's because we're quads. But I think it has more to do with the Big Bad. The headaches started with the first premonition I got of you guys. But being able to *feel* what was being done—that's new."

"But how could he even hurt Evan? He's still locked away."

"We've all felt him," Aria reminded her. "We know he's getting more powerful every day. Maybe he's strong enough now to affect us somehow."

"That's a comforting thought."

"Why did *you* feel it? I thought you said you could block it all out?" Aria threw an accusing glance her sister's way.

"I can," Anna confirmed. "But I dropped my barriers, so I could find out what was wrong with you." She made the left turn onto Beach Street. "How far down?"

"Pull up in front of the old motorcycle dealership."

Once Bike Week officially began, this stretch of road would be teeming with people and vehicles. For now, as the vendors began their set-up, only a few cars passed by.

Anna had barely stopped the car when they both jumped out on the run. Aria pointed around the side of the building. "Back there."

Aria hoped they weren't too late. The vision had ended before showing her the aftermath of the sudden attack. Was their brother dead? Would she find him covered in blood as she'd seen all those times before?

She refused to believe that and pushed herself faster. As she rounded the corner, she saw Evan. He was sitting with his back against the rear wall of the structure. Kneeling over him, with a bloody knife in his hand, was a huge man dressed all in black.

Without thought, Aria gathered the wind and sent it at her brother's attacker. The force of the gale sent him flying a good thirty feet away where he landed hard and rolled. She didn't even spare him a glance as she and Anna rushed to Evan.

His dark eyes looked up into her arctic-blue ones. "You shouldn't have done that."

"Shh, don't talk," she told him. "How badly are you hurt?"

"He was just—" Evan said through gritted teeth.

"Are you kidding me?" Aria cut him off.

"You don't understand—" Evan tried again.

"There's nothing to understand," she interrupted again. "I wasn't going to give him another chance to stab you and have my premonition come true."

"If you'd just let him finish, Pixie," a familiar voice sounded from behind her, "he'd tell you I wasn't the one to stick him."

~~~

As Law got back to his feet, he knew he should haul ass out of there. This meet had gone to shit, and he needed to distance himself from it before his cover was blown.

But the shock of seeing her again held him immobile. There was something about this woman that just wouldn't let go of him. He'd fought it since the night she'd nearly killed him on his motorcycle. But he'd learned it was a losing battle as, again and again, his mind had wandered back to her.

Even in the darkness of that night, he'd noticed her eyes. Blue so pale it was almost translucent. Skin fair and porcelain-smooth. And her hair, so light it reflected the glow of the moon and stars. That shining beacon had been the first thing he'd seen as he'd regained consciousness.

And just in that short amount of time, she'd gotten under his skin. She'd burrowed in deeper when he'd seen the instinctual fight every time he'd barked an order at her. Her heated gaze had told him what he could do with his abrupt commands. The fire of that temper had burned in her eyes and the few snide comments she'd let slip. But no matter what she'd felt, he could tell she'd held most of it back, out of guilt for running him off
~~~

the road.

If he hadn't been on such a strict timeline, he may have pushed her a little more. He'd had an overwhelming urge to see what it would take for her to lose control.

Instead he'd left her standing on the side of the highway. Knowing he'd never see her again had caused an ache in his chest he hadn't wanted to examine too closely. He'd hoped that as time went by, she'd loosen her grip on him and he'd forget her.

And now, here she was. Correction. Here *they* were. There were two of them, obviously twins, both standing guard over the man he was supposed to have met up with.

Law had parked his bike a block away and walked the rest of the way in, just to make sure he hadn't picked up a tail. He'd just caught sight of his local contact when some douchebag had come out of nowhere and slid a knife in between Evan's ribs.

Law had yelled out, and the attacker bolted as Evan had slid to the ground. Not sure of how severely he was injured, Law had run to the fallen man's side. As he'd dropped to his knees beside him, Evan's hands went to the hilt of the knife. Law had reached out to keep him from removing it, but he was too late. His hands were still wrapped around Evan's on the bloody blade when the women had found them.

He wasn't sure exactly what had happened after that, but somehow, he'd ended up on his ass.

Law carefully eyed the beauty he thought he'd never see again, side by side with her twin. The two were nearly identical, their petite builds and delicate features almost indistinguishable. But even with all that, Law didn't have any trouble telling them apart.

And she remembered him, evidenced by the stiffening of her body at just the sound of his voice. She slowly swung her head around towards him. A look of utter disbelief was written on her face.

"You." She rose to her feet and nailed him with a glare. Not so threatening when the top of her head only reached to his mid-chest. "What are *you* doing here?" Her jaw clenched. "And I've told you *not* to call me that."

There was that temper. Simmering just below the surface. "Yeah, well," he braced his feet and crossed his arms over his chest. He knew the move made his arms and shoulders look that much bigger. "We can't all get what we want now, can we, Pixie?" He winked at her and grinned when heat flared in her gaze. "As for what I'm doing here? I was just driving by and saw what happened." He shrugged. "Thought maybe I could help."

His size didn't seem to intimidate her, he noticed. The little spitfire put her hands on her hips, and her thin blonde eyebrows snapped together. "You expect me to believe that you just *happened* upon my brother getting stabbed, and you decided to be a Good Samaritan? What reason do you have for even being in this area?"

Brother, huh? That bit of information hit on both the good- *and* bad-news side of things. And it also answered the question as to how he'd ended up on his can. If she were Evan's sister, that meant she was a witch.

He and Evan had become friends through the tough weeks of training at the police academy. As it happened, they'd talked about where they'd come from and their families. But it wasn't until Law had a very near miss with some loose gravel on a steep incline that Evan had explained about his little something extra. Law had been well on his way to what should have been a serious injury, when suddenly the earth beneath him had stopped sliding out from under his feet and cradled him, keeping him from harm. With no other choice, Evan had disclosed what he and his family were.

It had been a little shocking at first to accept that witches and magic existed, but having been on the receiving end of that power, he'd slowly come to terms with it. They hadn't discussed it again, and it hadn't affected their friendship.

It had been shortly afterwards that Law was reassigned, and he and Evan had lost touch. Until this case had brought them back together again.

"Not that I owe you an explanation," he slid his hands into his pockets, "but I just got into town for Bike Week." He sent her an irreverent grin. "You *do* recall that I ride a motorcycle, don't you, Pixie?"

"Yes, I remember." She swung her head around to where her twin was tending to Evan. "You're positive he's not the one?"

Evan nodded and grimaced as Anna pressed harder on his wound to stop the flow of blood. "It was just as he said."

Little Miss Pixie spun back to face him. "Okay then. Be on your way." She even had the nerve to flip her hands at him in a 'go-away' gesture. "We've got it from here."

"Aria," Evan started before she cut him off.

"What?" she snapped at him. "He's not needed here. He should go." She turned to her brother, dismissing *him* completely. "Come on. We have to get you to the hospital and get you patched up."

Aria. Her name was Aria. It fit, Law thought. Beautiful. Powerful.

Law made a move to help the two women as they lifted Evan off the ground, but Aria sent him a mulish look that stopped him. He stepped back and let them handle it.

As they helped their brother carefully to his feet, Law sent him a look over their heads, relaying a silent message that they'd postpone this for another time. Evan gave him a slight nod and then limped off with his sisters.

4

They got Evan into the backseat of the car. Once he was settled, Aria slid in next to him as Anna got behind the wheel to drive to the ER.

"That was no ordinary perp." Evan braced his hand against his wound as Anna set the car into motion.

"No, it wasn't." Aria helped to steady her brother as Anna sped through the streets. "Our Big Bad did this."

Evan's gaze snapped to hers and his dark brows wrinkled. "How?"

"I don't know." Aria tried to think of the possibilities. "He can't physically come into this world yet. But what if he's gotten strong enough to affect people on the outside?"

"Although that would really suck, it might explain what I saw in that guy's eyes." Evan groaned as Anna took a fast turn. "They were unfocused and empty. He was *beyond* out of it."

"So you're thinking this was mind control?" Apprehension filled Anna's question.

"I can't see any other explanation." Evan looked down at the blood still flowing from his body. "Great. Just fucking great."

Aria pushed his hand aside, placed hers over the gash, and pressed hard against it.

Evan winced and swore. "That hurts, damn it."

Aria glared at him. "Would you prefer to bleed out?"

He held her stare and then asked a question of his own. "So, what was that back there? How do you know that biker?"

"I don't." Aria concentrated on stopping the bleeding, sending what little healing she could to his wound.

He sent her a scathing look but didn't take the hint to let it drop. "You recognized him. And he obviously knew you. Where do you know him from?"

Something in Evan's voice told Aria that her answer was important. "I don't know him at all," she assured him. "We ran into each other, *once*. That was it. I don't even know his name. He's no one."

"Ari," Anna admonished from the front seat. "If it hadn't been for him, your vision of Evan's death would have come true."

"Fine," she snapped. "I ran him off the road somewhere in North Carolina on my way down here. I fell asleep driving through the mountains and swerved into his lane. He was on his motorcycle and didn't have time to get out of the way. He ended up in the ditch. Unconscious."

Anna gasped, but the reprimand in Evan's eyes told her to continue.

She huffed out a breath at having to relay the details of such a stupid moment in her life, one that could have easily ended someone else's. But she told them everything. Except for the part where she'd ogled his fine ass.

"So that's it. I just didn't expect to see him here," she finished.

Anna gave her an odd look in the rearview mirror.

Shit. What does that mean? Had she sensed something?

Before she could think any more on the incident, they arrived at the entrance to the emergency room. The next few hours were filled with doctors and nurses, stitches, shots, and paperwork. And because Evan was a cop, even more reports had to be filed. By the time they arrived at his place, it was well after seven.

"Are you sure you don't want us to take you to Mom and Dad's instead?" Aria asked, once they'd gotten him inside. "I'd bet money that Mom can take care of you a hell of a lot better than you can."

Evan grimaced. "And have her fussing over me the entire time? No thank you. This isn't the first time I've been hurt on the job."

"Yeah, but this time it's not job-related," Aria reminded him. "It has to do with the prophecy and the fact that this evil bastard wants us dead."

"I'm fine." He held firm. "I can handle it."

Aria and her sister shared a knowing look. "Have it your way then. If you don't need anything else, we're headed out."

Once back in the car, Anna glanced over at her. "I think at this point, we could both use a glass of wine," Anna offered as they pulled out of Evan's driveway. "I have a nice red in the fridge. What do you say?"

"Definitely," Aria agreed.

Ten minutes later, Aria was settled into the navy-blue sofa in Anna's living room while her twin went to get the drinks. She studied the home her sister had created and felt a twinge of regret that she hadn't been around to help. What fun it would have been, shopping and decorating the cute little rooms. She'd deprived them both of years' worth of memories. And in the end, it had all been for nothing.

Aria's thoughts were interrupted when Anna came back carrying two glasses and a bottle. She set the stemware on the coffee table and poured. After setting the bottle aside, she passed one over to Aria.

"Thanks."

They both sat and sipped for a moment before Anna finally spoke.

"Don't get me wrong—I'm grateful to that biker for saving Evan. But I think you should stay away from him."

Puzzled, Aria turned to face her. "I have no intention of seeing him again," she answered truthfully.

"There's something about him…" Anna started and then stopped, dropping her gaze down to her glass. "I couldn't get anything from him."

"You tried to read him?" Aria was a little taken aback.

"What?" Anna's eyes shot up to pin hers. "You think you're the only one who gets to be protective? I wanted to make sure he was what he was claiming to be. But he had everything locked down." Anna gestured at Aria with her wineglass. "And that alone tells me not to trust him. Why would he shut everyone out if he doesn't have anything to hide? And how do we really know he has nothing to do with these attacks you saw?"

"Evan said he wasn't the one who stabbed him, so it seems to me that he's free of guilt."

"Maybe he and our Big Bad are working together, and it's a part of his job to get close to us. If even one of us goes down, we're done."

"I don't know. I just didn't get that vibe from him." Aria shook her head. "He's gruff and commanding, but he doesn't seem overly complicated. Just a rough, surly biker—the same as all the others we run into this time of year."

Anna didn't say anything, and Aria became a little uncomfortable with the way her sister was studying her.

"What?"

"I was trying to decide if I should be worried about this… *thing* you seem to have with this stranger."

"What? No." Aria rolled her eyes and shook her head. "There's no *thing*. I don't even know the man, Anna. And I have no desire to. There's more to worry about here than just some random guy."

"You're right. But it doesn't take an empath to sense something's going on between you; even Evan felt it. And that nickname. What's up with that?"

Aria sighed. "I don't know. He called me that the night of the accident. I told him to knock it off, but obviously he does it just to piss me off."

Annoyed now with the discussion, Aria redirected the conversation back to more important matters. "We need to prepare ourselves, because whoever this Big Bad is, he's getting stronger fast. In a little over a week, he's progressed from just sending visions and emotions, to now the possession and control of innocents. We may have lucked out with his attempt on Evan, but he's not finished."

Aria shook her head, overwhelmed. "And this is only the beginning. We've got a year until we face off, and he's already this strong? It's going to take everything we've got to put him down."

After a moment, Anna responded, "Do you think he knows about the prophecy?"

Aria was relieved her sister had finally decided to drop the subject. "That would be my guess. If he can take any one of us out, that'll be the end to the prophecy. We won't be able to unite and destroy him, and the evil will be free forever."

"How do we protect ourselves then?" Anna asked. "If he can control just any random person to the extent that they commit murder on his behalf, how are we to know where the threat is going to come from?"

"I don't have any idea."

"There's something else that's odd. Why have you never seen a vision of your own death? Why doesn't he seem to want to kill you?"

"I don't know that either. It could be as simple as just not being able to see my own future. Or..." Aria had a more disturbing theory and decided to share it with the one person who knew her best. "What if he knows I ran away, Anna? That I turned my back on my gifts, my destiny? What if he considers me the weakest link, and is only using these visions as a way to distract me, so he can take me out?"

Anna captured Aria's gaze and held it. "You are *not* weak.

If you were, you never would have come back here. Did you ever stop to think that maybe he's playing mind games with you? This could be exactly what he wants...for you to doubt yourself."

Anna pointed her finger at her as she spoke, her tone fierce. "Don't you dare let him do that to you, Aria. He has something else up his sleeve, and you have to be ready."

Aria felt a weight lift off her chest. Deep down, she *had* been insecure. Well, no more.

"So how do we guard against these attacks?"

"I wish I could have gotten some time with the guy who stabbed Evan," Anna said morosely, all her fire gone. "I'm sure I could have figured out exactly how the thing had hijacked him, and maybe gotten an idea of what his overall plan might be."

"Have you been able to pick up anything else from our Big Bad?" Aria asked.

Anna shook her head. "Just the hatred. I'll try to go deeper and see if I can sense anything else."

"No," Aria immediately objected. "It's not safe. If you connect with him, you'll be vulnerable to all his depravity and corruption. There's no reason to put yourself through that."

As far as Aria was concerned, the subject was closed, and Anna didn't argue. There was no way any of them would agree to that. Anna had only been exposed to the darker side of the human race, and that alone had almost been more than she could handle. Diving head first into centuries' worth of pent-up malevolence was an entirely different kind of evil—concentrated and undiluted. And no matter how desperate they became, Aria would make damned sure it never came down to that.

~~~
~~~

Law was dealing with his own version of evil. One he was all too familiar with, because he'd lived with it for what felt like forever. The gang he'd infiltrated had come to Daytona Beach under the guise of the annual gathering to distribute guns and drugs. This event was their single largest push of product to date. Thousands of people came from all over the country, all over the world, making it easy to deliver on orders already placed.

This year's trip had a double purpose, though. The MC was scheduled to take delivery on a large shipment of rifles and handguns in the next few days. He finally had a shot at the syndicate who supplied the weapons to this and a multitude of other clubs across the globe. If Law and the local authorities did their jobs, this whole operation could be shut down.

After that, he didn't know what he wanted to do. He hated the thought of going undercover again. He didn't know how many more times he could lose another piece of himself. There couldn't be much left now of the man he'd been at the beginning.

Law didn't normally let himself think about what came after. This world had consumed his life for the last six years, and he wasn't sure if he could ever go back to the normal guy he used to be.

At twenty-two, as a freshly-graduated rookie, Law had been recruited into a new, elite task force. One whose sole purpose was to send young, fresh-faced boys-in-blue like him undercover into some of the most dangerous criminal organizations in the country. There, they worked to bring them down from the inside. No matter how long it took. This was the longest of long cons.

His first assignment had begun the day he'd left the academy with his diploma and shiny new badge. Not that he even had them anymore. They, along with all other evidence of his previous life, had been taken and locked away.

Average guy Seth Lawson had ceased to exist. And Law, a

chronic troublemaker with an extensive rap-sheet, had been born. He'd spent months going through specialized training until his cover was more natural to him than the life he'd left behind. He was then sent out to do whatever it took to draw the attention of the right people.

The idea was genius, really. Why would these groups ever suspect a snot-nosed kid with a bad attitude of being a cop? If it worked as planned, the new recruit would be welcomed in and eventually brought into their inner circle.

And that's exactly how it had gone for Law. He'd been bouncing across the country, working his way into different organizations ever since. With the information he'd been able to provide, dozens of men had been sent to prison.

To further cement his own cover, he himself had spent over a year in jail after a raid he'd set in motion. It was while he'd been incarcerated that he was set onto his next target. He'd been told a member of a gun-running motorcycle gang out of Chicago was also serving time there. With his new assignment in mind, Law set about getting in good with the guy.

When they were released, coincidentally at the same time, the target had invited Law along and introduced him to his crew.

That had been two years ago. Law was now a full-fledged member of Satan's Chosen Motorcycle Club out of Chicago.

Throughout his time with the club, he'd learned what he could. But it wasn't until he'd received his patch six months ago that he'd been in a position to gather the really damning, and prison-worthy, evidence. And after years of painstaking work, he had enough to bust a lot of the key players in the club. He'd been ready to give it all over to his handler when he'd learned their supplier would finally be out in the open.

The opportunity to destroy not only the MC, but a heavy-hitter like the syndicate supplying them, had been too good to pass up. He'd immediately reported this new development to his superiors, and they'd agreed with his assessment. The decision was made to bring in, and work with, local law enforcement. Remembering his academy buddy, Law had requested Evan Burke, and after some extensive checks, contact was approved.

He'd worked it out so that he was sent down ahead of time to make sure the MC's accommodations were all set up. The club always rented an out-of-the-way house, so clients could come and go without notice. The meet with Evan was supposed to have taken place before the rest of the crew arrived, but that was now FUBAR.

The MC had rolled into town. Ahead of schedule. Law would have his work cut out for him—trying to set up a new place and time to meet Evan, passing him the info about the shipment, and helping to plan the Op. All while maintaining his role within the club, and without getting caught. Or killed.

No worries.

Thoughts of Evan brought to mind someone he had no right thinking about. But as was usual since the day he'd first seen her, she dominated every unguarded moment. Her face, her hair, her body. Everything about her was etched permanently into his brain.

But this particularly hot little pixie was off-limits on so many levels. If only he could convince his body of that.

For the first time since he'd signed on to the task force, he hated what he was doing. People judged on appearances, and the one he'd adopted was specifically designed towards violence and trouble. For Law, decent women like Aria Burke couldn't exist.

"Hey, Lawman, you with us?" Rat, his former jail partner, drew his attention from across the long table.

Rat got a kick out of calling him that. And he had no clue just how close to the truth he actually was. During his time as a prospect, they'd tried to saddle him with other names, but he'd refused to answer to any of them. It had cost him quite a few beatings, but eventually he'd become known only as Law. He'd heard it speculated that he used the name because of how much time he'd spent on the wrong side of it—that it was a way to stick it to the cops.

When in truth, it was a reminder of who he'd been and what he'd become. And why he was doing this.

Law glanced around the dining room table where the seven highest-ranking members of the club were seated and realized he'd missed some of the conversation.

"Sorry, what?"

"Where's your head at, boy?" Kane, the president of the club, intoned from the head of the table.

"Probably on some of that tight young cunt out there." The lecherous smile on JD's face made bile rise in Law's throat. "Gotta love it when Spring Break falls at the same time as Bike Week. All that fresh pussy out there, just ripe for the plucking."

As much as Law wanted to reach out and bitch-slap the nasty fucker, he held it in. It wouldn't do to screw things up now, not when he was so close. He held his tongue and let them think what they would.

Kane called the meeting back to order. "Is everything handled for the pick-up?" he asked the table in general.

Padre, Kane's lieutenant, filled him in. "I spoke with their representative not an hour ago. We're all set. The location's been scouted and secured by both sides."

"So we're a go for Thursday night." Law wanted to make sure no changes had been made to the information he'd already garnered. "You're sure you want Dickie and Ron in the vans? You know neither one of them can find their cocks without arrows pointing the way."

Kane cracked a grin. "They'll be fine. All they have to do is follow us in, stay in the vehicles while the inventory is loaded, and then follow us back out."

The discussion turned to how many men would be going and

where they'd be stationed as the exchange was made. When the meeting finally broke up, Law rose and headed for the front door of the rental house. He had his hand on the knob when Kane called him back.

"Is something going on that I need to know about?" Kane stood and watched him carefully. "You've seemed distracted since we got into town."

With so much on his mind, Law would have to make a bigger effort to not draw attention to himself. He was nearing the end of this, and if it were discovered what he was doing, he was a dead man.

"No, sir. Just want everything to go smooth with the pick-up. No surprises." Having proven himself during his time with the club, Kane had put him in charge of ensuring the security of the MC. As such, it was his job to make certain that nothing happened at the drop.

The irony was not lost on Law.

Kane relaxed. "I know this is your first big haul, but I've done this a number of times now. We've got it covered."

Kane grasped Law's shoulder and squeezed. "Go and see about getting some of that young pussy JD was talking about. We *are* here to have some fun, you know."

"Yeah. I might just do that." Law made himself smile and then winked. "Don't wait up."

Kane laughed as Law turned and strode out of the house. When he reached his bike, he threw his leg over and settled onto the hot leather seat. A push of a button had the Softail roaring to life.

As he headed off down the road, Law turned his thoughts to the problem foremost in his mind. Making contact with Evan. He decided there just wasn't time to wait for another meet to be scheduled. It was five days until the exchange, and they'd need every minute of that to coordinate the multiple law enforcement agencies and set up the sting.

He didn't like it, and the chances of being seen rose exponentially, but his only option was to go directly to Evan's house. Tonight. He'd wait until after midnight to lessen the odds of discovery, so that meant he had some hours to kill.

Law thought about losing himself in the chaos that was downtown Daytona during Bike Week, but just wasn't feeling it. Instead he cruised a stretch of road that took him along the water's edge. The setting sun sent red, pink, and purple streaking across the sky.

Interlaced in the hues, wispy clouds hung. Something about the combination of colors gave the clouds a pale blue tint. A blue that matched, almost exactly, the eyes that tormented him. Law pulled to the side of the road and shut his bike off. For several moments he just watched the play of nature's artwork at its best until movement down on the beach caught his notice.

He drew in a breath when he saw two women walking hand-in-hand on the warm sands. The long silvery hair blowing in the breeze was unmistakable.

Law didn't bother to wonder why or how he'd come across them. He just sat dazed as he watched Aria and her sister. He shouldn't have been able to tell them apart, especially at this distance, but his gaze kept being pulled back to the one he knew, without a doubt, was Aria.

The sisters strolled a few more yards when suddenly Aria's head whipped up and around. He felt the impact of her focus on him. It hit him right in the gut and took his breath away.

He didn't move. He couldn't. They continued to stare at each other until her sister, seeing what had distracted Aria, tugged her back down the beach. After a brief hesitation, Aria followed without looking back. Law drew air deep into his starved lungs. It wasn't until then that he realized he'd been holding his breath, only able to function again when the connection between them was broken.

Shit.

Law scrubbed his hands over his face. It was just as well she was gone. He had to stop this madness. His lifestyle just wasn't conducive to relationships of any kind. Aside from the fact that his future was so uncertain, the lies, danger, and disappearing for months or years at a time, would end it before it began. He had no right to bring a woman into that kind of situation. Even if she weren't his friend's sister.

When he finally brought his thoughts back to the present, Law noticed the sun had completed its descent beyond the horizon. Since it was still too early to show up at Evan's, Law went in search of somewhere to grab a drink and wait.

He found the perfect place in the little coffee shop four blocks from Evan's house. He would have preferred a shot of whiskey, but coffee would be better in this case. He finished off his third cup at one in the morning. He stood, slid some money out of his pocket, and threw the bills down onto the table.

Walking out the door, Law strode away from his bike. He'd leave it parked at the rear of the lot and make the trek on foot. Keeping to the shadows, he was at Evan's back door within a few minutes.

He was on his knees, working the lock pick when the door was jerked out of his hands. He looked up and into the large barrel of a .45 caliber pistol.

Law grinned and his gaze traveled past the gun to the man dressed in sweats and a t-shirt. "Is that any way to greet an old friend?"

"If he's picking my lock in the middle of the night?" Evan asked incredulously, lowering his weapon. "You bet your ass."

Law laughed as he stood and slipped around Evan to enter what he saw was the kitchen. "Close the door."

Evan arched a black brow at him but did as he'd asked.

"How's the side?" Law glanced down to where the knife had been buried.

"It's fine. All stitched up and good to go." Evan paused a moment, watching him. "It was dangerous for you to come here, Seth. What were you thinking?"

The name took Law aback for a moment. No one had called him by his given name in years. He no longer even thought of himself as that guy anymore. It was a whole different lifetime.

"It's Law now," he told Evan a little gruffly.

Evan gave a short nod.

"As to why I'm here, we're running short on time," he explained. "We don't have the luxury of waiting to set up another meet through the proper channels. We have too much to make happen before this shit goes down."

"All right then." Evan motioned to the small kitchen table. "Have a seat. But before we get started, there's something I have to know. What exactly happened between you and Aria?"

"I'm sure you asked her. What did she say?"

Evan's dark brows drew in. "Some story about how she ran you off the road."

"She did," Law confirmed. "Evidently, she fell asleep behind the wheel. Next thing I knew, I was waking up in a ditch with her standing over me."

"And that's all there was to it?"

Law bobbed his head. "Yeah."

"It seemed to me there was more going on when she saw you here. I sensed something between you."

"You'd just been stabbed, man. I think your detecting skills may have been a little off."

Evan cocked his head. "Pixie?"

"Yeah, that." Law grinned at the memory. "I was pissed off after having been thrown from my bike. Once I saw how much it irritated her, I stuck with it. And she is pretty small after all."

"Are you planning on pursuing anything with her?"

"There's nothing to pursue," Law declared. "Never was,

never will be. It was just a couple of chance encounters. And besides, you better than anyone knows I'm not in a position to offer a woman anything. Speaking of which, are we done with this? We've got more important things to discuss."

"Sure. You want a beer? Or coffee?"

Law nodded. "Coffee, please. Black."

When they both had steaming mugs in front of them, Law laid out his plan. "Okay, this is how I see this going down."

5

Aria was having a very pleasurable dream about a certain tall, broad-shouldered, ruggedly-handsome biker. Her imagination had picked up from where he'd come upon them the evening before. Only this time, she was alone.

As she watched him from the beach, he lowered the kickstand and slowly dismounted. Never taking his eyes off her, he started down the slight slope that led to the white sand where she waited.

He strode right up to her and cupped her face in his large, callused palms. His fevered gaze took in her every feature, and when it finally dropped to her mouth, Aria gasped. Using that to his advantage, he fused their mouths together in a hard, scorching kiss. Aria's unsteady hands went to the front of his t-shirt where they tangled in the soft material as her world spun away.

His touch roamed her body, leaving a streak of fire wherever it passed. Strong hands stopped to squeeze and mold her ass before sliding down to the backs of her thighs. She felt the shift of muscles in his arms, and suddenly her legs were wrapped around his waist, the bulge of his erection wedged securely against her aching core. Aria's arms encircled his neck, her sensitive breasts pressed tightly to his massive chest.

She was lost in the sensations until the kiss abruptly changed. Passion-filled urgency became a forceful and cruel attack.

Hands rose and fisted in her hair. They gripped painfully as his mouth mashed and ground against hers in a mockery of the previous kiss. Her soft lips were violently abused until the coppery taste of her own blood filled her mouth.

Aria instantly dropped her legs to push and shove at his unyielding bulk, trying to free herself from this vile embrace. To counter her movements, he lowered one arm to wrap brutally around her waist. With one hand securing her head for his assault and the other plastering her body to his in a rib-crushing hold, Aria was trapped.

Sounds of distress rolled uncontrolled up her throat as she fought him. Her suffering seemed to only encourage him more, her pain and fear arousing him further.

In the close confines of his grasp, Aria didn't know how much damage she could do, but she had to try something. This vicious assault had to stop.

Garnering her strength, she brought her knee up sharply and right on target.

The shock and agony of the strike loosened his grip, and she was able to back away from him. He recovered quickly though, and stood with an arrogant air. When he looked at her and smiled savagely, she knew this was not the same man.

Aria understood instantly who he was and watched him warily.

He licked his lips grotesquely, as if savoring the taste of her. "It has been *so* long since I had a willing," he bared his teeth in what she guessed was a smile, "or even unwilling woman in my arms."

The monster eyed her up and down lasciviously. "And you were so responsive. So aggressive in your passion. Are all women of this day and age so forward?"

He didn't let her speak. Not that she would have answered. "Oh, I am going to enjoy taking my fill when I'm finally free." He leered at her. "I've been watching you, witch, and I am intrigued. I wasn't sure what to do with you, but now that I've had a taste, I think I'll keep you for myself."

The thought nearly made her retch. "Free or not, you'll never have me," Aria countered forcefully. "We'll destroy you."

He threw his head back and laughed. "Haven't you learned yet? I am everlasting, and one way or another, I will end the Burkes. I will live again."

"Why?" Aria demanded. He seemed to be in a talkative mood. Maybe she could finally get some answers. "What did Burke witches ever do to you?"

"They cost me *everything*." All taunting was gone, leaving only madness and loathing. "My woman is gone because of the Burkes. And my sons with her. My *sons*. They belonged to me." He pounded his hand against his chest in a blatant show of ownership. "They were mine to do with as I pleased, and they took them and hid them from me. I will not stop until I wipe out every last one of you. You will all suffer loss as I did."

An eerie calm came over him, and a sinister glint lit his eyes. "Considering the moment I interrupted, it would seem this man means something to you." He looked down at the body he occupied. "But I cannot abide someone else taking what is mine." Menacing satisfaction settled over his face. "I will so enjoy watching him die."

Aria didn't figure the biker was in any real danger; she didn't even know his name. But just in case, she ought to at least try to throw him off the trail.

She pointed casually towards the hulking frame in front of her. "This guy? I don't even know who he is. I probably saw him on the street somewhere, and my subconscious did the rest."

He laughed at her protests. "As I said, I've been *watching* you. Therefore, I know all I need to know. Say goodbye to lover boy."

Blood blossomed across the front of his shirt, the shiny wetness obscene against the thin cotton. With a final sneer, the intruder was gone, leaving only the biker behind. He looked at her face, then down to his chest in shock. His hands came up to cover the growing stain.

Aria ran forward to help just as he slumped to his knees on the sand. She kneeled beside him and eased him down as he fell to his side. His blood soaked the white beach a deep, crimson red. Confusion and pain clouded his brown eyes, as the life slowly faded out of them.

Aria wrenched herself out of sleep and sat straight up in bed. She didn't know where she was, and it took her a moment to recognize Anna's moonlit guest room.

Once she had her bearings, she threw back the sheets and grabbed up her clothes. She was struggling into her jeans when Anna burst in and flipped on the light.

"Ari, are you all right? Your distress is so severe, it woke me up. What happened?"

"He's going to kill him." Aria pulled her shirt over her head. "All because he saw him in my stupid dream."

"Aria, what are you talking about? Who's going to kill who?" Anna reached out and grabbed her arm to stop her. "I want to help you, but you have to tell me what's going on."

"That biker. The one I ran off the road." She grabbed her phone off the bedside table and slid it into her pocket. "That evil son of a bitch is going to hurt him because of me."

"I'm assuming we're talking about our Big Bad," Anna guessed. "But why would he want to hurt a complete stranger who has nothing to do with us?"

"That bastard came into my dream." The ease at which he'd been able to invade her thoughts only made Aria more furious. She turned and left the room in search of her shoes.

Anna was on her heels. "Ari—"

"I was dreaming about that biker when that *filth* took him over. He used that man to attack me and send a brutal message. He said he's going to take everything away from us, like everything had been taken from him. Then he killed him. The guy died in my arms, Anna."

That memory shook her more than she let on. Shoes in hand, she sat on the couch to put them on.

Anna dropped down next to her, concerned. "He attacked you? Did he hurt you?"

"No, I'm fine." Aria dismissed that for her bigger worry. "But that guy won't be for long if I don't do something. I have to find him."

"You need to think this through, Ari," Anna stressed. "You don't even know who he is or where he's staying. How are you going to find him? And if by chance you do, what are you going to tell him?"

Fully dressed, Aria stood. "I don't know yet. But you were right when you said he has nothing to do with this. I can't let him get killed because he happened to star in my sex fantasy tonight."

Before Anna could interject, Aria stopped her. "Oh, don't give me that look. I can't control my subconscious any better than you can. And you can't deny how hot he is. I'm not going to jump into bed with him, but I can't just do nothing."

Aria took a breath and tried to think of what to do. How could she find him and warn him?

"Evan," Aria said as inspiration struck. "He or his cop friends will know what to do."

"Aria, it's the middle of the night. You can't go busting into Evan's house to ask him to find this guy."

"I have to, Anna." Aria took a deep breath and searched for a way to make her sister understand. "I can't let him die because of me. Big Bad has already proven he can get to us. Anywhere, anytime. We know he's coming for us but we can't predict where or when he'll strike. Add in that he can possess people now, and what chance would a perfect stranger have? He doesn't even know he's been targeted. He at least needs to know to watch his back."

"All right," Anna relented. "I get it."

Aria bolted out of the house and headed straight to her brother's place. She pulled into his driveway five minutes later and started up the walk. She could see a dim light coming from inside and vaguely wondered why he was still awake.

When she raised her hand to knock, he pulled the door open.

"Aria, what are you doing here? It's two in the morning. Is everything okay?" Evan looked like he didn't know whether to be surprised or concerned.

"I have to talk to you." She pushed past him and into his house.

He followed her in and closed the door behind them. "What's happened?"

"I need to find that guy—the biker who was there when you were stabbed." She paced the small area in front of the couch.

"Why? I already told you," Evan crossed his arms over his chest, "he had nothing to do with it."

"I know that." Frustration rang clear in her voice. "He's in danger. Our Big Bad is after him."

"What do you mean he's after him?" Evan narrowed his eyes. "He's out for Burke blood. Why would he go after some random guy?"

"It's my fault," Aria admitted. "He got into my head tonight while I was dreaming. He saw the biker there and assumed he was important to me. So he killed him. He died in my arms as an example of how he would take everything from us."

She implored him to understand. "Evan, this is the second time my actions have put this man's life in danger. First on that road in the mountains, and now I've put him on evil's radar. *An' it harm none*, Evan. You know how important our first rule is to me. If he dies and I didn't do anything to stop it, I wouldn't be any less responsible for his death."

~~~

When they'd seen the headlights pull into the driveway, Law and Evan had gone still. He'd sent a questioning glance to Evan but had only gotten a shrug in answer.

Evan had stood and gone silently to the living room window to peer through the crack in the curtains. When his tense shoulders relaxed, Law took a breath.

"It's Aria. Something must be wrong for her to come this late."

Evan rushed back to the kitchen and swept all their notes into a pile. Handing them off to Law, he instructed, "Throw these in that drawer over there, and then go out through the back door. The last thing we need is for her to find you here and see what we're up to."

Law had stashed the files, but there was no way in hell he was leaving. If something had her worried enough to come to her brother in the middle of the night, he wanted to know what it was.

Instead of leaving the way he'd come, Law stepped to the side and pressed up against the wall, hidden from the front of the house. He stood quietly, just out of sight, and listened.

Two things caught his attention right away. Someone was after him, and she'd been dreaming about him.

The first fact didn't concern him too much because, as an undercover cop, that just came with the territory. At any given time, he could die if his true identity were discovered. He accepted that as part of the job.

The more important of the two, as he saw it, was that he occupied her mind. Good to know, since she'd been tormenting his.

Law began to wonder who this person was they were talking about. And why he was after Burke blood, as Evan had put it.
~~~

Another point of interest was the way they spoke of the guy. It was almost as if he weren't human. Law didn't know what to make of that. He'd come across evil in many forms in the last few years, but every last one of them had been of the human variety.

But if Aria and Evan were both worried about this guy being on his ass, the fucker had to be something special. Worth watching his back for, definitely. But more, he felt the need to keep an eye on Aria. He could handle whatever came his way, but he'd be damned if she had to face whatever this was.

Hoping to learn more, he focused his attention back on the conversation going on in the other room.

"Walk me through what happened." He heard Evan's detective voice kick in. "What did he say, what did he do?"

Law heard the slight creak of springs and knew someone had just sat on the far end of the sofa. It must have been Aria, because when he'd sat in that exact spot earlier, it had protested much more loudly.

"I was dreaming the biker and I were on the beach by Anna's house, talking." Law smiled. Aria had just lied to her brother. He'd almost missed it, but there was the smallest of hesitations before the last word. It told him that 'talking' wasn't what they'd been doing on that beach.

A sex dream, huh? Cool.

"Then he changed, and he attacked me."

The smug grin fell from Law's face. *What the hell?*

"When I was finally able to fight him off," she went on, "and looked...really *looked* at him, I knew the biker was no longer there. Someone...some*thing* had taken him over."

He heard Aria take a deep breath. "I was able to get him to tell me why, Evan. He said the Burkes had cost him his family, and now he's going to take everything away from us." There was no humor in the laugh Law heard. "Except for *me*, that is. He plans on keeping me for himself. And then, just to make sure I knew he meant it, he killed him before crawling back into whatever hole he'd come out of."

Law felt his blood pressure rise. *Someone was planning on destroying their family? And taking Aria for his own?* This was sounding more like a nightmare, Law thought, and he couldn't help but wonder why a bad dream would send her running to her brother.

Law might be more worried if this weren't only a figment of her imagination, but he couldn't wrap his head around why they were both taking it so seriously...as though what happened in a dream could really be considered a true threat.

Before he could speculate further, Evan was speaking again. "I could feel him stirring, but I didn't think he would be this strong already. We're still a year out, and he's mastered enough control over someone to try and kill me. And now he's gotten into your mind and attacked you."

Wait. *What?* Law blinked. It sounded like they believed the assault on Evan was tied to Aria's dream. *But how could that be?*

"Now do you see why I need to find him?" Aria pushed.

"And how do you suggest I do that? You know how many people come into town for this particular week."

"I don't know." Her voice was heavy with frustration. "Maybe pass the word through the station? Have everyone keep an eye out for him?"

Yeah, that's just what he fucking needed—every cop in Daytona getting in his way. That would make his job a whole hell of a lot easier. Law shook his head. Evan would know that wouldn't work, and Law just hoped he could dissuade his sister from pursuing that avenue.

"Aria, you know I can't do that. As far as I know, he hasn't done anything wrong. I can't justify the resources it would take for that. Every cop out there is needed where they are. I'll think of something else, though. I promise."

Law took a deep breath and waited for her response.

"We have to protect him, Evan."

He wasn't sure how he felt about her declaration. It had been years since anyone had been concerned with his welfare. And now here was this little bit of a thing, wanting to shield him from whatever was coming.

"We will," Evan assured her. "Just give me a little time to come up with a plan."

Silence followed, and Law wondered what was happening. He was tempted to tip his head around the corner to see for himself and was about to do just that when Evan spoke up again.

"Why don't you take my bed, and I'll bunk on the couch? It's late, and there's no reason for you to drive back to Anna's tonight."

"Thank you," she sighed.

Law heard movement and listened as Aria's light footfalls faded away. Soon after, he heard Evan drawing closer to where he waited. He thought about zipping out the back door but decided against it.

He stood quietly until Evan had passed through the doorway, then shifted his weight to draw his friend's attention.

"What are you still doing here?" Evan demanded in a whisper, his gaze jumping back to the living room to make sure Aria was still out of earshot. "I thought I told you to leave."

"You did," Law replied in the same toneless hush. "I wanted to see what brought your sister out in the middle of the night."

"You, evidently." Evan crossed to the refrigerator and pulled the door open. Reaching in, he grabbed the gallon of water and after taking off the cap, drank straight from the jug.

"Do you guys really believe something from her dream is after me?" Law was sure there was skepticism written on his face, but it was just too hard to believe.

Evan wiped his mouth and set the container back in the

fridge. "Yeah, we do."

"How? That doesn't make sense."

"If you knew my family, it would," Evan answered cryptically.

"Does it have anything to do with the witch thing? I remember you telling me back at the academy about you and your family."

"Yeah, it does."

Before Law could toss him another question, Evan stopped him. "Look, it's late. I'll explain everything, I swear, but can we do it another time?"

Law checked his watch and saw it was almost three a.m. "Yeah. Sure." He glanced back through the doorway. "What are you going to tell her about me?"

"As little as possible," Evan answered. "This asshat's no joke, though, so watch your back."

"Always," Law assured him as he left.

Four blocks later, his ride was roaring to life, and he took off down the road.

6

When Aria awoke the following morning, she found herself alone in the house. Evan had already left for work. As she poured a cup of coffee, she prayed he'd find something that would lead them to the man who seemed determined to always pop up in her life.

In the meantime, she had some new information to hunt down. She called Anna and Ethan and told them to meet her at their parents' house. With the number of books and journals they had to go through, she'd need all the help she could get.

Aria arrived first and explained the situation to her mom.

"Have you ever seen any reference to a family being taken in and protected?" Aria asked her.

"Not that I recall." Mary's brow furrowed as she tried to remember. "I've been through all those books so many times, I could almost recite them from memory. But then again, I wasn't specifically looking for anything about a woman and her children."

"You should have heard the way he was talking about them." Aria shook her head. "Like they were his property. Fleeing to the protection of a coven of witches was probably their only option. I just hope there's a record of the incident somewhere."

"Well, we'll know soon enough." Mary eyed her with speculation. "But before we get into that, tell me more about this guy. The one he possessed and killed."

"There's really nothing to tell." Aria looked down at where her hands were clasped in her lap. "He had the misfortune of starring in my dream, and it put him on this nut-job's radar. I couldn't live with myself if I knew I got him killed. That's why I asked Evan to try and find him. I just hope we do before it's too late."

When Mary didn't respond, Aria brought her gaze up to find her mother studying her. "You have feelings for this man."

It wasn't a question.

"What? No," Aria denied. "Sure, he's handsome in a rough-and-rugged sort of way. And I obviously like the look of him, considering I was dreaming of beach-sex with him. But do I plan on pursuing him? No way. He is *so* not my type."

Aria had the feeling that her mom wanted to say something more, but at that moment, Anna and Ethan strolled in.

After that, the four of them were busy scouring dozens of old journals.

Ethan called for their attention an hour later. "Hey, listen to this. It's pretty vague, but it could have something to do with what we're looking for."

The three women stopped and looked over at him.

"'Isabel came today for her monthly herbal. It's not right what she's doing—what we're helping her to do—but no one can blame her for not wanting to bring more children into that household. Her horrible situation was never more evident than it was today. The proof of his evil was all over her face and body; she could barely lift and carry her little ones. We begged her to save herself and her children, but she is too scared. I only hope that one day she will come to us for the help she so desperately needs, to get away from that monster.'"

"When was that?" Mary set the book aside she'd been reading.

With his finger still in the page he'd just read, Ethan flipped to the front. "August, 1564."

"That has to be it." Aria's heart sped up. "Sometime after

this entry, she must have finally had enough and gone to them for help."

"Let's not get ahead of ourselves," Mary cautioned. "Though this does sound like it fits, we need to make sure. Those times were tough, and I'm sure it wasn't uncommon for men to be abusive back then. Ethan, you finish going through that journal. See if there's anything else, and we'll continue with these." She gestured to the books in front of her and her daughters.

Aria thought it was pointless to carry on with anything other than the one Ethan had. Something else was bound to be in there.

In her irritation, she almost missed what was on the page in front of her. It wasn't until the words *they're gone* jumped out at her that she took a closer look. Aria began reading again.

'We've done it. They're gone. He'll never find them. Isabel and her babies are safe. News came to us that when he realized they were out of his reach, he raged throughout the settlement, threatening great bodily harm to any and all who'd helped them to flee. We are not overly worried. Edrick Noor is no match for Burke witches.'

"I found it." Aria looked up, stunned. "I know his name."

Three sets of eyes flew to her, and she read the passage out loud. "It's dated April of 1565. She stayed with him for another eight months. Isabel. That *was* her in the first mention that Ethan found."

"How much worse did her life get to finally make her leave him?" Anna's soft, caring nature came through. "I wonder if he found out that she'd been preventing further pregnancies?"

"It's impossible to tell," Mary said. "I think the more important question here is, if our ancestors considered him nothing to worry about, how then, was he able to gather power and plague them for over a hundred and sixty years? By the time they finally trapped him, he'd become unstoppable and had already killed several Burke witches in his revenge."

"Yes, that *would* be a nice piece of information to have," Ethan agreed dryly.

"There has to be more here." Aria looked around at all the books. "We have to keep searching. But at least we know to focus on 1565 and later." She picked up the journal again at the same time her cell phone rang.

A glance at the screen, and she saw it was her brother. She hurried to answer. "Evan?"

"Yeah, I think I have a lead on our guy. He's a member of a hard-core motorcycle club out of Chicago."

"Where are they staying?"

"I have an idea, but I'm not sharing that information with you," he told her. "I'll handle it. I don't want you going anywhere near them."

Her brows furrowed as she turned away from the others. "Evan, you can't—"

"Yes. I can," he interrupted firmly.

Lowering her voice, she played her ace. "How's the side?"

After the efforts he had taken to hide his injury from their mother, Aria knew this was a low blow. But she wasn't going to let him shut her out of this.

He understood her meaning immediately. "You wouldn't."

"No?" Sugar dripped from her tone before she firmed it into steel. "Where?"

She heard a great sigh on the other end of the line. "They rented out the Whitaker place off of 95. But you steer clear of this, Aria. I mean it. This is a rough bunch of thugs, and they're dangerous. Just let me take care of it."

She hung up and laid the phone on the table.

"He found him?" Anna asked.

Aria nodded. "He rides with a club out of Chicago, and they're staying in a house outside of town."

"You're not really thinking about going out there, are you?" Ethan asked before shaking his head. "Of course you are. Who am I talking to here?"

"I don't like the idea of you walking into the middle of a biker gang's den alone," Mary protested. "You should wait for Evan."

Aria hated to see the anxious look on her mother's face, and she knew it would ease her mind if Evan were there with her.

"Okay, Mom," she conceded. "I'll call him on the way and have him meet me there."

Aria ran out of the house and jumped into her car. She called Evan as she was pulling out of the driveway.

"I'm headed to the Whitaker house now. Meet me there."

"I can't, Aria. I'm headed into court to testify on another case. Give me an hour—two tops."

"He may not have an hour, Evan." Aria mentally ran through her options. "Screw it. I'm going anyway."

"Damn it, Ari." She figured he must already be in the courthouse, because he didn't shout at her as she'd expected. In an adamant but hushed tone, he added, "Do *not* go out there without me."

"Sorry, Evan. I have to do this." Aria hung up before her brother could argue further.

Twenty minutes later, she found the road leading back into the woods where the Whitaker house was located.

She drove slowly, not sure of what to expect when she reached the end. As she pulled into the clearing, there were dozens of people sitting around in lawn chairs and at picnic tables. The men were all dressed in jeans and leather. The women, on the other hand, wore next to nothing.

Parking next to some bikes, Aria shut off her car and took a fortifying breath. She had no idea how she was going to find him in this crowd of people. She couldn't even ask for him by name.

But then it didn't matter, because she saw him. At the same time he saw her.

He was on the covered porch, sitting on the rail with a beer bottle in his hand. He, like all the others, had turned to see who'd arrived. She knew the instant he recognized her. His eyes registered surprise and then consternation before he lifted from the rail and straightened.

Aria got out of the car as he slowly set his bottle where his ass had been and stepped down into the yard. He made his way towards her to the sounds of cat-calls and whistles.

One voice rang out above all the others. "Go get her, Law!"

He seemed to ignore them as he approached her. He didn't stop until he had her crowded back against the hot door of her car.

"Get your little ass back in that car and get out of here. *Now*." His words were pushed through a tightly-clenched jaw, and his body language was aggressive and intimidating.

Aria swallowed back her nerves, and his gaze dropped to the movement in her throat. She shivered despite the warmth of the day.

"Law?" Her voice was raw and breathy. "Your name is Law?"

He gave a short, stiff nod to acknowledge her question. "You shouldn't be here, Pixie. You have to go."

The heat from his body competed with the metal at her back. "I had to find you."

Aria was beginning to think this hadn't been such a smart idea. But it had nothing at all to do with the gang of bikers across the yard. She felt a larger and more dangerous threat emanating from the man towering over her.

"Oh, yeah?" He stepped even closer. "And why would you risk your pretty little hide to do that?"

Aria's brain short-circuited at his words and nearness. She almost forgot why she was there. "To, ah, warn you."

"About what?"

Aria glanced to the side at the many pairs of eyes watching them. "Can we go somewhere to talk?"

Law stared at her for several moments before he nodded. "Yeah. Sure. Meet me at the end of the drive. I'll follow you out."

He finally backed away, and his sudden absence left Aria feeling like something had been stripped from her. She dragged air into her lungs as he headed back up to the porch. She saw him speak to one of the men there and then cross to where the motorcycles were parked.

She climbed in behind the wheel, started the car, and reversed to turn around. When she reached the main road, she stopped and waited. It was only a few seconds before she heard the sound of loud pipes coming up behind her.

Aria drove for a few miles until she found a shaded roadside park. There was a group of people at one of the tables. This would be perfect. She wanted privacy for this conversation, but she didn't want to be completely alone with him.

She stopped, turned the ignition off, and got out. As she made her way to a wooden bench, she heard him pull in and follow. She still didn't know how she was going to make him understand, but she had to try. When they were both seated, she began.

"This is going to sound crazy," she looked up into Law's chocolate-brown eyes, "but you need to listen to me."

He'd sat sideways on the bench. His right leg was curled under him, and his arm stretched out along the top edge, his hand resting just behind her shoulder.

"Okay."

"You're in danger. Someone is going to try to kill you."

His expression didn't change at all. He just sat there, looking intently at her.

"Did you hear me?"

"I did. But you haven't told me anything I don't already know."

"You know?" She wondered if Evan had spoken with him

already.

"Cops, rival gangs, outlaws. There's always someone on my tail."

"That's not what I meant."

"Well then, what exactly are we talking about?"

"I had a dream," she started, but he cut her off.

"About *me*?" He grinned at her, and a mischievous gleam lit his eyes. "Awe, Pixie. I didn't know you still thought of me."

Aria gritted her teeth. "I *don't*." She forcefully unclenched her jaw and tried a different tack. "Someone from my past saw us together. He warned me that he's going to kill you just to hurt me."

He tilted his head slightly, and his intense brown eyes drilled into her icy-blue ones. "And would it?"

Aria stood and crossed her arms over her chest in irritation. "Look. I don't want to see you get hurt. Just be watchful. He will…manipulate anyone he can to get to you."

Law rose, and Aria was again aware of his size. She backed off a few more steps. "I always keep my eyes open for trouble."

He kept advancing, and she continued to retreat, until she was abruptly brought up short by a solid object at her back. When her hands came down to grasp what it was, she felt the rough bark of a tree. Aria's gaze shot around, and she realized that all the people who'd been there before had gone.

She was totally alone with him in the deep shadows of the picnic area, her body trapped between his massive form and the thick oak behind her. Try as she might, she couldn't control the quiver of anticipation that racked her body.

As his head slowly descended towards hers, she saw that his pupils were dilated and his gaze smoldered. God help her, Aria could do nothing to stop what was about to happen. She was utterly incapable of moving as she waited for that first touch of his lips to hers. She knew it was madness to let this stranger kiss her, but she just didn't care. She was desperate to find out if his mouth felt as incredible in real life as it had in her dream.

Law didn't just lay his lips to hers; he possessed them and took them as his due. He demanded a response from her, and she willingly gave it. The angle of the kiss changed as they tried to take all they could from each other.

Aria's hands trailed up his muscled chest to smooth over his shoulders and wrap around his neck. She heard a low growl rumble in his chest as the action plastered her body against his. Before she realized his intent, his hands skimmed down her sides and hips to grab hold of her ass and lift her to better align their mouths.

She tightened her arms around him and tangled her hands in his hair as he held her aloft effortlessly and pinned her against the tree. Automatically and without thought, she wrapped her legs around his waist. She was completely lost to everything but the kiss until his hands, now free of holding her slight weight, fisted tightly in her hair.

Their entangled limbs and the pull on her scalp triggered something in the back of her mind. A frigid wisp of familiarity washed over her and stole the breath from her lungs. Aria's subconscious reacted to the pain and shock of the dream she'd tried so hard to repress, and dropped her right into the middle of a heaping pool of terror. She was suddenly, wildly, fighting to get out of his grasp.

"No, no, no! Let me go! Get away from me!"

~~~

Law heard the stark fear in her voice and instantly backed off. It had been stupid to give in to his overwhelming needs in the first place. But she'd just been too damned tempting, standing there looking up at him.

Still, he'd had no right. He shouldn't have touched her. And now that he'd scared her with his caveman tactics, he felt like
~~~

a total ass.

He held his hands up to show her he meant her no harm. "It's okay, Pixie. You're all right. I won't hurt you."

She was shaking her head and trying to catch her breath. "Don't touch me."

"I won't," he promised.

Now that there was space between them, she seemed to settle somewhat. She sucked in a big gulp of air and blew it out, making an effort to try and calm herself. Her delicate hand came up to push her hair back from her face, and he took note of how it trembled.

"It's not you." She wouldn't look at him as she needlessly adjusted her clothing. "I just...I, ah...never mind. I've gotta go."

Suddenly it hit him. That fucking nightmare. He didn't know exactly what had happened in that dreamscape, but from the little she'd told Evan, it wasn't hard to guess what direction the attack had taken. And the monster had worn Law's own face and body.

It was a wonder she'd even let him get close to her after that. And then he'd pawed at her up against a goddamned tree. Of *course* it triggered a horrifying memory and had her struggling to get away from him.

While Law was cursing himself for his stupidity, Aria sidestepped him. "Just be careful, please." She didn't look back as she all but ran to her car and tore out of the parking lot.

Law walked to his bike and straddled the seat. Seeing her panic and fear had shredded something inside him. And knowing he was the reason for it killed him. It didn't matter that he hadn't actually been the one to hurt her—in her mind, she saw him as the one who'd assaulted her in the worst possible way a woman could be.

Law looked down at his clenched fists. How he'd love to get his hands on that sick son of a bitch. A lot of Law's morals rode a shaky line because of what he had to do in his line of work, but one hard and fast rule never wavered. Women and children were not to be harmed.

He had no patience for anyone who victimized those smaller and weaker, and he would fight to the death to protect them. What was happening with Aria was just that much more frustrating because, if what she and her brother believed were true, there was nothing he could do about it.

How do you fight something like that?

Taking a steadying breath, he pushed the rage aside. Once he could think clearly again, another, more worrisome problem took hold of him. His hands, which had only moments ago shaken with anger, now tingled with the remembered feel of soft, pliant skin. His senses lingered over how sweet she had tasted, and his body was once again on fire with wanting her, his mind reeling with a desire to hold her again.

With an iron will, he shoved that away as well. It didn't matter what he, or his body, wanted. This could never happen again.

Resigned, Law revved his bike and headed back to the house. As it turned out, it was a good thing he'd told Kane that little lie before he'd left. The guys all gave him shit about having a chick come back for seconds, but he just laughed it off. At least his cover was still intact.

He was able to keep his mind on MC business, and the rest of the afternoon passed without incident. It wasn't until he went to bed that the torture resumed.

He dreamed of her. Hot, wet, erotic dreams that had him wrenching awake, hard and aching.

Law rolled to sit on the edge of the bed, naked. He spent several minutes trying to breathe away the need clawing at him. His whole body was covered in a fine layer of sweat, and his cock was so full and ready to thrust into Aria's silky heat that it twitched in anticipation.

Willing it away wasn't working, so he slowly rose to his feet. To cover the state of his body, he grabbed the towel he'd used after his shower earlier and made his way down the hall to the bathroom.

Reaching in, he cranked on the taps. He stepped in before the water came up to temperature and let the cool rain rinse his heated body. But no amount of cold water was going to ease his craving for her. Law closed his eyes and braced his left hand on the tile wall in front of him. The other wrapped tightly around his throbbing shaft and squeezed.

Law cursed the day he'd ever laid eyes on her, because he knew this wouldn't be the last time she starred in his fantasy as he jacked-off in the shower.

A few minutes later, towel again riding low on his hips, Law emerged from the bathroom. This early, the rest of the house was still asleep. Or it should have been. He frowned as movement drew his attention. Someone had just slipped into his room.

His bare feet silent on the carpeted floor, he made his way back to his doorway and peered into the dark room. He could just make out JD creeping toward his bed.

What the fuck? JD wasn't his fan on a good day, so why the hell was he even in here?

Coming into the MC, it hadn't taken long for Law to figure out that JD was one sadistic motherfucker. One that liked to hurt young girls. The younger, the better.

Law had caught him one night and beaten him to within an inch of his life. Just before he lost consciousness, Law had warned him if he ever saw him even look at another girl, he'd finish the job and kill him.

Kane knew something had gone down between them, but neither had divulged any details. And since then, they'd only dealt with each other when necessary.

So his being here now made no sense.

Law strode into the room and flipped the light on. "JD. What the fuck are you doing in here?"

As soon as the other man turned, Law knew something wasn't right. The biggest clue was the huge-ass knife in his hand. But aside from that, there was something...*off* about him.

JD didn't answer but just grinned manically as he advanced toward him. There was an unnatural glint in his eyes. Evil was the only way Law could think to describe it.

Until this very moment, he hadn't completely believed Aria's warning. But now, here it was, staring him in the face.

"You're not JD. You're the sick fuck who tried to hurt Aria."

"Oh, I'm not done with her yet." The thing in JD grinned. "I got a sweet taste of that little witch, and I plan on taking more."

"By lying and hiding behind someone else's face?" Law goaded him while watching him carefully. "Just like you're doing now? What's the matter—too much of a pussy to face anyone as yourself? Have to hijack other people's bodies to get it done? That's just sad, dude."

JD took a swipe at Law with the lethal blade, but he jumped out of the way just in time.

"But effective," JD returned as he circled Law. "Why waste my precious energy when I can simply use his own hate for you? And that hate is a thing of beauty." The voice coming out of JD was his own, but the words came from the impostor. "It made it so easy to slip in and give him a little push. He wants you dead as badly as I do."

"As much as I want to rip you apart for what you did to Aria, I'll have to bide my time until you're man enough to stand up to me on your own." Law side-stepped to keep out of reach of another strike.

"Just out of curiosity, what's the plan here? Kill me and then what? You think Aria will come running? I don't think so."

"I don't care if she comes willingly or not. It's exciting when they fight back." He sneered obscenely. "Your death will serve as a lesson that I will not be denied. I will have my revenge, and I will have all I desire. And I will take it all from those Burke witches."

It struck out again and this time, sliced a line down Law's forearm.

"Yeah, but that's where we run into a problem. A couple of those Burkes are friends of mine," Law taunted as he unwound the towel from his waist and wrapped it around his bleeding arm. Fighting naked probably wasn't the best idea, but he didn't have any other alternatives.

"You dare to defy me? I will disembowel you. And enjoy it." JD roared and the battle was on.

Law received a few more cuts, but he also got in a couple of good shots. As much as he hated it, he had to temper his urge to just kill the bastard. JD may be an idiot, but he wasn't responsible for his actions right now. And even in doing that, JD ended up with a broken nose, and his cheek was bleeding and sported a nice-sized bruise.

JD was launching another attack when a commotion filled the doorway. The crashing and carnage of the fight had roused the rest of the house. Kane and several others had rushed to investigate.

What they saw was a naked and bleeding Law, in a death match with a knife-wielding JD. Kane was the first to react.

"What the hell is going on here?" he bellowed.

Law didn't dare take his focus from JD, and he saw the moment when the other let him go. JD stood dazed for a moment, and then looked down at the weapon in his hand and the blood smeared on Law's body.

The blade clattered to the floor as he looked around frantically. "What's happening?"

"That's what I'd like to fucking know." Kane stepped into

the room and flashed a look at Law. "Get some pants on, for Christ's sake."

Snickers came from the rest of the crowd standing in the hall, but the three in the bedroom weren't laughing.

"All right, show's over," Kane told them before closing the door in their faces. When he turned back to Law, now wearing sweat pants, and JD, still looking confused, he crossed his arms over his chest.

"Someone start explaining."

"I...I don't know how I got here," JD stuttered. "The last thing I remember was going to bed."

Law knew the answer, but there was no way anyone would believe what had really gone down. So, thinking quickly, he came up with the most plausible excuse. "I think JD was sleepwalking or something. He didn't even know where he was. I think my room just happened to be the first he came to."

"Why was he trying to butcher you with that knife?" Kane wanted to know.

Law shrugged. "Don't know. Whatever dream he was having, he must have thought he needed it."

Kane and JD both thought it over and, evidently, neither could come up with a better explanation.

"JD, get your ass back to bed. I'll have Bear keep an eye on you. Make sure you stay put."

JD left without saying a word. Law didn't know if he'd been aware at all of being possessed, but if he had, he wasn't admitting it.

Once he was gone, Kane crossed to check Law's injuries. "JD's pretty good with that knife. You must have been quick on your feet to only suffer these few cuts. You're lucky." Kane studied him carefully. "I know you and he have some bad blood between you. Does this have anything to do with that?"

Law shook his head. "No, I don't think so. Like I said, I'm not sure he even knew what he was doing."

A few minutes later, Kane left and closed the door behind him.

Law sank down on the edge of the bed, scrubbed his hands over his face, and swore when the cut across his ribs pulled.

"Son of a bitch."

How the hell do you fight against something like this? Law had no doubt he could hold his own under normal circumstances, but this was a long way from normal. What would happen the next time this asshole possessed someone? What if it were an innocent woman or a cop? Someone he couldn't, *wouldn't*, be able to beat down like he had JD?

He and Evan were going to have to sit down and have a really long chat. Very soon.

But even more important than his own skin, he had to know how to protect Aria. This bastard had its sights set on her, and Law couldn't let that stand. It didn't matter that he wouldn't act on his own desires. He couldn't stomach the thought of that bastard getting hold of her again.

Meeting the beautiful blonde had thrown a huge wrench into his carefully-crafted existence. Up to this point in his life, he'd never had an emotional conflict like this. When his mind should have been on shutting down the MC and the syndicate supplying them, his thoughts were most often filled with her.

How she'd felt under his hands, how she'd tasted, and the sounds she'd made when he'd kissed her. It was imperative that he not let those feelings interfere with the way he did his job. He'd spent too many years getting to where he was to screw it all up now.

As he sat at the head of the bed with pillows propped behind him, Law thought of all the ways this could go sideways and backfire.

What the fuck. Just another day at the office.

7

Aria's night wasn't turning out to be very peaceful either. She'd dozed on and off, but her mind wouldn't settle enough to let her rest. She was mortified at the way she'd acted.

First she runs him off the road and accuses him of stabbing her brother. Then she tracks him down to tell him someone is out to kill him. In the next minute, she loses her mind and kisses him with more passion than she'd ever kissed anyone. And before he can even blink, she wigs out on him and runs away.

Yeah, he probably thinks I'm a total nutcase.

Motion in the doorway drew her attention. When she looked up, Anna was standing there. She came in and sat beside her. "Talk to me."

It all came rushing out. All of her fears and confusion. When she finally wound down, Anna drew her in and hugged her consolingly.

"I knew there was more to that damned dream." Anna drew back to look deep into her eyes. "Why didn't you tell me this before now? You shouldn't have to go through something like that alone."

"I thought if I ignored it, I could pretend it didn't happen," Aria told her. "It was only a dream. It shouldn't have affected me so much."

"He may not have laid hands on your physical body, but

the result is still the same. Call it what it was—he sexually assaulted you, Aria. And if you hadn't fought him off, he probably would have raped you. Just because it all took place in your mind, doesn't make it any less real or traumatic."

Tears were spilling down Aria's cheeks. "I just wanted to forget it happened."

Anna ran a comforting hand down her hair. "I know, but you need to acknowledge it and deal with it."

"What? You mean freaking out when someone kisses me isn't considered dealing with things?" Aria sent her a small, watery grin.

"Are you absolutely sure that Law's not involved in this? Because that sounded like more than a simple kiss to me," Anna asked. "I'd hate to see you hurt."

"I'm positive, Anna. He's not a part of Noor's plan."

"So, a biker huh?" Anna gave her a tentative smile. "Not the type I thought you'd go for."

Aria pushed her hair out of her face and leaned back against the headboard. "Yeah, me either. That first night on the road, I thought he was a jerk. A demanding, surly, overbearing dick, actually." She grinned up at her sister.

"And that's changed now?" Anna asked.

"No, not really," Aria laughed. "But when I'm with him, I forget all that."

"Do you want him?"

"There're too many obstacles to even consider that option."

"That's not an answer."

"But it's still true. Aside from the fact that we have all the prophecy crap hanging over our heads, he's a member of a biker gang that Evan has told me *repeatedly* to steer clear of. Out of Chicago, no less. That's not exactly down the street. And even if, by some chance, we got past all of that, who can forget how I flipped out on him the last time?"

Anna pinned her with a look Aria couldn't escape. "Do. You.

Want. Him?"

She fought it until she just couldn't hold it in anymore. On a blast of breath, she admitted to her sister what she hadn't even been able to admit to herself.

"God, yes."

Anna grinned at her emphatic answer. "So, what are you going to do about it?"

"Nothing." She pushed on when Anna would have spoken. "For all the reasons I just listed. My attention needs to be on Noor, and keeping my visions of all of your deaths from coming true."

"So you're just going to sacrifice something that could make you happy?"

"Maybe I'm meant to," Aria speculated sadly. "Maybe this is the sacrifice I'm destined to make in order to stop this monster."

"No." Anna adamantly shook her head. "I don't believe that. I won't. Turning away from your feelings to end him is no better than letting him kill us. We're meant to stop him *so that* we can go on and have meaningful lives."

Aria sighed. "I don't know what the answer is. All I know is that he occupies way too much of my mind, when I've got bigger priorities to worry about. It feels selfish of me to pursue anything with him, when we've already got so much going on."

"I still think you're wrong," Anna insisted.

They talked until Anna had to get ready to go train with her mystery man. From there she'd go straight to the elementary school where she taught. So that meant Aria had a few hours to herself. She decided to use that time to go to her parents' and look for more information on Edrick Noor.

She dove right in, but after hours of scouring notebooks and journals, she found nothing. It was like after his tantrum when his family had left, he'd dropped out of sight. No other mention was made of him until the night of the battle when he'd been imprisoned.

Now what?

The more Aria thought about it, the more she felt that knowing where his power had come from might prove to be the biggest piece of the puzzle.

But how to find that out? He was the only one who knew.

Aria began to wonder if she might be able to get it right from the horse's mouth. What if she lured him in somehow? Got him talking? Maybe he'd let something slip, like last time.

Did she really want to be that close to him again, though? *Hell no.* It gave her the willies just thinking about it. But if she could get the information they needed, wouldn't it be worth it?

She'd have to give that further thought. In the meantime, she was starving. Gathering her things, she set out to go to one of her favorite restaurants. It was a little place out on A1A that specialized in wings and shrimp.

When she pulled in, the front lot was full of bikes, so she parked on the side. This place was always busy, and when Bike Week rolled around, it was even more so. But the food was amazing, and she would wait however long it took.

Walking in, she lucked out and found an empty stool at the bar.

After ordering, Aria chatted with the owner, the father of a school friend. When he was called away, Aria took a sip of her iced tea and watched one of the many TV's mounted around the room. She'd just set her glass back on the smooth wood surface when she got that tingling feeling on the back of her neck. Someone was watching her.

There was no mirror over the bar, so she had to turn in her seat to scan the front of the restaurant. Nothing there drew her notice, so she slowly spun the other way and looked into the back section.

There, sitting at a large table, was Law with five of his friends. His deep brown eyes were glued on her as he sat slouched in his seat. He slowly lifted his bottle of beer, set it against his full lips, and tipped it up. All the while, his heated stare bore into her.

Aria was held in his gaze until a dark…malevolent feeling overtook her. Sliding her focus to the left, she caught one of the other bikers glaring at her.

She was shocked at the level of hate she felt radiating from him. Before she could examine it further, her food was brought out, drawing her attention. When she glanced back a few minutes later, both were involved in other conversations.

So conscious of the fact that Law was there, watching her, Aria wasn't able to fully enjoy her meal. She knew when he'd focus his attention on her again by a tingly, heart-racing feeling. She was helpless but to remember the roadside park and how he'd made her feel. And then she'd recall how she'd lost it, and embarrassment would move in. She was almost to the point of leaving when she heard his deep voice.

"You go on. I gotta hit the head."

She held herself still as, one by one, his crew walked past where she sat. The one who'd watched her so maliciously was the last to approach. As he drew even with her, she could feel his eyes drilling into her.

Aria turned her head and met his look with one of her own. His glower changed to a smirk as he continued silently out the door. She was still trying to figure out what his problem was when she felt *his* presence behind her.

With her pulse pounding, she swiveled her stool around and found herself face to face with Law. He was standing so close, the heat from his body warmed her. His intense gaze held hers for several beats before drifting away as he turned to walk past.

Without thought, Aria moved her left hand just enough to brush lightly over his arm. Despite all her warnings to herself, the need to touch him, to feel his skin, was more than she could withstand. As her fingers grazed over his forearm, she felt something she hadn't expected. Startled, her gaze dropped to see what her soft stroke had discovered.

Starting at his elbow, a bright red line bisected his muscled arm. It cut through the intricately-designed tattoo and ended a few inches above his wrist.

"What happened?" This wasn't there yesterday. She would have remembered. Aria felt compelled to run her hands over the wound. She didn't have much in the way of healing, but used what little she had to speed the process.

He didn't speak until she looked up at him.

"Sometimes working on a bike can be hazardous. Lots of edges and angles to catch the unaware."

"Oh," she murmured. "I'm sorry."

"No big." He shifted his weight. "I'd better go."

The muscle under her hand flexed, her cue to turn him loose. Slowly she released her grip. His intent stare had returned, lingering on her eyes before, unhurriedly, sliding down to her lips.

The bottom dropped out of her stomach, and her heart kicked heavily in her chest, fully aware that he was remembering their kiss. But before she could say or do anything, his lids dropped to sever the connection, and he was gone.

Why did he have such an overwhelming effect on her? No man had ever inspired these kinds of feelings. Granted, there hadn't been many, but she was by no means a virgin. What was it about Law that compelled her to be near him, to touch him, and be touched by him?

Is that how it was with her parents? That driving need to be close and connect? She'd always dreamed of having a relationship like theirs. Was this what they felt?

Why did it have to be with this man, though? And why right now? She had more on her plate than she could handle. The fate of her loved ones depended on her finding a way to stop what she saw in her visions.

All of her focus needed to be on discovering those answers.

Not on some outlaw biker with a dark, smoldering stare and ripped, hard body.

Frustrated with herself, Aria paid her bill and left.

She spent the rest of the day at the library searching old records, looking for any sign of Edrick Noor. By the time it was closing, she was no closer to finding him than when she'd arrived. It was looking more and more as if she'd have to try to lure him out somehow.

As she crossed the parking lot to her car in the fading light, she went over different scenarios in her mind. Distracted, she didn't see the dark form coming for her until it was too late. A strong, vice-like grip wound around her waist, pinning her arms against her sides as another clamped over her mouth, preventing the scream that tried to escape.

She felt herself being carried off into the darker shadows at the edge of the lot. Her slight build made it impossible for her to fight off her attacker. But what she lacked in physical strength, she more than made up for with her heritage.

Gathering the air around her, she used it to pelt him with sticks and debris off the ground. The cyclone she created tore at his hair and clothes, the force of it nearly knocking him off his feet.

When his grip loosened, Aria took her chance and spun out of his grasp. She was turning to lay into him when a much larger figure came barreling at him. They went down in a heap of black and leather.

Seeing her attacker's face for the first time, Aria recognized him. It was the man who had watched her with such hatred earlier in the day. She also knew the man who was currently pounding a large fist into his face. Law had come out of nowhere just in time.

When the other biker was an unconscious heap on the ground, Law shoved himself up and stood over him. The killing rage Aria had seen in him slowly faded, and he turned to her.

"You okay?"

"Yeah, I'm fine. How did you know?"

"I saw the way he was watching you. I thought it a good idea to keep an eye on him."

"Isn't he a friend of yours?"

He laughed humorlessly. "Not by a long shot. We've had issues before."

"But why did he come after me?"

Law looked down at the man lying at his feet, and she could see he was weighing how much to tell her.

"Law. He attacked me. I think I have a right to know."

"Yeah, you do," his voice rumbled. "Just not here." He looked over at her. "Give me an hour, and then meet me where we talked before."

"What about him?" Aria motioned to the man on the ground.

"Don't worry. I'll take care of him." Law speared the other man with a lethal look.

Aria told herself she didn't really want to know what Law had meant by that. She gave him one last look and a nod before she got into her car and drove away.

Exactly an hour later, when she pulled into the deserted roadside park, he was there waiting for her. In the darkness, she could just make out his large build sitting on top of one of the picnic tables at the back of the lot. Just beyond him was a dense wooded area.

He never took his eyes off of her as she made her way to him. Aria stopped a few feet away and folded her arms over her middle.

Being here brought back conflicting memories. On one hand, this is where he'd kissed the sense out of her, but on the other, it was also where she'd completely flipped out. Embarrassment warred with the need to taste him again.

"So, what's going on?" she asked him, hoping he didn't bring up the last time they'd been here.

He drew in a slow breath and blew it out. "I wasn't honest with you earlier." He looked down at the cut on his arm. "This isn't from my bike. JD, the guy who attacked you, came at me too."

Aria's brows came together in confusion. "Why?"

"I think it has something to do with what you told me. That guy from your past must have gotten to him. But it was weird. He almost didn't seem to be in control when he tried to slice me up."

Oh, God. He had no idea just how close he was to the truth. Aria shuddered at the thought of what could have happened.

"That *is* strange," she said vaguely. "How badly were you hurt?"

"A few cuts." She saw his hand go to his side and knew he'd suffered more injuries than just the one on his arm.

"I'm so sorry." Aria felt horrible that she'd brought this trouble down on him. "We're trying to find a way to draw him out and stop him, but he's covered his tracks too well."

"We?"

"My family." Aria considered how much she could tell him without sounding crazy. "He's hated us for...a long time."

"Why?"

"Many years ago, his wife left him and took their children. My family helped them to disappear, and now he wants revenge."

"He sounds like an epic ass. I hope they're well away from him."

Aria thought of the centuries that had passed and had to fight back a grin. "Oh, they are. He can't hurt them anymore."

"But now he's after you and your family."

"Yeah."

He slid off the table and closed the distance between them. When he was standing inches from her, she tipped her head back and took in his rugged features.

"What can I do to help?" He reached out and laid his hands

on her hips.

"Nothing. Just watch yourself. I hate that he's focused on you because of me." Aria's hands itched to mold themselves to his hard planes, but she held them tightly against her body. She needed to back away before she lost the battle raging inside of her.

They drank in the sight of each other for a few moments.

"Why can't I forget you?" Law asked in a low, sexy, frustrated tone. "How have you gotten so far into my system that I can't get you out?"

"Law…" Aria fought the pull to edge closer to him. "We can't…I can't."

"I'm sorry I scared you last time." His hand came up, and one finger traced the outline of her lower lip. "I would die before I ever hurt you, Pixie."

"I know," she assured him. "I'm not afraid of you, Law."

His eyes darkened to almost black. "I pray to God that's true."

He abruptly pulled her into his embrace and took her mouth in a kiss that blasted through her last bit of resistance. Her body went up in flames when he pressed the hard edge of his arousal against her stomach. Aria's head went light at the thought of what it would feel like to have him inside her.

She was barely aware that he pulled her with him as he backed up the few steps to the picnic table. He released her mouth as he sat on the bench, bringing his face even with her torso. When he spread his knees wide, she stepped into him and clasped his head in her hands.

Her fingers tunneled through his thick brown hair at the same time his came up to her breasts. As he squeezed and molded her ripe mounds, his mouth found her tight nipple through the cotton of her shirt.

Aria gasped as an answering need shot straight to her center. She moaned and arched her back, offering him more, her legs threatening to buckle at the sensation.

"Oh, God," Aria panted. She wanted...needed to touch him. Running her hands down his chest, then up and over his shoulders, she pushed his leather vest off. It landed under the table with a light sound. With that gone, she bent and gripped the hem of his shirt and tore it over his head.

With no more barriers, she glided her hands over every inch of skin she could reach. She caressed the tattoos that climbed up his arms and over his wide shoulders, tracing each pattern and following where they led. He groaned heavily in his chest in response, and she continued her wandering caress.

Well before she was finished, he stood. Taking her waist in his large hands he lifted her, turned, walked to the end of the table, and set her on the rough wooden surface. Raising his hands to her face, he held her for his possession.

Law's tongue swept across her lips and dipped in to tantalize and tease as he kissed her until her brain fuzzed out. To steady herself, Aria clutched at his hips where his pants rode low. She felt the muscles flex under her touch. Heady with the knowledge that she affected him the same way he did her, she pushed her fingers into the waistband of his jeans and slid them around to the front where his erection was straining to emerge.

A quick flick had the button on his fly open. When she grasped the metal tab of the zipper, his hands found hers and stopped them. He pulled them up, laid them flat against his chest, and held them there.

His breathing was ragged and his tone full of remorse. "If you do that, I'll have you naked and stretched out on this table before you can blink."

Aria shivered at the image of that. He saw her response and tipped his head back, inhaling deeply as if trying to gain control.

His eyes still burned hot when he brought his gaze back to her face. He looked deep into her eyes as he held her hands under his. "I want you to the point that I'll go crazy if I don't have you soon. You've become my obsession, little Pixie...ever since that night on the highway."

Her heart thudded heavily in her chest, her feelings echoing his.

"But there are just *so* many complications right now," he continued before she could respond. "Why did this have to happen now? Why couldn't I have met you in a few weeks?"

"A few weeks wouldn't matter either," Aria told him, finally finding the will to push him aside so she could slide off the table. "And in a year's time, who knows where we'll be." Until her twenty-fifth birthday came and went, she couldn't let herself be distracted from the destiny fate had dealt her. "We can't let this happen again. Like you said, there are too many things in the way."

She forced her feet to carry her farther away from him. The sight of him standing there, bare-chested with his jeans unfastened, tempted her as nothing else ever had. His washboard abs and broad, muscled chest gleamed in the moonlight. The intricate black ink-work on his arms and shoulders called to her to touch and taste.

Just before she turned and fled, she pleaded one more time. "Please. Just be careful."

8

Once again, Law watched her run from him. He knew it was for the best, but that didn't stop the tightness it caused in his chest.

He found his shirt and vest and pulled both back on as he thought about some of the things she'd said. Because he knew more than he let on, he was able to read further into her statements than she could have guessed. And what she'd said, and hadn't said, led him to some pretty unbelievable conclusions.

Whatever mess she and her family found themselves in, it was more than he'd first thought. And the comment about a year's time really had him wondering.

He and Evan needed to talk. Now.

Law jumped on his bike and set a course for his friend's house. As he'd done before, he parked his motorcycle elsewhere and walked the rest of the way in. He'd no sooner crossed into Evan's back yard than he saw Aria's car in the driveway.

Fuck. What was she doing here?

With no other choice but to wait for her to leave, Law found a comfortable spot on the ground and settled in.

Half an hour later, he watched as Evan walked her out to her car and saw her off. Law was up and across the yard in the blink of an eye. He stood in the heavy shadows at the corner of the house, and as Evan was about to pull the door open, Law sent out a low whistle.

Without missing a beat, Evan gave an almost imperceptible nod and went inside. Law snuck around to the back door just as it opened silently.

"I can guess why you're here," Evan said as he closed the door behind Law. "Aria just left. She told me you were attacked."

"I saw her. I figured it best to stay out of sight until she was gone."

Law helped himself to a beer out of Evan's fridge and sat down at the kitchen table. "I need to know what's really going on here. What happened with JD is like nothing I've ever seen before. He came at me with a knife, but it wasn't really him." Law took a quick drink before pushing on. "He was possessed, Evan. Just as Aria said I was in her dream. If I hadn't seen it with my own eyes, I wouldn't have believed it possible. You need to explain to me what the fuck is going on, and what the hell happens a year from now."

Evan grabbed his own beer and came to join him. He twisted off the cap and took a bracing drink to help with what he had to say.

"Aria, Anna, Ethan, and I are part of a prophecy that has been hanging over my family's heads for hundreds of years. Our births set in motion a way for an evil bastard to break out of the prison where he's been exiled, rise, and wreak havoc on the Burke line. And who knows what else."

Law tried to absorb what Evan was telling him. "How? Why?"

"Before I continue, just remember—you asked for this," Evan warned. "Back in 1565, my ancestors helped a woman and her children to escape from an abusive man. His name was Edrick Noor."

Over the next twenty minutes, Law's mind was completely blown. He looked at his friend in a whole new light.

"So that time you saved my ass—it was because you're linked to the earth?"

With his right hand, Evan reached across his chest and pulled the left sleeve of his shirt up.

Law followed the movement and saw the brownish-red birthmark in the shape of a circle. Spanning the inside from edge to edge was what looked like a drawing of a mountain range. It was the mark that tied his friend to not only the ground beneath their feet, but also to an age-old legend.

"Wait a minute. I've seen Aria's arm. There's no mark there."

"We each carry it in a different place. Ari's is on her right shoulder blade. She's air. Anna's water, and Ethan is fire."

"And come next February, you and the others will either have to come together somehow and take him down, or die trying."

"Pretty much." Evan took another long pull on his brew. "Though it's starting a lot sooner than any of us thought it would."

"What do you mean?"

"On the morning of our twenty-fourth birthdays, each of us started connecting with Noor in different ways. Through my bond with the earth, I can feel him moving and growing. Anna is an empath and is picking up on his hate and rage. Ethan says he's been dreaming, but that's all he'll say."

"And Aria?"

"She...ah...she's been having visions. Of our deaths."

"Empath, visions. So you all have other powers as well?"

Evan grinned at the awe in Law's voice. "We're still witches, so yes. Each of us has gifts that were handed down through our family. The association with the elements is part of the prophecy."

Law rubbed his hands over his face and then looked over at Evan. "Son of a bitch. You think you know a guy."

"Hey," he said on a half-laugh, "this isn't the kind of stuff you talk about with just anyone."

"Yeah, I get it." Law ran his hands through his hair. He

hated to add to Evan's already full load, but he needed to know what else had happened.

"We may have another problem to add to everything else we're dealing with."

Evan set his bottle down with a snap. "What?"

"JD, an asswipe member of the club, tried to attack Aria tonight."

Evan sat straighter in his seat, anger radiating from him. "She told me about your encounter with him, but she didn't mention anything about hers. Was she hurt?"

"No. I intervened and gladly beat the shit out of him."

Evan eyed him carefully. "Don't get me wrong—I'm glad you protected her, but why were you there?"

Law heard the underlying question. Evan still suspected he was interested in his sister, and was really asking if they'd been together at the time of the attack.

"A few of us from the MC were at Charlie Horse having dinner when she came in," Law told him truthfully. "I didn't like the way JD was watching her. He has a history with women, so I thought it would be a good idea to keep an eye on him."

"What kind of history?" The tone said he knew he wasn't going to like the answer.

"Exactly the kind you're thinking."

"Shit." Evan took another swig of his beer.

"Anyway, when he left, I followed him. He ended up doubling back and returning to the restaurant. From where I parked, I could see Aria's car was still there. When she finally came out and drove off, he tailed her.

"She ended up at the library, and he parked in the shadows and waited. I didn't really expect him to make a move on her right then, but that's exactly what he did. He grabbed her as she was walking back to her car."

"That doesn't make any sense." Evan's dark brows came together. "Why would he go for my sister? He doesn't even know her."

Law voiced a concern he'd been thinking about since it happened. "I wouldn't put it past him to have done this on his own. She's the type he'd go for, but after what occurred last night, I have to ask. Is it possible JD could have been aware when Noor took him over? Could he have heard us talking about her, or could he know what's in Noor's mind while he's possessed?"

Evan considered the possibility. "To be completely honest, I don't know. There's a lot we still don't understand about this guy. We have no clue as to what kind of power he has or what he's capable of."

"But we already know that Noor wants Aria for himself, and that he's after me because he sees me as an obstacle. He believes we're lovers."

"And aside from your presence in her dream," Evan eyed him suspiciously, "does he have any other reason to believe that?"

"I've already told you," Law was getting tired of repeating himself. "I am not looking to start anything with your sister. Can we move on now please?"

Evan studied him for a second and then nodded. "What I don't get about this is why JD would be interested in Aria in the first place?"

Law gave Evan a little backstory. "To say JD and I have never seen eye-to-eye is an understatement. The truth is we actively hate each other, so we try to stay out of each other's way. But at the same time, if he found something he thought he could use against me, I think he'd jump on it without hesitation. If he assumed, as Noor did, that Aria and I are close, I wouldn't put it past him to hurt her just to get at me."

Evan pushed away from the table and paced around the small kitchen. "Just fucking great. As if having one psycho fixated on my sister wasn't bad enough, now another one pops up out of the woodwork. Awesome."

Law rose as well. "You let me worry about JD. If he tries to hurt her again, I'll kill him."

As soon as the oath left his mouth, Law knew he'd put too much of his emotions into it. Evan turned to him with a thoughtful look on his face.

"You know this is the worst possible time to be distracted."

Law didn't need Evan to tell him what he already knew. He finished off his beer and set the empty bottle back on the table.

"I have no intention of letting that happen," Law said as he rose to his feet. "Nothing will stand in the way of me finishing this job and putting these assholes away." He crossed to the back door and then stopped. "Speaking of which, you got all your shit ready to go for the bust?"

Evan nodded. "Yep. We're all set."

Closing the door behind him, Law knew Evan was right; he couldn't afford to be preoccupied. He had to lock down whatever feelings he had for Aria and put them away.

On the return drive to the rental house, Law couldn't help but smile in satisfaction as he thought back on the brutal lesson he'd given JD in the parking lot.

After Aria had left the library, Law had stuck around and waited for JD to regain consciousness. When the scumbag had finally come around, Law was there, hovering menacingly over him. From his prone position on the ground, JD's eyes widened, and he immediately attempted to scramble away. But the injuries Law had inflicted were severe enough to limit the quick movement, and JD groaned as he slumped back to the asphalt.

Law crouched down and settled a knee onto one side of JD's torso. He gradually leaned his weight on ribs he knew were cracked. When JD broke out in a pain-filled sweat, Law pinned him with a look, letting all his rage and hate show through.

"I told you the next time you assaulted a woman, I'd kill you, you sorry piece of shit."

"You can't—" JD gasped out.

Law laughed. "Oh, I *can* and I *will*. But luckily for you, we've got too much riding on this shipment, and killing you now would only jeopardize that. So I'm giving you a reprieve. But your days are numbered, motherfucker."

He applied more pressure to JD's ribs. "When this is over, I'll be coming for you." He left JD crumpled in a heap, gasping for air and clutching his battered side.

Bringing his thoughts back to the present, Law was still grinning when he turned up the long drive and parked. Walking through the front door, he saw JD sprawled in a recliner in the living room, asleep.

He was tempted to dump the son of a bitch out of the chair and finish the job right now, but what he'd told him earlier had been true. Everyone had an assignment in the coming meeting, and Law would do nothing to put this Op at risk.

~~~

After three more days of searching through every family record, the internet, and any other miscellaneous documents she could find, Aria's plan to draw Noor out was looking more and more like the only way to get the facts they needed.

As Thursday afternoon gave way to evening, a strange anxiousness settled over her. A terrible feeling kept haunting her. It wasn't a premonition, exactly. It was more of a dark weight that pressed increasingly heavier on her. She'd never felt anything like it before and didn't quite know how to interpret what it meant.

After going to bed, she tossed and turned for hours until finally, disgusted, she threw the covers aside and got up. She crossed to the window in her room and looked out into the moonlit night.

A few moments later, behind her on the bedside table, her
~~~

phone started to vibrate.

Calls in the middle of the night were never good. Would this be the one to tell her what was causing this uneasiness?

She rounded the bed and picked up the phone. Seeing it was Evan, she unplugged it and, with a swipe of her thumb, the call was connected.

"Evan? What's wrong?"

"Law's hurt. It's serious. He—"

"Where?" she demanded with a voice that shook.

"Ari—"

"Where is he, Evan?"

She heard a deep sigh. "We're at Halifax."

"I'm coming." She hung up and threw on some clothes.

She left a quick note for Anna and ran out of the house. She was able to make good time as she rushed to the hospital and tore into the parking lot. At this hour, the only entrance open was Emergency, so that's where she headed.

As soon as she blew through the doors, she saw Evan. His shirt and pants were covered in blood, and her insides twisted painfully.

"Are you hurt?" she asked in a panic as she drew closer to her brother.

He held her gaze. "It's not mine."

Aria's stomach plummeted further and her heart clenched in her chest. *That meant...* "What happened?"

He didn't say anything but took her by the arm and led her into a small room off the waiting area.

Oh God. Oh God. Was he...? She didn't let herself finish the thought.

"Tell me." Her voice was a raw whisper.

"Sit down," he told her.

She didn't want to sit, but she flung herself into a chair, just to hurry things up.

Once he was also seated, he began the explanation. "The

news channels will know about this very soon. But they won't have the whole story. I wanted you to hear that part from me." Evan reached out and took her hand.

"Evan, please. Just tell me what's going on."

His dark eyes begged for patience. "There are a few things you need to know. Law's alive, but it doesn't look good."

Aria bit back the sob that wanted to fall from her lips. She couldn't lose it now; she had to hold on. She remained silent and took a deep breath, waiting for her brother to finish.

"The group Law rides with took possession of a large shipment of weapons a few hours ago. I was part of a joint operation between local and federal law enforcement, whose objective it was to take down both the motorcycle club, as well as the syndicate that was supplying them. We were working off of information given to us by an undercover agent inside the motorcycle club. With what he gave us, we set up near where the meet was to take place. This was a once in a lifetime bust, Aria, and everything was planned out to the last detail."

His slow reveal was killing her, but she held her frustration in check. "Okay."

"It went off without a hitch." Evan dropped his eyes to their clasped hands. "Or so we thought."

He cleared his throat and shifted in his seat, and Aria could tell that this was where it was going to get bad. She braced herself for whatever he was going to say next.

"We already had everyone in custody and were in the process of loading them all up. What we didn't realize though, was that someone had gotten away. He'd made it to the tree line and was hiding there. I had Law handcuffed and was about to put him into one of the transport vans when we heard four quick gunshots.

"We all dropped to the ground for cover. When no more shots were fired, we looked around to see where they'd come from. That's when I saw Law. He'd gone down with the rest of us, but not in the way I'd thought. That's when I saw the blood."

Aria felt a direct blow to her heart as her composure started to slip.

Evan's fingers rubbed her trembling hands in comfort.

"I immediately assessed him, and that's when I saw that all four rounds had struck him…in the back."

Aria couldn't hold back the gasp at his words or the tears that rained down her cheeks. "Did you…did you catch him? The one who shot him?"

Evan shook his head. "No. He was gone by the time the agents reacted and searched the woods. I did what I could to stop the bleeding, but there was so much." He looked at his own clothes still stained with blood. He took a breath and let it out. "Aria, Law was…*is*," he corrected, "the undercover agent. He works from the inside of these clubs to take them down. This was *his* Op. This bust was set in motion weeks ago, though I've actually known him for years—we went through the police academy together. But we lost touch when he got called into this specialized task force."

Aria couldn't believe what she was hearing. She slowly pulled her hands out from under her brother's and sat back in her chair.

"You knew." Her voice started out as a strangled whisper but rose with each sentence. "All this time, you knew who he was. You let me go on and on about how we had to find him and warn him. And all that time, you *knew*."

She rose and paced the small room.

"Ari, I couldn't tell you. I couldn't tell anyone." Evan pleaded for her to understand, but she was too overwhelmed by grief to care.

"But I'm your sister, for God's sake!" She rounded on him. "And I…" She stopped abruptly, the flow of words cutting off before she said any more.

He stood and came towards her. "It didn't matter. Letting

anyone in on the secret could have blown the whole operation. We had a lot riding on this going exactly the right way. Law has worked for years…*years*, Aria," he stressed, "to make this happen. He's had to live and breathe and work right alongside these people. If any of them had found out what he was, *who* he was, they'd have killed him on sight. That's why I was arresting him, along with all the others. So his cover would hold, and he could go on to the next job."

"So what happened then? Why was he shot? Did someone find out anyway?"

"We don't know." He plowed his hands through his black hair, sending the long locks into total disarray. The irritation in his movements and voice told her he was as frustrated and worried as she was. "Until we know who shot him, we won't know the answer. Which means he's still in danger. Those weren't just random shots, Aria. Whoever pulled that trigger meant to kill him."

Aria couldn't wait another minute. "Where is he? I want to see him. Now."

"The last I heard, he was still in surgery. Let's go see what we can find out." He started for the door.

"Evan?"

He stopped and turned back towards her.

"Why did you tell me this?"

Evan sighed as his shoulders slumped. "Ari, I hate to say this, but honestly, I don't think he's going to make it. I can see there's something between you, and I didn't want you to go on thinking he was one of those thugs."

She absorbed that blow and nodded. "What's his name? His real name?"

He paused, obviously trying to decide whether or not to divulge that information.

"If he's that bad, what could it hurt? I need to know, Evan."

Her brother finally nodded. "Seth Lawson."

Well, Seth Lawson, Aria thought, stiffening her spine, *if I have anything to do with it, you won't be dying any time soon.*

"Take me to him."

She followed her brother out and through another set of doors. She lost track of the turns they made, but soon they were standing in front of a desk, and Evan was asking about the man who'd been shot.

The nurse knew Evan and told him that the doctor was just finishing up and would be out shortly. They could speak with him then.

Aria and Evan moved across the wide hall to stand against the wall. They had a clear view of the doors leading back to where the operating rooms were.

Half an hour later, a tall black man in scrubs came out. He wearily slid the surgical hat off his head. Aria was the first to reach him.

"The gunshot victim, how is he?"

"Are you family?"

Before Aria could lie, Evan stepped in and flashed his badge. "I'm Daytona police. We need an update on his condition."

The doctor eyed Aria for another moment but then turned to Evan and spoke. "I don't know how, but he pulled through surgery. The bullets caused a lot of damage. One is still lodged in his back. It was too close to the spine for us to attempt removal."

The surgeon pulled the face mask off his neck and wadded it up in his hand. "He'll be in recovery for a few hours. He's listed as critical right now. If he makes it through the next twenty-four hours, we'll revisit the possibility of a future surgery, or whether it's even necessary."

"Can I see him?" Aria asked.

"Like I said, he'll be in recovery for quite a while. Once he's moved to ICU, you can see him for a few minutes every hour."

9

The next three hours passed in a haze of exhaustion and fear. Aria refused to leave the surgical waiting area. When they finally came in and told her they were moving Law, she immediately went to that floor and waited for them to wheel him in.

Her first view of him tore her heart out. Tubes and wires were attached to every part of him. But the one that scared her the most was the ventilator. Knowing he was so badly wounded that he couldn't breathe on his own almost paralyzed her.

She stood back as they hooked everything up and got him situated. As the last nurse left, she told Aria she could stay for ten minutes, and then she'd have to wait until the next hour.

Aria nodded and slowly approached the bed. He looked so pale, which made the flecks of dried blood on his neck and arms stand out obscenely. She turned and left the room. Going to the nurse's station, she asked for a basin of warm water and a washcloth.

After the nurse promised to bring one right in, she returned to his side. She bent down and whispered into his ear.

"I hope you can hear me. I'm here, and you're not alone. I'm not going anywhere. They may kick me out for a little while, but I'll be back. I'll always be back." She ran her hand through his soft brown hair.

Just then, the nurse came in with the items she'd requested.

She set about gently washing him. Starting with his face, she stroked the white cloth over his forehead and around his eyes. After a quick rinse, she smoothed it over his stubble-covered cheeks and around his neck.

Aria dipped it back into the water and rung it out. Next she concentrated on his arms and hands. It wasn't much, but she felt like she was doing what she could to make him more comfortable.

Once all the traces of blood were washed away, she pulled a chair up close to the bed and sat. She leaned forward so that she could grasp his hand in hers. She silently studied their differences. Where his was large and broad, hers was petite and narrow. His darkly-tanned skin stood out in contrast to her fair complexion. His palm was rough and calloused against hers where they lay, fingers entwined.

Wrapping her other hand around their clasped ones, she sat with him, sending him what energy she could until she was told she had to go. They showed her to a waiting room down the hall. When she couldn't be with him, this is where she'd wait.

Every member of her family had come to check on her, but she eventually sent them home. She was still under strict orders from Evan to not say anything about who and what Law really was. His job and life depended on the secret remaining intact.

So, on and on it went throughout the day and into the evening. Every hour she'd retrace her steps to his room, hoping that this time he'd show signs of waking up. He never did, and she continued to share what she had with him. His recovery reached a turning point when, between one visit and the next, they'd removed the breathing tube.

But still he didn't rouse.

At one point in the waiting room, it was just her and Evan, and he spent some time filling her in a little more about what Law had been doing since he'd seen him last. She was still stunned to know he put himself in such terrible danger over and over in order to put the worst kind of criminals away.

What kind of life could he possibly have? None, she'd concluded. No wonder he'd kept pushing her away. He couldn't possibly pursue anything with her, or with anyone else outside the motorcycle clubs he infiltrated.

Thinking back over the conversations they'd had, Aria was able to look at them in a new light. The disparities between what he'd said and his actions made more sense now. Like her, he could hold steady to his resolve to stay away until they were thrown together again. Then the attraction they felt would override whatever good intentions they'd had to forget the other.

Discovering his true identity hadn't changed how she felt about him. He was still who she thought of first thing in the morning and last at night. But that didn't alter the impossible situation they still found themselves in. His dangerous and highly secretive work, as well as the coming battle her family faced, remained major roadblocks.

And neither was going away anytime soon.

But no matter the obstacles between them, she couldn't leave him here to suffer alone. She'd just have to find a way to protect her heart when the time came to walk away for good.

Sitting there watching him, Aria reassessed what she knew of this man. He wasn't the outlaw biker he'd portrayed himself to be. Instead, he was the exact opposite—risking his own life daily to ensure that the safety and freedom of others came before his own.

She couldn't help but notice the similarities between how they lived their lives. Aria had dedicated herself to one steadfast and true law—An' it harm none. Just like the laws that he upheld, hers was meant to control against the misuse of power and defend innocents from those who would do them harm.

She contemplated all the good he'd done for so many people. By taking these men off the streets, Law had prevented them from hurting countless innocents. He was waging a war on evil, just as she was.

Aria gasped as the weight of her realizations sunk in. This man was the epitome of the very edict she'd lived her entire life by.

Her thoughts were interrupted when Law shifted on the bed and groaned in pain.

Aria was on her feet instantly, still a little shaken by her sudden revelation. She didn't know what it would mean for her, but she couldn't think about that right now. Law needed her.

"Don't try to move. You were shot, and you're in the hospital."

When he licked his dry lips, Aria grabbed the plastic water cup and brought the straw to his mouth.

"Here, try this. Take it slow."

He drank a few sips and then relaxed back against the pillow. His lashes started to flutter as he tried to open his eyes.

She grasped his hand in hers and waited for his brown gaze to find her and focus. "Hi," she murmured and smiled.

"Where?" His voice was raw and hoarse.

"You're in the hospital," Aria repeated. "You were shot. But you're going to be fine."

He seemed to be taking that in. Then she saw him grimace. "Are you in pain? Do you want me to get the doctor?"

He shook his head slightly and tightened his grip on her hand in answer. "Stay."

"I will." She ran her free hand through his hair.

She knew the moment he fell back into the darkness of sleep. His hand still clutched hers, but the tension around his mouth and eyes slackened.

Aria sat with him until the nurse told her she had to leave. She took a moment to let her know that he'd woken up for a few minutes. The nurse smiled and went to the computer station to note it in his chart. Aria made her way back to the lounge and called Evan first and then the rest of her family.

Law slept through her next visit and when she came out, Evan was there.

"Has he said anything?"

"No. He was only awake for those few moments."

He nodded and walked her down the hall. "Why don't you take a break? Go back to Anna's, have some dinner, take a shower, get some rest. I'll stay."

Aria refused with a shake of her head.

"I need to talk to him, Ari. If he's awake, I need some answers. We have to find out who did this."

She hated to miss what little time she had with him, but they all needed to know. "You can take the next hour, but I'm staying here."

~~~

When Law surfaced again, he was alone. He lay there in the dim light and tried to figure out what was real and what were dreams.

He could have sworn he'd heard Aria talking to him, caring for him, but that may have been his pain-riddled mind playing tricks on him. His whole body throbbed. It was almost impossible to say what hurt more, but his back seemed to be edging into the lead.

When he heard the door open, he swung his head around to look and bit back a moan as it set off jackhammers in his brain.

"Don't get up on my account." Evan strode in and came to the side of the bed.

"Fuck you." Law closed his eyes and willed the construction crew to cease and desist. When they backed off some, he took a chance and opened his eyes again.
~~~

"What the hell happened?" he asked. "The last thing I remember...was you cuffing me."

"Yeah. Evidently, someone got away and took up a position in the woods. Whoever it was got off four rounds. All of which landed in your back."

Law tried to think, but his mind was fuzzy. "Who, ah, who all did you pick up that night?"

Evan took out his notepad and read off the twenty or so names of the people they'd arrested.

"Don't know...about the syndicate's side," Law finally got out after he forced his mind to focus on the task. "But from the MC's...JD is missing from your list."

"You think it was JD that got away?"

Law nodded.

"That's the same guy who attacked you and Aria."

Even the small nod had set the crew back to work in his head, so Law just made an affirmative sound this time.

"Do you think he found out you're a cop? Is that why he tried to kill you?"

"Doubt it," Law said after some thought. "Either because...I kicked his ass or..." Law tried to zero in on another thought. "Noor?"

"You think he got to JD again?" Law was thankful Evan was able to interpret his scattered thoughts.

"Maybe." Law could feel himself slipping back under. Evan must have seen it too.

"Look. That's enough for now. If I tire you out too much, they won't let me back in. Aria reluctantly let me have this visit, but she'll be back the next time you wake up. In the meantime buddy, you get healed up. There's a guard on the door. He's actually there to protect you, since we haven't located the shooter, but it also continues the ruse that you're a criminal bad-ass and have to be watched."

Law grinned.

"One other thing." Evan was still standing next to the bed. "I told Aria the truth."

Law nailed Evan with a killing look. "Why?"

"It didn't look good, dude. If the worst happened," Evan only shrugged at the frown Law sent him, "I thought she deserved to know."

"Dangerous."

"She won't say anything to anyone. We Burkes are pretty good at keeping secrets." Evan smiled and turned to leave.

Law wanted to think through the ramifications of Aria knowing who he really was, but sleep pulled him under too quickly.

The next time he woke, she was there. He willingly got lost in the sight of her until his conversation with Evan came back to him.

"JD," he grunted.

She was on her feet and next to the bed before he could blink. She held out the cup of water for him. Once his mouth didn't feel like it was full of sand, he tried again.

"JD shot me. Still out there."

"Shh, I know." She combed her fingers back through his hair, and he marveled at the sensation. The lingering headache faded away under her touch. "I know what happened. You just rest."

The pain that had beat at him during Evan's visit had lessened. Whatever they were giving him must be some good shit. And his mind felt clear—not fuzzy and disconnected like most of the pain meds made him feel.

Aria continued to stroke her hand over his head. Law closed his eyes and sank into a peaceful kind of place. Nothing reached him but her soft touch. With each caress, more of the throbbing throughout his body eased.

With his ability to think slowly coming back, Law was able to discern a few things. He forced his eyes open, and he looked up at the blonde beauty standing over him.

She looked worse than he felt. Dark circles ringed her pale blue eyes, and her skin looked sallow and almost translucent. She was very obviously tired and worn out. More so than she should be if she'd just been sitting vigil by his bed.

What she was doing finally clicked.

Whatever witchy power she had, she was using it on him. She was burning herself up to heal him.

"Stop." Law slid out from beneath her hand.

Aria, startled by his movement and the order, pulled her hand back and clutched it to her chest. Her eyes went wide.

"Did I hurt you? I'm sorry. I was just trying to ease your pain."

"At your own expense," Law rebuked. "Evan said he filled you in on who I was, that we've known each other for a while."

Aria bobbed her head and watched him quizzically, as if trying to figure out where the conversation was going.

"Then it stands to reason I know who you are. Or should I say *what*."

She froze, as if waiting for him to cast her out.

"The fact that you're a witch doesn't bother me, Pixie. What I don't like is seeing you suffer in order to fix me."

"I wasn't actually healing you." Some of her spark was coming back. "Just sending a little extra energy to help speed up the process."

"Well, don't." He realized his words were a little harsher than he'd intended when she flinched. He took a breath and tried again. "You've been doing that the whole time I've been here, haven't you?"

Aria nodded. "Yes."

"You've got to stop. You're wearing yourself out." He reached out and took her hand in his. "Whatever you did helped, and thank you. But I can take it from here."

A thought occurred to Law. "How long have I been here?"

"You were shot early Friday morning. It's Saturday now, just after seven a.m."

Just then a nurse came through the door. "Well, looks like we'll be moving you to a regular room sometime today. The doctor says your recovery has been remarkable."

Law resisted looking at Aria. "How soon before I'm out all together?"

The nurse checked his vitals and went to the computer to make note of them. "That depends on if you continue to improve as you have up until now." She backed out of the program and looked at Aria. "He's awake and well on his way to recovery. Why don't you go home, eat a decent meal, and rest? You've been here since he came in, and you look exhausted. If you're not careful, you'll end up right here beside him. When you come back, check with the main information desk to see if he's been moved yet." She walked out with a slight squeak of her rubber-soled shoes.

When they were alone again, Law brought the subject back to the outlaw biker. "Have they found JD yet?"

Aria stepped close to the bed again. "Not that I know of. But I'm kind of out of the loop here." She sent a quick glance towards the closed door before turning back. When she spoke, her voice was almost a whisper. "Do you think he found out you were undercover?"

"I don't think so." He was having a hard time talking about this with her. The only people he'd ever spoken to freely about any of this were his handler and Evan. Aria knowing the truth was going to take some getting used to.

"As I said before, he and I have had issues for years. What I don't know is if he acted on his own, or if Noor possessed him again and made another attempt to take me out."

The shock on her face told him his knowledge of her nemesis surprised her. "How long have you known about all of this?"

"About him being a meat-suit for your friend?" Law decided

to be completely honest with how much he knew. "I was at Evan's the night you had that dream. I heard what you told him, and I couldn't understand why you both thought some douchebag from your nightmare could come after me. But then JD, or who I'd thought was JD, tried to carve me up. Then when we ran into him again at the library, I went back to Evan and made him tell me everything."

"I was there."

"I know. I waited outside for you to leave."

"I see." She crossed her arms over her middle and paced a few feet away. "So you and my brother have not only neglected to tell me you knew each other, but you've also been talking about our family business."

Law gingerly adjusted himself to an upright position. He wanted to face her head-on—not as an invalid from flat on his back.

He'd just shifted his weight when she swung back around to face him. She ran her hands up and through her long hair. She also let out a tired sigh.

"I know, I know. Neither of you could risk what you were doing. And Noor isn't just our problem anymore. He's yours now too."

She dropped her head back on her shoulders and looked up at the ceiling. Her long silky hair flowed down her back to reach the rounded curve of her butt. "Ugh, what a fucked-up mess."

Her use of the f-bomb made him smile. It was kind of jarring to hear such a harsh word coming from his little pixie. But she was right. This was a fucked-up mess.

10

Law didn't end up being moved until the following morning. The doctor wanted to take another look at his back and the bullet that remained. He was pleased with what he saw and decided another surgery wouldn't be necessary.

He signed off on the transfer out of ICU but it took close to an hour to move him and all the miscellaneous equipment monitoring him. By the time he was settled into his new room, he was exhausted. They no sooner had everything plugged back in than he slipped into sleep.

Sometime later, Law knew he was no longer alone. Years of living a dangerous life had his lids parting just a fraction to judge the threat level. He saw Aria was standing next to the bed staring down at him. He sighed in relief and opened his eyes fully.

No, not Aria. Anna. Immediately, his guard went up.

Her head tilted to the side, causing her silvery-blonde hair to slide over her shoulder. Her perfectly-arched brows dipped in, considering. "You know I'm not Aria. Interesting." She moved around to the foot of the bed, never taking her eyes from his. "She's talking with the nurse and should be here any minute, but I wanted a moment alone with you."

Law hit the button to raise the head of the bed. "I take it there's something you want to say to me?"

"There was," she said cryptically. "But as I watched you

sleep, I was able to…understand a few things."

Oh, shit. Law suddenly remembered Evan telling him this sister was an empath. If he had a handle on it right, that meant she picked up on feelings and emotions. He had to wonder what she'd seen in him while he'd been unaware and exposed.

"Oh, yeah? And what was that?" He laced his tone with skepticism. If Evan and Aria had kept their mouths shut, then Anna would only know he was a part of a criminal biker gang. His stint with this MC may be over, but there would always be another assignment. Unless he chose to throw in his towel.

But that decision hadn't been made yet.

"There's more to you than I first thought." Anna's blue eyes may have been an exact match to Aria's in color, but they differed in their measure of him. He had a feeling Anna didn't really like what she saw. "There's something underneath the facade you show to the world. A piece of you that's locked tightly away."

Fuck. Law didn't like how close to the truth she'd come in her assessment. "You know, if I'd wanted a psychic reading, I would have called a nine-hundred number."

She quirked a grin at him. One that said she knew he was bluffing his ass off. How the hell had he gotten involved with a bunch of nosy witches?

He was still staring coolly at Anna when Aria came in looking refreshed, and reminded him why he'd ignored his better judgment in the first place.

"What's going on in here?" Aria eyed her sister and him warily.

"Just getting to know each other." Anna crossed to Aria and kissed her cheek. "I'll see you at home later."

A look passed between the twins before Anna left, one that contained an entirely silent conversation. And one that Law had no hope of understanding.

As Anna's footsteps faded away down the hall, he looked at

Aria. "I think for the duration, it's a good idea for your sister and me to steer clear of each other."

"Why?"

"She's an empath, right?"

"Wow, Evan really did run off at the mouth, didn't he?" Aria shook her head. "Don't worry, she can't read you. She told me she tried that day Evan was stabbed, but couldn't get anything."

"Well, she picked up on something while I was sleeping." Law was uneasy and needed her to understand how bad this could get if someone slipped up. "I can't take the chance that she'll learn the truth, Aria. The more people that know who I am, the less likely I am to stay alive."

"I really don't think you have anything to worry about, but I'll talk to her."

Aria came close to the bed, and he caught her unique scent. All other concerns drifted away as something floral and delicate saturated his senses and seeped into his pores. He knew he'd never again get that fragrance out of his system. She'd managed to become a part of every cell in his body, and right now he was too tired and too sore to fight against the pull that was Aria.

He shifted until he'd slid to the opposite rail. He reached out, grasped her hand, and tugged her until she was lying beside him.

"We shouldn't do this," she protested as she snuggled into him. "I could hurt you. Or someone could come in."

"I don't care." No truer words had ever come out of his mouth. The feeling of her body pressed to his was better than any meds they could have given him.

They lay quietly for a long time. His arms were wrapped around her waist, her face buried in his chest. They took comfort in the chance just to be close. He knew once he was on his feet again, he'd have to give her up.

As if reading his mind, Aria tilted her head back. "What

happens now? Since your plan was successful and everyone, other than JD, is behind bars, I'm assuming you'll be leaving soon."

"I won't know for sure until I can get in touch with my bosses. But, yeah. They'll probably have another job lined up."

"The only bright spot I can see in this is that Noor will think he succeeded in driving you away and leave you alone. You'll be safe." She wrapped her arm around his waist and held him tight.

Law could barely take the sense of finality that swamped him. He wanted to argue back, to tell her he'd stay and help her fight. But he knew he had to let her go. And if he were never going to see her again, he wanted to take with him whatever memories he could. Raising up on his elbow caused pain to shoot down his back, but it was worth it to be able to look down into her clear blue eyes.

The sadness he saw in them matched his own despair.

"Seth."

The soft murmur of his name on her lips caused his heart to stutter in his chest. He took the sound of it into himself and held it close.

"You shouldn't call me that," he whispered, staring into her beautiful face.

She smiled gently. "I know. But I needed to, just this once."

Law brushed the stray strands of her silky hair back. He lowered his head and pressed his lips to hers with more gentleness and passion than he'd ever felt for anyone. She responded instantly and brought her hand up to the side of his face. He loved the intimacy of her touch, and the gesture warmed a place inside of him that had been cold and lonely for a very long time.

They were completely absorbed in each other when a loud knock sounded on the door. Before they had time to react, it pushed open. "The Daytona Beach Police Department has a few more questions for you, sir," Evan said loudly in the open doorway before he strode in and closed it behind him.

He stopped and frowned at them lying in each other's arms. "I don't think that kind of activity is good for your health," Evan said. "Or mine, since that's more than I ever wanted to know about my sister's personal life."

Law, who'd been startled by the sudden intrusion, relaxed and grinned. He looked back down at Aria lying next to him and caught a sparkle of humor in the blue depths.

"So turn around and leave."

"Can't." Evan strode across the room. "Got a message from your boss."

Shit. Already?

"What did he say?" With a soft sigh, Aria rose from the bed, and Law rearranged himself until he was seated. He breathed away the pain that spanned his entire upper body. Aria's ministrations had done wonders for his wounds, but his back was still full of half-healed holes, and if he moved the wrong way, it was quick to let him know.

"Wait a minute. Why did he contact *you*?" Aria spun around to ask her brother.

It was Law who answered. "We never have direct contact. All communication is done through third parties. You can imagine what would happen if I were seen speaking with law enforcement."

She nodded. "So that's what Evan's little act was about. In case anyone happened to be listening."

"Yup," Evan confirmed.

If he'd been assigned elsewhere, Law wanted to know sooner rather than later. "What's the message?"

"That you're to stick around and catch the asshole that shot you." Evan half-laughed. "I think your superior knew you'd want to finish up that bit of business yourself."

"You've got that shit straight." Law was looking forward to

getting his hands on that bastard. "Has there been any sign of him?"

Evan shook his head. "No. We've got men stationed around the house, but there's been no sign of him. Some activity as the lesser members and women were packing up and heading back to Chicago, but nothing else. JD must have found somewhere else to hide out." His gaze landed on Law. "Can you think of anywhere he'd go?"

"I can't." Law gave it some thought. "But I know someone who might." He grinned as a plan took form in his mind. "You, my friend," he said to Evan, "will get to arrest me after all. And you'll need to make sure I'm in a cell next to Kane."

The rest of the day was spent going over the details. When Evan left, Aria came to stand next to Law.

"Think you can get the information you need?"

"If Kane knows where JD's hiding, he'll tell me. Or he will, once he learns what JD did to me."

"You're still hurt, though," she protested. "Can't you wait until you're in better shape?"

"If I were an actual criminal, I'd *already* be in jail. Thanks to you, my recovery has been miraculous."

"Then let me finish the job. That way you'll be able to protect yourself if something doesn't go as planned."

"No. I can't show up perfectly healthy, two days after getting hit by four bullets. I need Kane to see I'm legitimately hurt for this to work."

"I hate the thought of you being in jail."

"It won't be the first time." He held her gaze to convey how important this was. "This is my job, Pixie. I do what I have to do to put these people away. To maintain my cover, sometimes I go away with them for a while. When I'm released, I move on to the next assignment."

"Have you ever thought about getting out and having a life of your own?"

Should he tell her the truth? That since he'd met her, that's all he'd thought about? Or did he lie and save them both the heartache?

He found the thought of lying unbearable. "Yeah, I have. But I just don't see that being possible right now."

She slowly nodded in understanding. "How long do you think you'll have to stay there?"

"As long as it takes. But don't you have your own bad guy to find? Visions to stop? Siblings to save?"

"At this point, I don't know how to accomplish any of that," Aria said in disgust as she paced to the window to look out. "The only plan I can come up with is to lure Noor out somehow. Let him come after me, so I can try and work some more clues out of him."

Law's gaze followed her progress. "I don't like the sound of that. Have you discussed this plan with the rest of your family?

"No. Not yet." She turned back to face him. "I was trying to find another way, *any* other way, but this is all I'm left with."

"Please tell me you won't do this on your own. Assure me you'll have some kind of backup in place to help you."

"Do *you* ever have backup?" she shot back at him.

"Aria, you know it's not the same. The monsters *I* go after can't take over someone else's body. You have your whole family ready and able to help you. I don't have anyone."

"Yes, you do," she whispered as she came to his bedside and took his face in her hands. "You have me." She leaned in and kissed him.

As much as he hated to do it, he made her leave a short time later. Evan would be coming back with a couple of uniforms to haul him in to jail, and he didn't want her to see him that way.

<p style="text-align:center">~~~</p>

Aria fought back tears on the drive over to Anna's house.

She'd probably never see him again. He was on his way to jail, and once JD was caught, he'd leave.

When she walked into her sister's house, Anna was sitting on the couch. There was a pint of their favorite ice cream sitting on the coffee table. It had two spoons sticking out of the top.

Aria smiled and dropped her purse and keys to the floor. She crossed to the couch and plopped down as Anna picked up the carton and held it between them.

"Thought you could use some caramel therapy." Anna scooped up a bite as Aria took her spoon and dug in.

The cold vanilla and gooey sauce hit her tongue and she sighed. "So good," she said around the bite. "I did need this. Thank you."

They enjoyed the sweet treat for a few moments before Anna spoke. "So...a cop, huh?"

Aria choked on the bite she'd just taken. "How—"

"I finally figured out what he has buried behind that block I can't see through."

"What?"

"The same thing Evan does when he's on a big case that he can't discuss with anyone. There's a wall they put up to compartmentalize what they have to do. Law's is more substantial to account for the bigger secrets he's hiding."

"He was afraid you'd seen too much today," Aria told her, taking another bite. "This has to stay a secret, Anna. No one can know what he is."

Her sister nodded. "Don't worry, my lips are sealed." She scooped out another gooey spoonful. "So, he knows about us? What we are?"

"Yeah. Evan gave him a pretty heavy crash course in it. Edrick Noor possessed one of the others in the motorcycle gang and tried to kill him the other night. That same guy, JD, is the one who shot him. We're trying to figure out if he did it on his own, or if Noor got to him again."

Aria explained the events from the last couple of days, finishing with the plan they'd implemented this morning.

It felt good to have someone to talk it all out with.

"There's something else I wanted to pass by you," Aria started. "I think I have an idea of how to get more information on Noor."

"How?"

"From him." Aria stuck the spoon back in the carton and looked directly at Anna. "I want to draw him out. Make him come to me. If I can get him talking again, maybe he'll give up some clues—something that will help us to take him down."

Anna set the ice cream on the table and then turned back to Aria. "You want to use yourself as bait. After what he did to you the last time?"

Aria had known this wasn't going to be easy. "I'll be ready for him. He won't hurt me."

"And you know this, how? He's already tried to kill our brother *and* the man you're falling for."

Aria opened her mouth to argue that point, but Anna held up her hand. "Save it. It doesn't take an empath to pick up on the hormones flying around you two."

She left Anna's statement alone. "Noor's attempts on their lives are precisely why we need to do whatever we can to stop him. He's not going to quit until you're all dead. And I refuse to let him win."

Anna sighed in what sounded like defeat. "You really think you can get him to give up some hints about where he got his power?"

"I do," Aria nodded. "From what I saw in my dream and what Law described, he likes to run his mouth. This is the first time in centuries he's been able to interact with someone. He's bound to let something slip as he's spewing his shit."

"We'll need to have a family meeting about this," Anna said. "We all have to be in agreement, and we have to find the best way to keep you safe."

"I have no problem with that." Aria smiled.

They put out the call. The gathering would take place at their parents' house in a few hours. It would take Evan that long to be able to break away from arresting and processing Law.

Since Aria didn't want to think about what was happening downtown, she grabbed up the ice cream again and sat back against the cushions. She turned the conversation to the one member of her family that had her worried.

"Ethan still seems distant."

Anna took her spoon and dug in too. "He still blames himself for Honor's death."

"It's been four years. I thought he'd put that behind him. When I talked to him on the phone, he sounded fine. But now that I see him in person, I can see he's not."

"He loved her."

"I know, but her death wasn't his fault."

"He doesn't see it that way." Anna shook her head. "He believes that since fire is his element, he should have been able to control the one that broke out in her family's home."

"He wasn't even there. From what you told me, by the time he got there and saw what was happening, the structure was completely engulfed. There was no way he could have taken on a blaze that size, and even if it *were* possible, it still would have been too late."

"He doesn't see it as the fire being too big. He sees it as *him* being too *weak* to save her."

Aria hurt for her brother. He and Honor Andrews had started dating in eighth grade and had been inseparable until the day she died. She'd never felt that kind of loss. The pain she was experiencing over Law didn't even compare. She would always know he was out there somewhere. Living, and as safe as he could be.

Ethan didn't have that. The one person he loved most was completely out of his reach. Forever. Honor was never coming back. And that knowledge still haunted him.

"Has he said anything about the dreams he's been having of Noor?"

Anna's hair swung as she shook her head. "No. He's never talked about them."

"We should probably nudge him a little there. They might provide us with more insight."

"We've asked him repeatedly, but he always says he can't remember them." Anna paused in thought. "I don't think he likes to talk about them."

"Well, he may not have a choice. I think we need to know. Anything pertaining to the prophecy needs to be examined and discussed."

"You can ask him tonight. Maybe you'll have better luck."

Aria set her chin. "I think I'll do that."

11

While Aria was deciding on the best way to probe into her brother's dreams, Law was being locked into a jail cell.

Evan gave him a shove that was a little too helpful. It had Law propelling across the small room and into the opposite wall. The stumble was real, as was the pain it caused. He didn't bother to hide it as he turned to drill Evan with a look that promised he'd return the favor if he ever got the chance.

"Welcome to your new digs." Evan slammed the door shut and then glanced into the next cell at Kane. "And look, you already know your neighbor."

Evan sauntered away as Law braced himself against the wall and let the throbbing take him over. He knew it would wash out his skin tone and make the fact that he was seriously injured more evident.

He gingerly sat down on the bunk and took a couple of deep breaths.

"I heard the shots. I saw you go down." Kane rose and came to stand at the common wall of bars between their cages. "I thought you were dead."

"I should be—no thanks to that coward, JD." Law made a show of fighting back the pain. "Instead, I've spent the last two days in the hospital, under guard."

"What does JD have to do with that?"

"He's the one who shot me," Law said through clenched

teeth. "In the fucking back."

"It was probably one of the cops or feds."

"No. It was him. I saw him as I was lying in the dirt, bleeding out." Law told the lie he and Evan had worked out beforehand. "He was hiding like a pussy. He couldn't take me on face-to-face, so he fucking ambushed me."

Law came up off the bed and took the few steps needed to put him right in front of Kane. He let all his anger and hatred loose as he glared at the leader of his club. "Being laid up in that bed, I had a lot of time to think. And I'm betting JD *did* know what he was doing that night in my room. Then, when he got caught in the act, he played stupid."

Kane eyed him. "What is it between you two, anyway? Something's been going on for a long time."

"It's because I got in his way. I had a problem with him raping and killing young girls." Law saw a flash of recognition in Kane's eyes.

"You knew what he was doing and did nothing?" He'd never known for sure if Kane was aware of JD's activities, but it gave him a perfect opening to turn Kane against JD. "It was probably his little sideline that brought the cops down on us. Only so many girls can go missing before someone notices. The Feds have probably been watching him for years, and that's how they found out about the weapons shipment."

Law returned to his bunk and gently laid back, putting his left arm beneath his head. "I'm getting out of this cage, and when I do, I'm going to kill that son of a bitch with my bare hands."

That was enough for now. He could see Kane was soaking it all in and knew a fire was smoldering in Kane's belly. Law hoped it caught quickly and burned down his resistance.

The subject of JD didn't come up again until the next day. As pre-arranged, Evan came to Law's cell and watched him through the bars.

Law was sitting with his back against the block wall behind the cot. He eyed Evan disdainfully. "What can I do for you, Officer?"

"That's Detective to you, asswipe."

Law laughed derisively but said nothing else.

"I thought I'd give you another chance to help find your... well, I guess he's not really a friend, considering what he did to you," Evan taunted with a grin.

"Wow." Law shook his head ruefully. "He must really have you chasing your tails if you're asking *me* for help. Well, sorry, Offic...whoops, *Detective*," he corrected purposely, "I can't help you."

Evan lost the good-guy façade. "I would think you'd want to see the man who tried to kill you brought to justice."

"Oh, he will be. You can bank on it," Law said in a dangerous voice.

Evan tried for a few more minutes, but when Law refused to answer, he stormed off. Kane roused himself from where he sat on his bed. "You really think you can get out of here and find JD on your own?"

Law sat up slowly and turned a look of steely determination on Kane. "That all depends on you."

"How?"

"He's not stupid enough to go back to the house, which means he's holed up somewhere else. And I'm betting you know where that is."

When Kane said nothing more, Law rose and came to the wall separating them. "Why are you protecting him? He's the reason we're all sitting in these goddamned cells."

"Even if you knew where to find him, you can't get out of here."

Law held himself in check. This could be just what he needed. "Tell me where he is, and I'll tell you exactly how I plan on getting out of this shit-hole."

Kane finally relented and told him about a safe-house he'd rented. "I like to have a backup plan, just in case things go to hell. JD knew about it, but I don't know if that's actually where he is."

In return, Law laid out his strategy to get himself out of jail. It was going to hurt like a bitch, but it would get him out without blowing his cover.

An hour later, Law was on his way back to the hospital. The sutures in his back had ruptured, and the wounds were open and bleeding. The guards had come running when they'd heard a commotion in the cell area.

What they'd found was Law held in a choke-hold against the bars, with Kane's fist hammering into Law's side. Each hit tore at the still-healing wounds.

By the time they'd gotten them separated, Law was a mess.

When they had him out and loaded into an ambulance, Evan was there. "Dude, a little overkill, don't you think?"

Law breathed through the pain. "Had to look good."

"Ari finds out about this, she'll have my ass."

"So don't tell her."

Once Law had been seen to and his back redressed, he filled Evan in on what he'd learned. Evan immediately called the station and set up a team to go in and apprehend JD.

Law pushed himself off the bed.

Evan caught the movement and held his hands up. "Whoa. And just where do you think you're going?"

"With you." Law shrugged into the scrubs shirt the hospital had provided for him.

"Oh, hell no," Evan protested. "You're not getting anywhere near this. You were just sewn up again."

"I'll be numb for a while yet," Law told him. "I'm good to go." He stopped and held Evan's gaze. "I won't be kept out of this. I have a score to settle with this motherfucker."

"You're still a cop, Law," Evan cautioned. "You need to keep that in mind when we find him.”

"I won't kill him," Law promised. "But if he happens to resist arrest..."

Evan just shook his head.

Half an hour later, they were headed to the small house Kane had told him about.

Once everyone was in position, they busted through the door and swarmed the place. The rooms were empty, but there was evidence JD had been there recently.

They'd only just missed him.

The entire structure and surrounding area were searched until they ran out of light. But there was no other trace of JD. He'd slipped through their fingers.

"Son of a fucking bitch!" Law punched the doorframe of the room JD had been in just hours before.

The search resumed at first light the following day, but when a week had gone by with still no sign of JD, Law wasn't holding out hope that they were going to find him.

Monday evening, he sat on Evan's couch and tried to think of what he could have done differently. Evan was in the kitchen grabbing them both a beer when Law heard Evan's phone ring.

"Hello?...No. We haven't located him yet...Yeah, okay. I'll get word to him."

Evan came over, handed Law one of the bottles, and sat down on the opposite end of the couch. "Your boss is calling it. He wants you back for debriefing tomorrow."

Law nodded and took a long drink of his beer. He'd known this moment was coming. He stared into the brown bottle in his hand and tried not to think about all the things he would be walking away from.

Out of the corner of his eye, Law saw Evan picking at the label on his own bottle. "You know...I could be persuaded to put in a good word for you, if you ever wanted to try your hand at being an ordinary detective. I'm sure Daytona could use a good cop like you." He paused a moment. "Think about it. No more moving around. No more solitude. No more living a life that isn't really yours. It wouldn't be the excitement you're used to, but we get some action every now and then."

Evan took a swig and smiled as he lowered the bottle. "Detective Seth Lawson kind of has a ring to it."

Law clamped down on the yearning for what Evan was offering. He snorted out a half-laugh. "You wouldn't want me around showing you up. And besides, I've still got a job to do."

"Just something to think about." Evan sent him a hooded look.

"Do you mind me crashing on your couch one more night? I'll be out of here first thing."

"Not at all. You're welcome to it any time."

True to his word, Law was up and out of the house before dawn. Since he'd already put his bike into storage, he took a cab to the airport. Within the hour, was putting hundreds of miles between himself and Daytona Beach, Florida.

<div align="center">~~~</div>

Aria's phone rang early Tuesday morning. She rubbed the sleep from her eyes as she reached for it.

"Hello?"

"He's gone."

Aria's heart stopped. "What?"

"We lost JD. It looks like he skipped town. Since there was nothing left for Law to do here, his boss called him back in. He flew out this morning."

Tears burned her eyes and throat. She reached up and squeezed the bridge of her nose with a finger and thumb, trying to hold them off. She needed to hang up before she lost it. "Okay. Thanks for letting me know."

She'd taken the phone away from her ear when she heard

Evan's voice come through the speaker. She slowly pulled it back.

"If it's any consolation, he didn't want to go. I could see it in him last night." His tone was soft and sympathetic. "I all but offered him a job working with me here in Daytona."

Aria swallowed back the tears. "What did he say?"

"Made some offhand comment about showing me up, but I could tell it was killing him to leave. You both have denied having feelings for each other, but it's easy to see what's really going on." Silence hung in the air between them. "Maybe he'll change his mind and come back."

"Yeah." Aria disconnected the call before Evan could say anything else. She dropped the phone on the bed and rolled to her side. She pulled her legs up close and wrapped her arms around her middle, physically holding herself together from the shattering pain of losing him.

No matter how many times she'd told herself this was for the best, the agony she was suffering, now that he was truly out of her life, felt like it would rip her apart.

After a while, Aria forced her arms and legs to move. She refused to lay here and wallow in self-pity. The reason she'd had to say goodbye to Law was still out there. Edrick Noor had to be stopped.

When she'd pressed Ethan about the dreams, he'd said he couldn't really remember them. He recalled that they were dark and nasty, but after waking, the details would slip away. Aria had a feeling that he was holding something back—something he didn't want the rest of them to know. But no matter how many times she'd asked, he'd given her the same response.

She'd explained to her family the plan to try and draw Noor out. They hadn't liked it at first, but as the days passed, the idea had started to sink in, and they'd agreed it warranted further discussion.

Noor had been suspiciously quiet lately. No new attempts on

any of her siblings. No taunts. No visions. No other sign of him.

The general consensus was that he'd expended his energy possessing JD at the time of the shooting, and now had to lay low to build his stores back up. Maybe that was true, but Anna was still able to sense him off and on. What concerned them most was that she'd been picking up on glee and satisfaction instead of his usual anger and rage.

It didn't bode well for anyone if he'd found something that excited him.

Aria pushed the covers aside and sat up on the edge of the bed. But before she could stand, she was overwhelmed by a vision.

Early morning light barely illuminated the scene, but she could just make out a young girl walking ahead of her. She looked to be in her late teens—maybe a little older. She carried a backpack slung over one shoulder, and her blonde hair was pulled back into a ponytail. *Was she a student?*

Aria looked past the girl to see where she was going. She seemed to be headed to the lone car in a parking lot. Aria tried to turn her head to discern where this girl was, but it appeared she was only along for the ride. She had no control of whoever's body she was watching from.

And then she heard it. A voice in her head, talking directly to her. Noor's voice.

"Well, well, well. Look who should happen to show up. And perfect timing too. You get a little preview of what you'll have to look forward to when I'm finally free."

"Keep dreaming. You won't live long enough to get that far."

The woman was approaching her car, not noticing that evil lurked behind her.

"Hey! Turn around! Run!" Aria screamed in her head.

"She can't hear you, little witch," Noor laughed. *"Oh, we're going to enjoy our time with her."*

"We? We who? Who have you possessed this time?"

The girl reached out to grasp the door handle, and Aria knew she had to do something before it was too late.

Thinking frantically, she concentrated all her energy on the air surrounding the unsuspecting innocent and sent it her way.

The wind swirled and turned until it caught at the long tail of her hair. Her head swung to the side, enough for her to catch sight of the danger stalking closely behind her.

Though her eyes registered shock, her body was already in motion. She let the bag slide down her arm to land in her hand. She gripped it tightly, and on a powerful swing, had it connecting with her would-be attacker.

She didn't wait around. Once the blow had landed, the blonde took off running.

Aria smiled in her mind, knowing the girl was safe.

Two deep voices rang out in her head, both filled with rage at being deprived of their prey.

Before she could say anything, she saw a reflection in the car window. The face staring back at her was JD's.

Noor and JD were working together. The pairing of these two would mean a torturous end for all those in their path, a union made only more deadly by the morbid pleasure they took in the pain and suffering they inflicted on others.

One more wrathful shout rang out in her mind, just as she was wrenched out of the vision. She found herself still seated on her bed, but she wasn't alone. Anna was kneeling in front of her.

"What happened?" Anna rose to sit down next to her. "You were yelling."

Aria knew instinctively that there would be more incidents like this one. They had to find a way to stop them and destroy Noor forever.

"We've got a huge problem." Aria took a calming breath and explained what she'd just seen.

"And that happened this morning?"

"Yeah. I don't know how I tapped into them—maybe because I was thinking about Noor, but I'm glad I did. That girl would be dead otherwise. Or worse."

"We need to tell the others." Anna paused before continuing. "Evan may want to call Law back in, since JD is a part of it."

Aria had purposely stayed away during their search for JD, and now her pulse raced at the thought of seeing him again. She'd love nothing more, but one goodbye was enough. She didn't think she could survive another. No. They'd take care of it on their own.

"We can handle this." Aria got up and walked to the dresser, opened a drawer, and started to pull out clothes. "There's no need for him to return."

She ignored Anna's watchful gaze as she dressed, and her sister finally left to change clothes and make a call to their brothers.

Ten minutes later, all of them were gathered around Anna's living room, Anna and Ethan on the couch, and Aria and Evan facing each other in the side chairs. Each held a cup of freshly-brewed coffee.

The boys listened intently to Aria's vision. When she finished, Evan rose and paced the small living room.

"Son of a bitch." He plowed his fingers through his shaggy black hair. "The thought of those two joining forces makes my skin crawl."

He turned back to face Aria. "You know Law's going to want to know about this."

She shook her head. "Like I told Anna, we can handle it. He's already moved on to something else, and there's no need for him to get caught up in this mess again."

"And you think he's just going to forget what JD did to him?" Evan's black eyes widened incredulously. "I know for a fact he won't appreciate you withholding this from him. As he sees it, he has a score to settle."

She tried to get her brother to understand. "He's out of it now. He's beyond their reach."

"So you're trying to protect him by keeping him in the dark?" Evan asked her in disbelief.

Aria was losing patience, and her voice rose because of it. "He never would have been hurt in the first place if it hadn't been for me."

"How can you possibly know that?" Evan shouted in frustration before reining it back in. "You know as well as I do that Law has had problems with JD for a long time. What's to say JD hasn't been planning to kill him all along? It may have nothing to do with our problem."

"It doesn't matter." Aria wouldn't be moved on this. "He's safely away from here, and that's where he needs to stay."

Ethan spoke into the tense silence. "What the hell are you two talking about?"

Shit. Aria hadn't even realized how out of the loop Ethan was while she was arguing with his twin. And by the look on Evan's face, he hadn't either.

She had no choice but to tell her brother the truth. When she finished her explanation, Ethan only sat back and muttered, "Wow. Yeah, I agree with Evan. He's gonna want to know about this."

Before Evan could put up another argument, Aria cut him off. "Can you both just please help me figure out how to find these two before they kill someone?"

Thankfully, they finally let it drop. When Evan spoke again, he'd slipped back into cop-mode. "Did you recognize where they were? My guess would be that JD is staying within a couple-mile perimeter of where the attack took place."

"No." Aria had been away for too long. The landscape of Daytona Beach had changed a lot in that time. "I don't."

"She probably called it in." Evan leaned forward and rested his elbows on his knees as he thought it through. "I'll check with dispatch when I get into work. See who caught it. With a close call like this one though, he may move again. If he *was* in the area, this may well have pushed him out."

"I see what Noor's getting from this partnership," Ethan offered. "By the sounds of it, he's found a kindred spirit in JD. He can experience the torment and humiliation of others again, something he's missed out on since our ancestors locked him away. But what's JD getting out of it? From what we know, he doesn't need any help to attack and hurt women."

"Maybe he doesn't know he's being possessed," Anna suggested.

"Oh, he does," Aria answered. "When I was in his head, they both expressed their fury at having been deprived of their victim. That tells me JD is fully aware. I think they play off of each other. I don't know what kind of deal they have worked out, but we need to end it. We need a plan that will neutralize JD and stop Noor from taking over anyone else."

"We *do* need a plan," Anna chimed in. "But it just occurred to me that we haven't made any attempts to combine our magic since Aria got back. We have no hope of truly stopping Noor until we can figure out how to accomplish the 'four into one' part of the prophecy."

"Anna's right," Ethan nodded. "Why don't we meet back here later to work on our elemental magic?"

"Sounds good," Aria and Anna answered together.

Aria followed Evan out of the house, and once they were outside, she cornered him one last time.

She waited for him to look at her. "Evan, promise me you won't call Law. I don't want him pulled back into this."

"That's not really your call."

"It is when Noor and JD are trying to kill him," Aria said, frustrated. "He knows nothing of magic, Evan. JD has a huge advantage on him now."

She was gathering herself to argue further, but Evan went

off on her before she could.

"Why don't you just stop obsessing over JD and focus your attention on Noor? *He* needs a magical solution. Not JD. Leave him to me—to the police. We're on it. We'll find him."

Aria was shocked by his outburst. His reticence towards using magic was something she was going to have to think about.

She bit back any further argument and simply said, "Fine."

Evan turned to walk away, but she needed to know for sure. "Are you going to leave Law out of this?"

He stopped and looked back at her. "I won't say anything to him, as long as you let me do my job and find JD."

"Deal."

12

When she returned to the house, Ethan was also taking his leave. With nothing but waiting and thinking to fill her day, Aria cajoled Anna into letting her tag along for her mysterious self-defense class.

She borrowed some of Anna's workout clothes and fifteen minutes later, they pulled into the gym parking lot. Before Aria could open the door and get out of the car, Anna turned in her seat.

"No third degree," Anna warned. "I know you think I shouldn't be doing this, but this is what I want. So no threats of retaliation if he hurts me."

"Fine," Aria said, but she'd reserve judgment on the guy until she saw him. "Let's go."

When Aria got her first look inside Knight's Place, her first thought was, *Oh, hell no.* This was not the type of place her sister needed to be hanging out in. Knight's was a straight-up guy's gym. This was a no-frills facility where men came to sweat and train.

If music were ever played, Aria was sure it would be hard-driving and testosterone-laden. Bright fluorescent lights had been passed over for large industrial fixtures with wire frames that hung at even intervals throughout the room.

Aria didn't think of herself as a girly-girl, but she would have never stepped foot in this place without an armed escort.

But since Anna had, she was here to see what it was all about. She took a moment to look around at all the equipment.

Taking up a large portion of one side of the room was a red, white, and blue boxing ring. Beyond that was a sizable circular cage. Noticing the tall chain-link walls that would keep the fighters in, Aria shivered. She'd never understood how two grown men could beat the living crap out of each other for no reason.

Her gaze swept the space and noted the other half of the room was littered with heavy bags, dumbbells, and weight benches. There was also a good-sized matted area where men were rolling around trying to pin each other down. At the opposite end, she caught sight of an enormous tire that had to have come off of some kind of farming machinery. She wondered briefly what the hell they did with that and then remembered seeing a video of a man lifting and flipping it over and over.

Aria wrinkled her nose a little. This was definitely a man's-man type of place. And as with most areas occupied by this kind of man, the smell of musk and blood hung in the air.

She followed Anna to the ring and set her stuff down when Anna did. Two guys were already in there sparring. A well-fit black man held up large padded mitts and barked out orders. He shouted out a quick succession of punches before changing it up to kicks. He was relentless but got everything he demanded out of the fighter.

They waited for the men to finish before approaching the side. When the trainer turned and saw them, he smiled, pulled off the pads, and came over.

"This must be Aria." He ducked under the middle rope and jumped down to introduce himself. "Joe Conrad."

"Not a Knight?" Aria asked, a little surprised.

Joe laughed easily. "I've been called many things, but never a knight. That's the guy who used to own the place. When I bought it, I just left the name."

When he focused on Anna and started talking to her about her training, Aria took a moment to check him out.

He looked to be about six feet tall, early thirties maybe. He wore nothing but baggy dark-blue cotton shorts, leaving a good majority of his milk-chocolate skin on display. His black hair was cropped extremely short, almost shaven. Black brows rose above eyes the color of rich amber, and a dark goatee framed his full mouth.

Joe Conrad was ripped. His shoulders and chest were well-defined, and his cut abs looked like solid stone. His legs were thick and muscular, and he carried himself with confidence and ease. All in all, he was a handsome man. He reminded her more of an actor than the ex-MMA fighter Anna claimed him to be.

"So, grab your gear and get warmed up, baby girl," Joe told Anna, drawing Aria's attention. "I've got a new move I want to show you, and we need to work on your take-downs."

Anna nodded, snatched up her bag, and with one last warning look at Aria, walked over to the matted area to do as Joe had instructed.

When Aria brought her gaze back around to him, he was standing before her with his powerful arms crossed over his chest. His head was tilted to the side, considering her.

"What?" Her tone was a touch belligerent.

"You've already decided you don't like me. Why is that?"

He seemed to prefer it straightforward, so Aria would play it the same. "It's not that I don't like you. I just don't think this is the best setting for my sister."

His dark brows came together. "Oh, yeah? How do you figure?"

"She's too..." Aria looked for the right description.

"Fragile? Soft? Naive?" Joe supplied when she took too long. His intriguing eyes took on a fierce, defensive edge, and his arms dropped to his sides. Almost battle-ready. "Were those some of the words you were looking for? She's told me a little about how you all treat her."

Before Aria could refute his assumption, he stepped in close, towering over her. "If that's where you were going, then you don't know Anna at all."

Aria didn't let his tactic cow her. She stood her ground and leaned in. "We're identical twins. If anyone knows her, it's *me*."

"You'd think so, wouldn't you?" He reached out to grab the small towel off the edge of the ring floor and then looped it around his neck. "But somewhere along the way, you stopped *seeing* her. Now, if you'll excuse me, I have work to do. I'll send Jay over to help you."

He walked away from her and over to where Anna was stretching out. Aria wasn't sure of what to think about this man taking her to task over her sister. He didn't know Anna like she did. He'd never seen what she'd gone through growing up because of her empathic power.

Jay did indeed come over. He was tall and gangly, probably fifteen or sixteen, with short, sandy blond hair and a just-developing physique.

After introductions, he took her through warmups of jumping jacks, sit-ups, and push-ups. Aria did as he asked but kept an eye on Anna and Joe.

"She's fine, you know," Jay said when he noticed her attention was more on the couple than on her own training. "We don't normally get women in here, but all of us know Joe would skin us if anyone gave her a hard time. She's kind of become a favorite around here."

They watched as Anna snuck under Joe's punch to wrap her arms around his legs and over-balance him.

Jay's next words were spoken with a note of humor. "She's a little bit of a thing, but she gives him a run. What she lacks in size and strength, she makes up for with speed, agility, and downright sneakiness."

For the next half-hour, Aria was too busy to do anything but remember how to breathe as she punched and kicked until she thought her arms and legs would melt into a flesh-colored heap. Jay ended up taking pity on her when it became evident she hadn't worked out in a while. He called a halt after Aria completed one last round on the heavy bag.

Grateful, she grabbed her bottle of water and turned just in time to see Joe take Anna down hard. Aria felt the impact of her sister hitting the barely-padded floor from where she stood. Straddling her, Joe reached down and grabbed her by the throat. He held her to the mat in a move that looked impossible to escape.

Before Aria could decide whether to interfere or not, Anna was in motion. She pushed her hands up through Joe's arms, grabbed his head, and yanked it down into her chest, at the same time that her legs came up to lock around his waist. After that, it became a blur of action until Anna had somehow gotten the upper hand and rolled Joe to his back. And proceeded to throw punches at his face and head.

When she pushed up off of him to stand, she did a little booty-shaking victory dance. Joe laughed as he got to his feet.

"Nice. You didn't hesitate at all."

Aria was at a loss. Until this moment, she hadn't believed her sister when she'd said this was something she'd needed. She hadn't trusted Anna to know what was good for herself.

As Aria had watched Joe use and abuse her sister—and her sister give it right back—she'd gained a new insight into who Anna had become in the time she'd been gone. And it was *not* someone who needed to be coddled and protected.

And her opinion of Joe Conrad elevated a few notches too.

They worked for another half-hour before ending the session. Aria smiled at Anna as she approached where she sat.

"What?"

"Nothing." Aria grinned. "Just wondering when sweet little

Anna became a kick-ass bitch."

Anna laughed as she ran a towel over her face and neck.

Joe walked up behind Anna, obviously overhearing Aria's comment. "My best student. She's learned fast."

"Not fast enough to miss out on a few bruises," Anna groused. "I had a nice-sized one on my ass that took weeks to heal. Felt it every time I sat down."

If Aria hadn't been looking directly at Joe in that moment, she would have missed the heat that pooled in his eyes as they dropped to Anna's rear end. If she were reading him right, he would've loved the chance to kiss it and make it better.

So, that's how it is, huh? Someone has the hots for my sister.

Aria glanced at Anna. *And if I'm not mistaken, the recipient of that affection is oblivious.*

Aria waited until they were in the car to test the waters. "So, how did you meet Joe?"

Anna pulled out onto the road. "There had been a few attacks reported in the area, and he offered one free self-defense class to show women how they could protect themselves. There were probably about ten of us who took it, but I was the only one who chose to come back. I really liked it. It made me feel…I don't know…empowered, to learn the moves and be able to use them, so I stuck with it."

"He's kind of handsome."

"Yeah, I guess so," Anna agreed, distracted. "I never really noticed."

"You never noticed," Aria muttered with a shake of her head.

Anna glanced at her and then back at the road. "What?"

"Anna." Aria turned in her seat to face her sister. "That man would love nothing better than to be your knight in shining armor. Not to mention, kissing all those bruises you're so proud of."

"What? No way." Anna sent her a surprised look. "Really?"

Aria nodded and grinned.

Anna seemed to be thinking it through when she suddenly burst out, "Great! Now it's going to be all awkward the next time I go in there. Do you know how often we're body to body when he's showing me something? Oh, God," she moaned. "That move today. His face was buried in my chest. You just couldn't have kept that to yourself, could you?"

"Hey," Aria laughed, "it's not my fault you're deaf and blind to hot guys drooling all over you. Ease up on those shields. Live a little."

"Just great," Anna repeated and drove on towards home. Aria laughed, enjoying how flustered her sister had become.

After arriving back at the house and having a quick bite for lunch, Anna got ready for work and left. Now that she was alone, Aria wanted to seriously think about a way to stop JD and Noor. It was all well and good that Evan was working on it from his end, but Aria wanted a backup plan if that failed.

But first, she needed a long, hot shower to soothe her sore muscles.

Thirty minutes later and feeling a lot better, she stood in the kitchen pouring a pop over ice when she heard a metallic sound. She turned to the back door and saw the handle jiggle as if someone were trying to get in.

Without a sound, she set the can down. On silent feet, she cautiously backed out of the room.

If she could get through the front door and around the house, she could surprise whoever it was. And outside was better anyway. Anna wouldn't appreciate any destruction done to her house, and the force Aria intended to use would definitely wreak havoc.

Once out of the kitchen, Aria pivoted and ran for the front door, glad she'd taken the time to dress in worn jeans and a blue tank. She was barefoot, but that wouldn't hinder her.

She jerked the door open and sprinted around the side of the house. Reaching the rear corner, she stopped and peeked her head around to get a view of her would-be intruder.

JD, head bent to his task, was working on the lock. He'd gain entrance any minute. She had to act. Aria stepped out of cover and shouted. "Hey!"

He jerked upright at the sound and glared. Aria slowly made her way around him to the middle of the back yard. She started gathering power, asking her old friend for aid.

Startled at first by her appearance, JD quickly recovered and advanced towards her. He clearly didn't care that it was the middle of the day and that anyone could see them. Being thwarted that morning must have really pushed him over the edge.

"Alone at last. And your guard dog isn't around to protect you." He smirked. "Last I saw him, he was face down in the dirt."

She ignored his reference to Law. She didn't know if JD knew that Law had survived his bullets, but it didn't matter. He was gone and out of harm's way. Now, she just had to do the same for herself.

"So where's your master?" Aria taunted. "What'd you do, slip your leash? What's he going to think when he finds out you've come here without his permission?"

"No one tells me what to do, you stupid bitch!" JD shouted, crazy lighting his eyes.

"Oh, really?" Aria pulled on her magic, ready to strike out at a moment's notice. "And here I thought you were just his tool. Content to walk around with his hand up your ass, controlling your every move."

"I'm no one's fucking puppet!" JD roared out in anger. "I agreed to let him tag along once in a while, and for that, he's promised me unimaginable power. As soon as that happens, no one will *ever* stop me from taking what I want again."

"He'll never give you anything, because my family and I will end him long before that can happen."

He smiled grotesquely. "You won't be able to do anything by the time I'm through with you."

"Don't count on it, asshole." Aria let loose the gale-force wind she'd been holding. It took him completely off his feet and dropped him a good twenty feet from where he'd been standing.

He got up and shook himself off. "What the fuck?"

"I'm a witch, dipshit," Aria shouted. "Didn't Noor share that little tidbit with you? I won't be so easy to rape and kill as that other girl would have been."

Heedless of her warning, JD launched himself at her. Just before he would have grabbed her, she knocked him to the side with another blast of air. He fell into the dirt but was right back on his feet. Before she realized his intent, he chucked a handful of sand into her face and eyes.

He took advantage of her sudden vulnerability and hit her mid-body like a tackling dummy. Aria felt her feet lift off of the ground as they flew backwards. They landed with enough force to knock the breath from her lungs.

Blinded and gasping for air, she fought to free herself from his grasp. He laughed as he pinned her to the ground and straddled her waist. She smelled his acrid stench as he leaned down onto her. The hot, foul odor that panted out from between his lips nearly made her gag as it wafted over her face.

Aria desperately pulled more of her magic. She knew what she was creating would be dangerous, but she had no other choice.

So intent on his mission to rip and tear at her clothes, JD didn't hear the wind rising around them until it was too late. The funnel that hit him plucked him right up and hurled him away. Once the weight was gone, Aria jumped to her feet and surrounded herself with the cyclone.

She flinched when he suddenly screamed. She thought it might have been out of frustration and anger at being bested yet again, but she wasn't sure.

Protected from another attack, she frantically wiped the debris from her eyes. Once she could open them, she watched and listened for any movement that would give away his position or what he was doing.

She heard and saw nothing.

Though her eyes still watered, she slowly allowed the wall of storm to dissipate.

There was no sign of JD. What she did see, however, was a small tree limb completely coated in blood. And underneath was a large pool of darkness staining the ground.

From that, she could only conclude that in the wake of her tornado, JD had been flung and impaled on the branch. Regardless of whether it had gone completely through him or he'd only been stabbed, he was injured. It was a significant amount of blood, but since he wasn't lying dead at her feet, he'd evidently been alive enough to run off.

Making her way back around to the front of the house, Aria stepped inside and locked the door behind her.

She went immediately to the bathroom to flush the remaining grit from her eyes. Her next order of business was to call her family to let them know what had happened and what she'd learned.

It was decided that instead of meeting at Anna's later, they'd all go to their parents' for dinner and discussion.

13

Aria was the first to arrive later that afternoon. After kissing her dad on the cheek, she went directly to the kitchen where her mom was, no doubt, already preparing dinner.

"Hey, Mom."

Mary set aside the burger patty she was shaping, wiped her hands, and wrapped Aria in a tight hug.

"You okay?"

"Yeah," Aria smiled in reassurance. "I'm good."

She stepped out of her mother's embrace and crossed to the fridge to grab a pop. "I just wish that stick would have caused enough damage to slow him down. That way he'd be behind bars and out of the picture, and we could concentrate solely on our other problem."

She pulled the tab on the top on the can and sat down on one of the tall stools at the island as Mary resumed her preparations.

"As it is, we don't know when they'll show their faces again." Aria took a quick sip. "I just hope that JD is out of commission enough that Noor can't use him for a while."

"That may not have any bearing," Mary offered. "He'll just possess someone else."

"I know." Aria didn't want to think about how hard it would be anticipate an attack when you had no idea where or from whom it would be coming. "But I think Noor knows he has it good with JD. I'm hoping he'll wait until his preferred meat-suit is healed."

Mary shook her head. "Saying it like that sounds so bad. *Meat-suit.* It brings to mind that movie about the serial killer who would kill women and wear their skin."

She shuddered and Aria grinned. "I heard it said recently and thought it fit the situation pretty well."

"It does," Mary smirked over at her. "I could just do without the visual."

Aria shook her head. "Is there anything I can help you with?"

"Now, that you mention it..."

Aria was finishing up the salad when Anna and Ethan came in.

"Evan will be here in a few." Ethan picked a cherry tomato off the top of the lettuce and tossed it into his mouth.

"Ethan Burke," Mary scolded from where her head was buried in the refrigerator, "get your hands out of that food and set the table."

He sent a quick glance at his mother's back before turning to Aria and mouthing, "How does she do that?"

Aria shrugged, enjoying his discomfort. She mouthed back, "I don't know."

Mary, arms laden with condiments, closed the door with her hip and sneered over at her son. "It's no big secret, my dear boy. Ever since you were little, when you'd walk into this kitchen, you'd snitch a taste of whatever I was cooking."

"I did not." He stood up straight and acted offended. In the next second he was laughing. "Okay, I did." He sidled up to her and pressed a kiss to her cheek. "It's because you're the best cooker there is."

Love shined bright in her mom's hazel eyes. Aria knew she was remembering how, when they'd been about three years old, Ethan had told her that she was a good cooker. For many years after that, they'd all said it, but as they'd grown, it had faded away. Aria could see how much it meant to their mom to hear it once again.

Mary cupped the side of Ethan's face and then picked a cucumber slice out of the salad and handed it to him.

As he chewed and smiled, Anna teased, "Suck up."

They were still laughing when Evan and their father came in.

"What'd I miss?" Evan asked.

"Ethan brown-nosing," Aria supplied.

"Oh, that's nothing new."

"Hey, don't blame me because I have a way with the ladies."

Then it registered what he'd said, and he instantly sobered, turned, and walked out of the room. The others were caught off-guard by the abrupt shift, but they all knew the cause. Undoubtedly, his thoughts had turned to Honor.

It had been so nice to have the old Ethan back for a minute, but he was gone now.

"She would want him to laugh and smile again." Anna stared at the doorway he'd escaped through. "This guilt is killing him."

Paul wrapped an arm around Anna's shoulders and pulled her close in comfort. "He knows that, but actually forgiving himself is something else."

Mary got everyone back on track, and soon the meal was on the table. As they ate, Aria recounted her confrontation with JD that afternoon.

"We should probably check with hospitals and clinics," Evan suggested. "If his injuries are severe enough, he may have sought out medical help."

"And if he didn't?" Mary asked. "Something needs to be done. This man is too dangerous to just leave out there." She looked at her son. "Are you guys any closer to finding him?"

"No, but we're not giving up," Evan stressed. "He's wanted in association with multiple crimes, plus he shot and nearly killed a law enforcement officer. And now that he has some kind of hard-on for Aria, we won't rest until we find him. *I* won't rest."

Once the dinner mess was cleared away and the kitchen put to rights, they gathered outside on the back lawn. The four formed their circle as they'd always done—hands clasped, each set of twins facing each other.

As their parents looked on, one by one, they called to that which was theirs by birth.

As eldest of the four, Aria began.

"Still and calm or a raging storm
We are as one, from the day I was born
I am Air and Air is me
As I will, so mote it be."

She felt the immediate rush as the element that was as much a part of her as her hair and skin, answered and joined with her.

Across from her, Anna began her call.

"From the heavens above to the oceans below
Together always as you ebb and flow
I am Water and Water is me
As I will, so mote it be."

Aria's gaze slid to the next in order of birth, Evan.

"Sand and soil, dirt and stone
Neither you nor I shall stand alone
I am Earth and Earth is me
As I will, so mote it be."

And finally Ethan.

"Smoke, spark, ember, flame

You and I forever the same
I am Fire and Fire is me
As I will, so mote it be."

They'd spoken those same words countless times throughout the years. They were the calls to the elements that were theirs through the marks on their bodies.

Only this time, Aria felt the birthmark on her shoulder blade burn white hot before it gradually faded away. From the surprised looks on her siblings' faces, they, too, had felt the same reaction in their marks. This ritual had always been a gentle communion of spirits. The symbols of that connection had never before become active.

What did it mean, she wondered. Why now? Was it because this was the first time they'd worked together in so many years? Or would this have happened sooner if Aria hadn't left? Was this the natural progression their magic would have taken?

Another thought crossed her mind. They were within a year of the time when they would have to face Noor for a final showdown. Maybe now that he was gaining strength, he'd triggered their own powers to expand in response. Was this the first stage in finding the way to end him?

"Keep going." Aria suddenly wanted to see if this change signaled a progression in their magic.

Four voices continued the spell.

"We call to our elements for protection and grace
Gather now in this blessed place
Grant us your strength and your power
On this night and in this hour."

A force more powerful than Aria had ever felt blasted through her. The wind swirled around her and filled her with such energy and strength, she thought she might burst from the sheer volume of it.

She could just make out her siblings through the current of air and saw that they too were enveloped within a storm of their own making.

All she could do was hold on and ride the high.

Long before she was ready for it to end, the surge of magic faded away. Aria was left standing in shock and wonderment.

Ethan was the first to speak. "Holy fucking shit."

"You can say that again," Evan laughed, looking down at his hands. "I have never experienced anything like that before."

"Still buzzing?" Aria smiled because she was feeling the same.

"Yeah." Evan flexed his fingers.

"Me too, and I feel so energetic," Anna bounced on her toes, "like I could fly."

They were still reveling in what had happened when their mother spoke from the door.

"Before we get too far into what just took place," Mary looked at each of them, "you'd better close your circle."

The four of them clasped hands again and said the words which ended the rite.

"A circle cast for a favor asked
Closed now that the need has passed
Our thanks and blessings be to thee
As we will so mote it be."

Afterwards, they all gathered at the patio table to discuss everything from the zing of their marks to the rush of power from their elements.

Her twin echoed her thoughts from earlier. "What do you think it means?" Anna asked. "Why such a big shift?"

Aria shared her thoughts from earlier. "Since Noor is getting stronger, it makes sense that our own powers would elevate to counter his."

"I hope you're right about that," Anna said. "I'm ready for a little good news."

~~~

With JD out of commission and no sign of Noor, there was a lull the last few weeks of March. But as April arrived, all that changed.

Aria started to see JD. Everywhere. She'd be going about her day and there he'd be, standing a few blocks away, just staring at her. In the next instant, he'd be gone—sucked into a crowd of people, or lost behind a passing truck.

She'd reported each incident to Evan, but by the time he could get there, JD would be long gone.

Noor had resumed his old tricks as well, invading her mind while she slept and sending vile and disgusting images. On the nights he would come, he'd describe in lurid detail what he'd do to her when he was finally freed from his prison.

Through it all, she and her siblings continued to work together to hone their magic. The marks would still activate and the elements would flow, but no matter what they did, there was no further indication of what they needed to do from there.

By mid-April, it was all becoming too much for Aria. The double assault was taking its toll on her. They never left her alone. And even when Noor was absent, her sleep wasn't restful, because on those nights, she would dream of Law.

He'd been gone for a month now, and the hole in her heart was still there—if not even larger, as the full ramifications of never seeing him again settled in.

She knew he was probably off on another assignment somewhere, working to put yet more criminals behind bars. And denying himself all forms of attachment in order to do the
~~~

job.

But wasn't that exactly what she'd done? Pushed him away for the greater good? She had to remind herself over and over that she'd done the right thing—as had he—but that knowledge didn't help to heal the part of her that missed him desperately.

Her dreams of him tempted her with hot and steamy encounters. She'd wake in the throes of an orgasm that never fully satisfied her.

This was one such morning, and as she lay in bed trying to catch her breath, she wished she'd had a chance to sleep with him all those weeks ago. At least then her imagination wouldn't take off running with what could have been.

Over and over, she'd told herself to forget him. But on the nights they were together, she'd wake up missing him too much, and each new day was like saying goodbye all over again.

Aria threw the covers aside and got out of bed. She headed straight for the shower and the soothing spray that would wash away the remnants of the dream, and her own turbulent feelings.

Clean and refreshed, she'd just finished brushing her teeth when she heard knocking at the front door.

Anna was already up and gone, leaving only Aria to see who it was. A quick glance in the mirror told her she was mostly presentable, and that the silk robe she'd donned after her shower covered her appropriately. Smoothing her damp hair back, she left the bathroom and wound her way through the small house.

Caution made her check to see who was on the other side of the door before opening it. When she looked through the peep hole, she saw a tall man standing with his back to her. He was dressed in a tan sport coat and jeans. In the slightly distorted image, she could see his hands were tucked into the front pockets of his pants as he looked out over the neighborhood.

The breadth of this man's shoulders gave her a moment's

pause, but the dark hair was too short, so she pushed the thought aside. Pulling the door open, she stepped back.

~~~

Seth heard the sound of the door opening behind him and closed his eyes. He knew who stood there, as he'd purposely waited until Anna had left to make his approach.

For weeks he'd wondered what his first sight of Aria after so long would feel like. And as he'd stood there waiting for her to come, he'd actually been nervous. That wasn't a feeling he was used to experiencing.

Not a single worry had plagued him when he'd walked into his boss's office to begin the debriefing that had taken the better part of a week. None were present as he'd requested time off to figure a few things out. And they were blessedly absent as he'd typed up his resignation letter and handed it to the man who'd recruited him straight out of the police academy.

He'd never wavered when he'd finally called Evan a week ago to take him up on his offer of a job. Even the new DBPD badge in his pocket didn't cause alarm.

But this…seeing Aria again as himself…as Seth Lawson, scared him to death. Would she accept him? He knew the fight she and her family were preparing for still hung over their heads, but he hoped he could change her mind about going it alone.

If she let him in—into her life and into this fight—he knew he could convince her she'd made the right choice.

So here he was. Almost afraid to face her.

He took a deep breath, firmed his resolve, and slowly turned around.

Her beautiful blue eyes went large in recognition. She drew in a gasp but remained silent.

"Hi." He shifted his weight slightly and stuffed his hands
~~~

deeper into his pockets to dispel the need to reach out and touch her.

Her hand came up to rest on her chest even as the other held tightly to the door. "What are you doing here?" Her voice was whisper-soft and raw.

"I came back." He paused, but when it didn't look as if she were going to move, he took the next step. "May I come in?"

Wordlessly, she backed up and allowed him to pass. When the door closed behind him, he turned to face her.

She looked so damned good. Her long, silver-blonde hair hanging loose and tousled down her back. Small, pert breasts, free beneath the thin silk of her robe. Narrow waist that tucked in enough to showcase the flare of her hips. He wanted his hands on her, but he knew that would have to wait until she was more certain of him. Or he just lost his mind and took her. Whichever came first.

He was taken completely off-guard when she launched herself into his arms, but he recovered quickly and caught her tightly against his body. Her bare legs instantly wound around his waist and locked at the small of his back. Her arms wrapped around his neck at the same time she took his mouth in a scorching kiss.

He held on to her lush little body and tried to retain control. It was nearly impossible as his blood went lava-hot and rushed to more southern locales.

Grudgingly, he finally found some sense and tore himself away from her mouth.

"Aria." He tried to keep a sane thought in his head as she attacked his chin and neck with her teeth and lips. "I think we need to discuss a few things."

"Later." She blew away the rest of his reserve with a grinding movement of her hips against the hard edge of his erection.

He spun around with her in his arms and headed for the hall. There was a bedroom in each direction. "Which way?"

"Left."

Seth swung left and through the door, stopping long enough to push it closed with his foot before taking her to the bed.

Before he could lay her down and cover her body with his, she unhooked her legs from around his waist. She reached up, removed his jacket, and let it drop. She grasped the edges of his button-down shirt and pulled, buttons flying as the thin threads holding them gave way. The shirt joined the coat in a pile on the floor.

Seth stood there, bared to the waist as she leisurely ran her hands and gaze up his arms from wrists to biceps. Her touch left a trail of fire as she skimmed over the curve of his shoulders and down his pecs to lightly brush through the hair there. She continued down his abdomen, tracing the line of his ribs until finally they stopped at the fly of his jeans.

When her fingers dipped into his pants to unfasten them, he broke out in a sweat and his heart went into overdrive. God, he wanted her hands on him. He desperately needed her to reach in farther, take hold of him, and grip him hard. But he knew if she did that, it would be over before it began.

To take his mind off of what she was doing to him, he set to unwrapping her luscious body. Grasping the knot at her waist, Seth slowly unwound the ties and let them fall. The edges of the dressing gown parted to reveal the mid-line of her body, all the way down to the juncture of her thighs. She smiled up at him, and he fell into the promise he saw in the pale blue depths of her eyes.

She leaned forward and kissed the dead center of his chest. With her face still buried there, she breathed in deeply, taking the scent of him into her body.

God, that was sexy. He'd never thought about how he smelled to women. The knowledge that Aria found it to her liking made his pride, and other things, swell.

That hot mouth of hers traveled the expanse of his torso,

leaving a trail of searing bites over every inch of him.

When he didn't think he could take any more, Seth lifted her chin with a single finger and bent low to take possession of her lips. His tongue sank into the depths of her mouth in a preview of what would come later when he possessed her body.

Sliding his hands over her shoulders, Seth stripped her out of her robe. With a hand against her back to steady her, he laid her back onto the bed and followed her down. He broke away from the kiss to nibble his way down her body. He paused to lavish his attention on each of her breasts in turn, licking and sucking each pebbled nipple until she writhed beneath him.

Her ribs and stomach were given the same thorough treatment, her lithe body in constant motion now as she begged for more.

As he moved lower to her hips, Seth groaned in his chest when he saw how ready she was for him.

Starting at her feet, he kissed his way up until he came back to her center. He threaded his fingers through the short, trimmed hairs that guarded her entrance.

"Please, please, please," she panted out as her hips lifted and searched. "You're killing me."

Without a word, Seth draped her legs over his shoulders and lowered his mouth to her. The contact and pressure sent her over the edge, and she was still convulsing when he stripped out of the rest of his clothes and drove, full-length, into her.

The sudden friction and fullness set off her next orgasm. He held himself completely still as her body pulled and squeezed at his shaft. He was drenched in sweat in the effort it took to hold back his own release. When he finally felt her relax underneath him, he started with long, slow thrusts.

He set a pace that gave her time to reach that pinnacle again. As her breathing sped up, so did his movements. Her moans and gasps were so raw and intense, he stayed in a constant state of readiness. He found his own pleasure was tied to hers now. He couldn't let himself go until she'd peaked again.

Aria's head was thrashing back and forth on the bed. "Seth. Please."

The sound of his name on her lips, uttered in such passion-filled bliss, broke the last shred of his control.

Seth gritted his teeth, plunged deep, and pressed against the little nub hidden in the folds of her sex.

Aria screamed and came apart in his arms. He rode the storm for a heartbeat and then slammed into her over and over until, with a moan, his own release took him over.

14

They lay sprawled across the bed. Seth only had enough brain power left to roll slightly so he didn't collapse right on top of her. He was so much bigger than she was, and that was never more evident as they lay in each other's arms, his big body enveloping hers.

And when she started to shiver, he pulled her closer into his warmth and wrapped himself around her.

He didn't realize he'd dozed off until he felt her shift against him. When he opened his eyes, she was staring at him.

"Hi." He grinned at her.

"Hi, yourself."

He wasn't really sure how to proceed from here. He'd wanted to talk and plead his case, but things had taken a turn he hadn't expected. Her face seemed somewhat cautious right now, and he couldn't decipher what was going on in her mind.

"I hadn't intended for this to happen," he started.

"I know. I attacked you."

"Not that I'm complaining, but why did you?"

Her gaze dropped to his chest. "I had just woken from a dream about you, and it pissed me off. I was trying so hard to forget you, to block you out of my mind. You were gone. You were away from all the crap that surrounds me. I hoped I'd never see you again."

Seth felt the punch to his heart. "I didn't mean to—"

"But when I saw you standing on the porch…" Her blue eyes came back to his, and what he saw in them blew away all the pain her previous words had caused.

"I knew I'd been lying to myself. I couldn't live without you, and my mind and body have been trying to remind me of that since you left. You are the only man who has ever made me feel this way."

She leaned up and kissed his lips gently. "If you hadn't come back when you had, I'm sure it wouldn't have been long before I'd have come and found you."

Seth pulled her in close to the heart that was beating with happiness in his chest. "It killed me to stay away, but I had to make sure I was making the right choice for me. I've known for a while that I didn't want to be that man anymore. Then I met you, and that was the push I needed to make the change. I needed to find Seth Lawson again. And that's what I did.

"Once my mind was made up, I wrapped up all the loose ends of Law's life, and I handed in my two-week notice."

"You're not a cop anymore?" She pulled back enough to see his face.

He laughed at her assumption. "I'm not on the task force anymore, but I'm still a cop. Wherever my pants are, there's a brand new Daytona Beach Police Department badge in one of the pockets. I guess they liked how Evan and I worked together on the last case. They made me his partner."

Aria sat up. "Oh, my God, so you're staying?"

He propped himself up on his elbow and smiled. "As long as you'll have me."

"Is it safe? You were undercover for a long time."

"Anyone around here who knew me as Law is gone. They're either in jail, or they skipped town." His eyebrows drew together. "I really wish I could have finished things with JD, but I guess that's over now."

When Aria shifted her gaze away, Seth had a hunch she was

keeping something from him.

"What? Did something else happen?"

She was silent before taking a deep breath and looking up at him. "JD never left."

Now Seth sat up on the bed. "What?" His tone was ominous, but he didn't care. If that asshole was still here, why had no one told him?

What she said to him after that had him up and off the bed and jerking on his pants. Before he even got to the button, he lost his hold on his temper and swung back around to face her. "Are you fucking kidding me? Why the *hell* didn't you tell me about the attack when it happened? And now he's stalking you?"

Seth ran his hands up through his hair in frustration and anger. He turned, trying to gain some control over the compulsion to hunt the bastard down and kill him. But he was trying to put that way of life behind him, so he fought and finally pushed the urge away. When he thought he could speak without shouting, he turned around and asked, "What's being done to find him? And more importantly, what's your family doing to protect you?"

Aria pulled the sheet around her naked body. "I've called Evan every time I've seen him, but JD's always gone by the time he gets there. He hasn't tried anything—he only watches me." She took a breath and pushed her hair away from her face. "And as for the other, it was *my* choice to leave you out of it. You were gone and out of their reach. When I found out they were working together, I was never more grateful you'd already left."

Seth ran his hands through his cropped hair in frustration before spinning around to confront her again. "JD is *mine* to deal with."

She came up to her knees, still clutching the cover. "If it had only been him, it would have been different. You've dealt with the likes of him before, and I don't doubt you could have handled him. But it isn't just him anymore. He has Noor behind him, *inside* him. You have no clue how to fight something like that."

"Oh, that's just bullshit, and you know it," he flung back at her. "Or did you forget that I held my own against Noor once already? I'm not that easy to kill, Aria."

"I couldn't take that chance." The misery in her words nearly broke him. With an effort, he reined in his irritation.

He sat down next to her. "Aria, if something had happened to you, if he'd touched one hair on your head, I would have gone to jail for what I'd have done to him. Either that, or died trying." He shook his head. "I still might."

Aria threw her hands up. "See? That right there is why I didn't tell you. I was trying to protect you."

Seth ran his hands up through his hair again. "It's not your job to protect me. It's *my* job to protect *you*. And I should have stayed. I should have made sure he was either gone for good or dead."

"It wasn't your fault." She reached out and took his hand in hers. "You were called back. You had to follow orders."

"I can't believe Evan went along with this. He knew how I felt about JD. Why would he keep this from me too?"

"I made him promise not to contact you. He didn't like it, but he stuck to his word."

She shifted around until she straddled his lap and brought both hands up to capture his face. "I almost lost you when JD, or Noor, shot you. I couldn't go through that again. At least with you gone, I knew you were out there somewhere. I could lie to myself and say you were better off."

Seth wrapped his arms around her waist and pressed his forehead to hers. "I definitely was not better off without you."

She smiled sadly. "Neither was I."

"So what happens now?" He pulled his head back far enough to see her face. "They're both still out there. When they find out

I'm back, they're going to come after me."

She nodded. "I know, but I can't give you up again." She rested her head on his shoulder. "We'll figure it out as we go."

Seth held her close as he thought it through. He knew they had a lot to do, and that he had much to learn about the world that Aria and her family came from. Witches and magic and ancient evil weren't things he was used to dealing with, but he vowed to learn fast, because the alternative wasn't anything he could live with. He would not leave her again. He was in until the bitter end.

His thoughts were interrupted when she started to nibble on the underside of his chin and neck. "When do you have to report to work?"

Seth smiled. "Not until Wednesday morning."

"Tomorrow," Aria grinned. "Perfect."

They made love again, and when Anna came home later, they all shared dinner. They tried watching a movie together, but he and Aria couldn't keep their hands off of each other. Shortly after the title sequence rolled by, they escaped back to her bedroom.

~~~

They shared a shower in the morning, and while she made breakfast, Seth ran out to his car to get his bag. As she stirred the eggs, she thought about everything they'd discussed the previous night. They'd lain in the dark and talked for hours.

She knew so much more about him now. He'd told her of his childhood. How, at the age of four, his parents had been killed by a gang of bank robbers. He'd explained that while he'd been tucked away at pre-school, they'd stopped off at the bank to make a withdrawal for the vacation the three of them were leaving on that afternoon.

He'd learned later that five masked gunmen had stormed
~~~

the bank and shot everyone inside. Traumatized and alone, a young Seth had been taken into the state's custody while they tracked down a relative who would take him in. Eventually, his maternal grandfather had been located and came for him.

He hadn't been the most loving of men, but he'd provided a roof, meals, stability, and all the necessities. And by the time Seth had hit his teenage years, they'd gotten on pretty well. But at seventeen, Seth's world had been rocked once again by his grandfather passing away in his sleep.

The state had stepped in once again. But since he was only within a few months of legal age, he was able to talk them into letting him remain where he was.

Seth had never given any thought to what would happen upon his grandfather's death, or how he'd make ends meet. But he should have known his grandfather would ensure he'd be taken care of. Everything included in his estate had come to him free and clear. So at seventeen, he'd begun a life on his own.

Because he knew his grandfather would have wanted it, he'd finished out high school. Afterwards, with no clear purpose, he'd floated around for a few years. It wasn't until he'd finally sorted through his grandfather's belongings that he'd found the old clippings of the day that had changed his life.

An old need resurfaced. A drive to make sure that what had happened to him didn't happen to anyone else. So at twenty-two, he'd joined the police academy. It was pure luck that he'd been tagged to join a task force that would give him the chance to fulfill that dream.

Aria couldn't imagine what growing up like that had been like. She'd been one of four her entire life. Her parents had been sure to treat all of them as individuals and not as a set, but still, as one of quads—and especially with two sets of identical twins—she was always a part of someone else. And she knew she was never truly alone.

She'd never known what it was like to be that isolated in the world. But she hoped the love she felt for Seth now would ensure that he'd never feel that way again.

Her hands stilled on the frying pan. Did she really love him? She'd only known him a little over a month, and most of that had been spent apart. Could she have fallen for him that fast?

Aria searched deep into her heart and came to an easy conclusion. Yes, she did. She'd begun that journey on the side of a dark, deserted highway, and now loved him with everything in her.

As soon as she admitted that to herself, she was instantly filled with a warmth and contentment she couldn't contain. She let it wash over her and reveled in the glow.

Seth came in at that exact moment. Still giddy with discovery, she looked over at him with a full heart, her emotions brimming. He couldn't possibly know what had put her in such a good mood, but he came directly to her, pulled her up onto her toes, and into his solid body. The chocolate brown of his eyes darkened as he ravished her mouth.

Eggs forgotten, Aria poured her feelings into the embrace, the words ready to spill out when he relinquished possession of her lips.

When she heard the front door open and close, she knew her declaration would have to wait. When she told Seth she loved him for the first time, she didn't want any distractions. And Evan's arrival was one such interruption.

He stopped in the doorway to the kitchen. "I take it you two worked it all out?"

Seth straightened away from her but held her gaze. He smiled tenderly at her before turning to where Evan had taken a seat at the table.

"You could say that." Seth sat down across from him, all business now. "So fill me in on what you guys have done to find JD."

Over the food she'd prepared, the two men discussed their options for tracking their rogue psychopath.

Shortly after they'd gone, Anna returned from her morning workout. She sat down at the table while Aria finished cleaning up the kitchen.

"This is the first chance we've had to talk," Anna said. "What are your feelings about Seth coming back? I know last night you seemed happy, but what are you thinking today?"

"You were right." Aria joined her sister. "I don't have to sacrifice my happiness to fulfill our destiny. Seth is in my life for good. We'll deal with the rest when it comes, but I'm not giving him up again."

Anna smiled. "I'm glad. You deserve someone special in your life."

"Speaking of," Aria grinned slyly, "how's Joe?"

Anna huffed out a breath, blowing the loose strands from her ponytail out of her face. "Thinking I've lost my mind."

"What?" Aria laughed. "Why?"

"After that day you came to the gym, I got so nervous around him, I froze up every time he tried to show me something. If he touched me unexpectedly, I'd almost jump right out of my skin. We haven't worked together in weeks. Jay's the one who's been training me."

Aria covered her mouth with her hands. "Oh no. What are you going to do?"

"I have to find a new place to work out." Anna nodded decisively.

Aria only stared at her.

In a dejected tone, she added, "Or I have to have it out with him." Anna set her elbows on the table and slid her hands back over her hair, slicking it back to where the tie held it.

"I think before you run out to find a new trainer, you should decide how you really feel about him. If there's any possibility you could return his feelings, I think you owe it to the both of you to sit down and talk."

"I've just never thought about him that way." Anna's hands dropped to the surface in front of her. "Now, all I *do* is think about him."

Aria felt bad for her. She sounded so confused.

"And where do those thoughts take you?"

Anna scowled at her. "Let's just say you're not the only one having sex dreams anymore."

"Oh. Okay." Aria fought to stifle the chuckle that wanted to burst free. "Well in that case, I would say you know your answer then."

"Yeah, I do." With a sigh, Anna sat back and jerked the ponytail holder out of her hair. "Now I just have to work up the nerve to approach him before he writes me off as a lunatic."

Before Aria could say anything else, Anna stood. "I gotta take a shower, or I'll be late for work." She was almost through the doorway when she stopped and turned back. "I'm really glad it's worked out for you and Seth."

"Thanks, sis. Me too."

Anna left, and Aria was still humming with happy thoughts about her own life, and Anna's, when she was slammed with a vision. It showed Seth and her brother driving right into a wall of fire and being engulfed by it.

She hadn't realized she'd screamed until Anna came running back into the kitchen, still in her workout clothes.

"Aria!" Anna gathered her up in her arms. "What is it? What did you see?"

Aria was in a panic. She had to do something. She had to warn them. "My phone! Where's my phone? I have to stop them!"

She took off out of the kitchen in search of her cell.

"Stop who?" Anna followed close. "What did you see?"

"Seth and Evan. Fire." That's all she could choke out as she barreled into her bedroom.

Thankfully, Anna didn't question her further, and Aria grabbed up her phone from the bedside table.

Her fingers shook so badly she could barely hang onto the small device, let alone operate it.

She suddenly realized she didn't have a phone number for Seth. She'd never thought to ask him for one.

Frantically, she hit the button for her favorites and found Evan's name. She stabbed it with her thumb and waited for it to ring. Her hand was trembling as she counted the seconds before she heard it.

But then it just rang and rang with no response. "Pick up, pick up, pick up."

She hung up and called again. Still, no answer. She was tempted to throw her phone in frustration but curbed the impulse. She turned tear-filled eyes to her sister. She didn't know what to do now.

"Tell me what's happening," Anna demanded.

"I had a vision. I saw Evan's car driving into a wall of flames. He and Seth were both in the car. And now I can't get a hold of them."

Anna shocked her by grabbing her arm and dragging her out of the room. "Anna, what are you doing?"

"We're going to find them."

Anna's quick thinking jump-started her own brain and helped to clear the panic in her mind. Anna snatched up her purse and keys on the fly, and out the door they went. They jumped into Anna's car, and Aria barely had time to fasten her seatbelt before Anna was tearing off down the road.

"How do you know where to go?"

"Evan picked Seth up this morning, right?"

Aria nodded but realized Anna's full focus was on the road, so she said, "Yeah."

"Then there's only one way they could have gone to get to the station from here."

Aria just hoped they could catch up to them in time.

15

Seth waited for Evan to pull out onto the road before letting his question fly. "Why the *fuck,*" he turned to glare across the interior of the car, "didn't you call me when it was evident that JD was still around? Let alone when he attacked Aria?"

"I wanted to tell you, man," Evan swore. "Aria wouldn't let me."

"And you gave in to her?"

Evan flashed him an incredulous look. "You've *met* my sister, right?"

Seth conceded. "Yeah. Yeah, I have. Sorry, I'm more pissed off at myself than anyone else. I just left her here with that monster still at large."

"Don't go there, dude. We searched. We thought he was gone. There's no way you could have known. Every indication was that he'd taken off for greener pastures."

"And instead, he teamed up with your Big Bad."

"Yup." Evan let the p pop. "Makes for an interesting situation, I'll tell you that. But even though JD is apparently on the mend, Noor has been suspiciously quiet."

Seth picked up on his tone. "You think he's planning something?"

"We're not sure," Evan said with his eyes still on the road. "The going consensus in the Burke clan is that between possessing JD when you were shot, and that attempted abduction Aria witnessed, Noor blew his wad. That he had to slink away to recharge. The premise holds, as JD was definitely working on his own when he attacked Aria."

"And you know for sure that JD was acting as Noor the night I was shot?"

"No, but that's the theory we're following. With Noor out charging his batteries, we're just waiting to see what happens next."

Law could hear in Evan's voice how much that disturbed him, but before he could ask anything else, the road in front of them erupted into a fiery ball of twenty-foot tall flames.

Evan stomped both feet on the brakes, throwing them forward as the tires locked up and squealed as they tried to stop the momentum of the heavy vehicle.

It was pure luck that no one was behind them. Otherwise, they would have plowed straight into the ass-end of Evan's car.

When they came to a screeching halt a good fifteen feet short of the inferno, Law breathed a sigh of relief and assumed they were in the clear. But before Evan could reverse farther out of the way, the fire jumped forward to completely engulf them. Seth shot a look at Evan and saw the same fear mirrored in his eyes.

The heat was tremendous. He could actually see the plastic on the side mirrors melting away. Smoke was filling the car, and they started to cough, covering their mouths with their shirts.

Law made a frantic grab for the door handle, but it was too hot and blistered his hand before he could let go. They were trapped, and the fire was eating away at the car around them.

Four loud pops sounded as the tires exploded from the extreme heat. It was getting harder and harder to breathe as the noxious fumes filled the interior. Seth leaned towards the center console to get away from the scorching metal of the door.

The sound of maniacal laughter began to echo all around him, growing louder as the flames grew and the heat intensified. It sounded as if it came from the fire itself. He looked at Evan to see if he'd heard it too. In unison, they spoke.

"Noor."

But there was nothing they could do. Seth's last thought before it all went black, was of his pixie.

~~~

Seth came back to himself when the car door was abruptly wrenched open. He looked up and was surprised to see Aria standing in the opening with tears staining her cheeks.

"Are you all right?" she demanded as she pulled him out.

Law looked around, shocked to see the fire gone and Evan's vehicle undamaged and whole. His gaze immediately shot across the roof to where the other man stood with Anna.

"What the fuck just happened?"

"Looks like Noor's powers have recharged." Evan shook his head.

Seth looked down at the woman in his arms. "What are you doing here?"

"I saw what happened in a vision," Aria told him. "We got here as soon as we could. I was so scared. I expected to find you both dead, but when we pulled up, you were just sitting here, parked in the middle of the road. I called to you, but it looked like you were in a trance or something."

"I think it's pretty obvious what happened," Anna said.

"Well, it's not to me," Seth said. "Could someone please explain what the hell is going on?"

Evan interrupted. "How about we get out of the road first? We were lucky no one rammed us before, but let's not push our luck."

The next few minutes were spent moving cars off the road and into a parking lot a short distance away. The time gave
~~~

Seth a chance to think through what had happened.

He was still trying to wrap his head around the fact that the ordeal they'd experienced hadn't even been real. He could still remember the heat and pain of being burned alive. Then to see everything back to normal, not a scorch mark anywhere, blew his mind.

The answer struck him. It had all been a fucking illusion.

Once they were parked and had exited the vehicles, Aria came to him.

"Are you okay? How are you handling this?"

"I admit, I'm a little freaked." He smiled down at her. "But I'm good." He turned his head to address Evan. "You heard that laughter too, didn't you?"

"Yeah, I did," Evan nodded. "The fucker was enjoying it."

"I get what he did now, but how did he make it seem so real?" Seth asked. "I felt the heat, I was choking on the smoke. I had blisters on my hand, but they're gone now."

"Every day, we get closer to the big showdown," Aria explained. "The stronger he gets, the weaker the bonds that hold him become."

"So we can expect *more* of this?"

"Count on it," Evan warned. "If he can get rid of just one of us, the prophecy can't be fulfilled, and he'll finally be free for good."

"This was a pretty big show of power," Anna interjected. "What are our chances that he has to crawl back under his rock for a while?"

"I wish I knew." Aria sighed. "I guess we'll have to wait and see. But I, for one, am just glad a show is all it was."

"Seth," Evan called to him. "I wish I could give you more time to absorb this, but we really need to get to the station. The girls can fill in the rest of the family on what happened."

"Yeah, okay." Seth knew there would be little else he thought about today, but Evan was right. It wouldn't do him any good to be late on his first day at a new job. Especially with an excuse that only those standing here with him would believe. "Let's go."

He gave Aria a brief, hard kiss. "I'll see you tonight." He ducked and got back into Evan's car. He looked around one last time, just to confirm there really was no evidence of the blazing inferno from only moments before.

Reclining back into his seat, he was actually glad to be putting the unexplainable away for a while. A return to the normal and mundane was just what he needed.

And that's exactly what he got. The first half of the day was spent meeting the rest of the crew and then studying the open cases on Evan's desk. He needed to familiarize himself with the specifics of each one if he were going to be of any help. After that, they got down to what they were paid the mediocre bucks for and started to do actual police work.

On the personal front, the rest of the day passed uneventfully. Seth wasn't sure how he felt about that. On one hand, it was good that Noor didn't try any more tricks, but on the other, it meant there was no news on JD's whereabouts. Other than when he was seen by Aria, he seemed to disappear.

Seth vowed he'd find that motherfucker if it took the rest of his goddamned life.

He and Evan were just getting ready to pack it in when someone called out, "Hey, Lawson."

It took him a moment to realize they were talking to him. Even though he'd already gotten used to being called Seth again, it was still strange to be addressed by his last name. It'd been so many years since he'd heard it spoken aloud. But if he truly wanted to embrace this new life, he was going to have to let go of his outlaw identity, and start thinking of himself as Seth Lawson.

"Yeah," he turned and called back.

"Captain wants to see you in his office."

Seth looked at Evan. "Wonder what that's about?"

Evan shrugged. "Don't know. I'll meet you at the car."

"Okay."

Seth retraced his steps across the squad room and knocked on the open door of Captain Reynolds' office. "Sir, you wanted to see me?"

His boss sat back in his chair and gestured to the seat across the desk from him. "Have a seat."

Seth sank into the chair and waited.

"This department is glad to have you, Seth. Your unique… talents will be a definite asset to our team. However…" He left it hanging for a moment. "I'm worried we might have a problem when this joker JD shows up again. I know you and he have a fuck-ton of issues, but I can't have you going all renegade and taking matters into your own hands. You've done things on your own for a long time now. Are you going to be able to put that aside and do it by the book from now on?"

Seth didn't blame the captain for his concern. His question was valid. He'd just a few minutes ago sworn to do that very thing. But here, now, he reassured his new boss.

"I understand. I wouldn't want to do anything that put a bad light on this department. It's going to be an adjustment, I'll admit, to get used to this new dynamic, but I promise I'll do my best. And as far as JD goes," Seth worded his answer very carefully, "getting him off the streets before he hurts anyone else is my first priority."

By the look on Reynolds' face, he knew exactly what Seth had really meant. But thankfully, he let it go and didn't press him on it.

"Good to know. Dismissed."

When he slid into the passenger seat next to Evan a few minutes later, his partner turned to him. "What'd he want?"

"To make sure I wasn't going to go rogue on JD."

"What did you tell him?"

"What he wanted to hear."

"You know that no matter what, if JD turns up dead, they're gonna look at you."

"Can't be helped."

"The girls called while you were in with the captain. We're meeting up at Mom and Dad's to talk about this morning."

Evan must have picked up on his discomfort and the reason behind it. He grinned. "Buck up, dude. It's time to meet the parents."

Meeting parents was something Seth had no experience in. He'd been undercover for so long, it just hadn't applied. Before the police academy, he'd had his fair share of women, but none had ever progressed to the point of family introductions. The women he'd been with had only lasted one, maybe two nights.

He supposed it was better to be meeting the rest of her family now, as opposed to a month ago. At least now they'd know him as Seth Lawson, the cop—instead of Law, the lowlife, miscreant biker.

Fifteen minutes later, they pulled into the driveway of a nice family home. As he got out of the car, he heard the sounds of waves lapping against the shore. As he looked around, he noticed that this house, and all the others nearby, backed up to the water.

He followed Evan in and saw that everyone else was already there. When they saw the last of the group had arrived, an older gentleman came forward.

Thanks to the late-night talk between him and Aria, he knew this to be her father, Paul Daniels. He'd wondered why her mother hadn't taken her husband's name and had asked her about it. She'd explained how the Burke name spanned centuries of magical history, and each generation of witches wanted the next to carry that history forward. And so the tradition began: if you were born a Burke witch, you stayed a Burke witch.

Seth had thought about it and decided it would take a very strong man to marry into this family without caring that his own name wouldn't be passed on. Looking at the man before him, Seth knew he fit the bill.

He accepted the hand Paul offered to him and shook it firmly. "Sir."

Aria's father took his measure. "So you're Law."

"No sir, not anymore. It's Seth. Seth Lawson."

"Well, Seth, it's nice to meet you. I understand you had quite the display today."

"Yes sir, I did."

"Paul, please." He paused when his wife approached. "And this is my bride, Mary."

"Ma'am," Seth greeted.

She laughed. "None of that. Please, call me Mary." She reached out and touched his arm. As soon as he felt the contact, her warm hazel eyes went blank. But before Seth could ask if she was okay, she was talking again as if nothing had happened. "Welcome to our madness." She smiled at him, but there was something else behind it now. "Come on in and have a seat. Dinner will be ready shortly. In the meantime, there's a lot we need to discuss."

"Thank you, Mary."

Seth was still watching her retreating back when Aria came to greet him with a quick kiss. "Nothing like being dropped into the middle of a family meeting as an introduction, huh?"

He realized she'd seen nothing of what had transpired with her mother. Maybe it hadn't been anything after all.

"Is there ever a good time to meet your girlfriend's family?" he teased, brushing off the odd incident.

"Is that what I am?" she murmured.

"I certainly hope so."

She smiled up at him. "Sorry about that. With everything going on, I forgot to tell them about the name change."

Seth grinned. "That's fine. No harm done."

They turned and Aria guided him to the couch where she'd been sitting.

"So he's back, and he's upped his game again," Mary started the conversation.

"What did he hope to accomplish with this demonstration?" Paul looked at Evan and Seth. "He wasn't actually able to hurt you."

"To prove he could get to us. Into our minds," Anna answered. "I felt his satisfaction at having made us believe he'd killed them."

"There're a few things here I find troubling," Mary said through a frown.

"Only a few?" Evan countered.

Anna shot her brother a dirty look and sat forward in her seat. "What has you worried, Mom?"

Mary's gaze slid to Seth.

He didn't know what she was going to say, but internally he braced.

"I don't think Aria's encounters with Seth were as random as we first thought. I've thought it interesting just how much he's tied into the Burkes. It goes all the way back to when Seth and Evan first met in the academy. Then there's the night with Aria on the highway, the day Evan was stabbed..." She gave her son a pointed look, and then, "Yes, I know about that."

Evan hung his head and said nothing.

She returned her attention to Seth. "And now, as things are really stirring up, he's smack in the middle of it."

He'd been right to steel himself. Did she actually believe he'd had a hand in what was happening to her family? He'd never do anything to hurt Aria, or anyone else.

"Ma'am, I hope you're not implying that I'm somehow involved with Noor."

Aria rushed to his defense. "She doesn't think that."

The seconds seemed to tick by before Mary answered, although he knew there'd been no hesitation.

"No, I don't think Seth is working with our enemy. But I do think there's something else to consider. Was it simply a coincidence that Noor struck today? Or was it because Seth returned?"

The thought of that set him back a moment. He hadn't really considered who the target had been. He'd known Noor would come for him—it had only been a matter of time, because he still saw him as an obstacle to Aria. In the back of Seth's mind, he'd just assumed it had been a two-birds-with-one-stone type of deal.

He shared that thought with the group.

"Whatever the reason, we're just lucky no one else happened to be on that road." Evan glanced around the room. "A fire that big could have caused widespread panic, and we'd have had a mess on our hands."

"But there was." Anna had spoken up, and Evan's gaze snapped to his sister. "A van passed us in the oncoming lane before we caught up to your car. They were laughing and talking and drove right by like it was any normal day. If they'd actually been able to *see* the fire, there's no way they could have just driven on by. It was too big to miss."

"I saw it." There was a sick feeling in the pit of Seth's stomach. "I felt it."

"He probably wanted you to." Aria grasped his hand in hers. "You both said you heard him laughing as you thought you were dying."

"What if there's more behind Seth's ability to interact with Noor?" Mary added, causing everyone in the room to go still.

"What are you trying to say, Mom?" Ethan's gaze narrowed in on Mary.

"I think Seth has his own connection to him."

Aria was skeptical, but she decided to give her mother the

benefit of the doubt. "What makes you say that?"

Mary looked on patiently. "I'm just saying that I think Seth was put in our path for a reason."

Paul, who'd been quietly watching, addressed his wife. "You know something, don't you?"

She nodded. "It's going to take some digging though, to verify if what I saw is right."

"What?" Seth barked. "If you know…"

Mary said one word that brought a collective gasp from every other person in the room. "Isabel."

"No, impossible." Aria shook her head adamantly from beside him. "The only reason Noor even knows who Seth is is because he saw him in my dream." She sent him a quick, apologetic look. "And besides, how do we know Noor can't make his presence known to anyone he chooses? The way you say it, he needs a personal connection to whomever he makes contact with, so does that mean he's related to JD too?" Aria heaved out a sigh. "The point is, he gets stronger every day. We don't know what he's capable of, or what kind of reach he might have."

Seth's gaze shot around to all the different faces. Everyone was staring at him, but no one was saying anything. "Wait, what are you talking about? And who's Isabel?" he demanded.

Aria tightened her grip on his hand. When he glanced down, he saw distress clouding her eyes.

"Tell me, damn it."

"She was Edrick Noor's wife back in the 1500's. They had two small boys when our ancestors helped her disappear with them."

Seth pulled his hand out of Aria's and rose. He couldn't sit. He had to move as the implication of what she'd said sunk in.

Evan had told him about the wife and kids. Kids that would grow into men and have families of their own. Generation after generation. Down to *him*? Was it possible? Yeah, it was…but what were the chances?

He was halfway across the room when he spun back around and addressed Mary. "You really think I could be descended from that nut-job?"

"It *would* explain the connection." Mary's tone was gentle. "But like I said, it's something we'll need to investigate further to be sure."

He didn't know what to say or think.

Mary rose, and Seth eyed her warily. She came to stand directly in front of him. When she reached up and cupped the side of his face in her hand, all the tension and anger he'd been feeling drained away.

The caress was something Aria had so often done. He saw now that it was an indication of how much they cared.

"Even if it turns out to be true, it won't change the man you are," she promised. "And although we *know* he's a nut-job, as you put it, that is not a reflection of who *you* are. You're a good person, Seth, or my daughter wouldn't have feelings for you."

He looked at Aria over Mary's shoulder, and she smiled softly at him.

Mary dropped her hand and looped it around his elbow as she turned to face the others. "We have a lot to think about. Let's take a break and get some food going."

Half an hour later, they were all seated at the table. Bowls of steaming spaghetti, cold salads, and garlic bread made the rounds as they discussed Seth's history.

"Do you know anything about where your family came from?" Mary asked.

"No. I lived with my parents in Michigan until they died when I was four. After that, I came to Florida to live with my grandfather. He wasn't one to discuss much, so I have no clue."

"Is there any way to find out?" Aria asked. "You told me your grandfather left everything to you. Could there be documents or family records somewhere that might hold some information?"

"I sold most of it when I joined the task force—the house, the furnishings, anything that couldn't be easily packed up. They advised me to hide away anything that might link me back to my old life, so what I kept, I put into storage."

"Where's it stored?" Evan popped a meatball into his mouth. "It might be worth it to go through it all."

"It's back in Michigan. The town where I lived with my parents is pretty small, and I thought it was a good place to leave Seth Lawson. Law had no ties there, and no one would think to look, so it seemed like the perfect place. There's a storage facility just outside of town. Payments are made out of an account that has no association with my undercover persona."

"Why don't we fly up on Friday?" Aria suggested. "We can see what's there and fly back on Sunday."

Before he knew it, he was buying plane tickets and packing a small bag.

He was surprised at how fast the two days had passed. Suddenly it was time to go, and he and Aria were buckling their seats on the airplane.

16

They landed at Bishop International Airport at ten on Friday night. April in Michigan was still brisk, so he was glad they'd thought to bring jackets. Since the storage facility wouldn't open again until morning, they picked up the rental car and drove to some cottages about halfway between the airport and the small town of Genesee.

After a quick stop at the main office to pick up the key, they parked in front of the third cabin. Seth grabbed their overnight bags while Aria unloaded the take-out they'd bought on the way. They stepped into the small building, and Seth gave it the once-over.

It consisted of one large room with a bed off to one side, and the kitchen and living areas on the other. It wasn't anything fancy, but it would work for a couple of nights.

He dropped the bags on the couch as Aria set out the food. Seth thought it best to caution her again.

"There's no guarantee we'll find anything tomorrow."

"I know. But we still have to look. If my mom is right and you're tied to this in some way, we need to know."

He ate the food in front of him, but he didn't really taste it. He'd nudged the remains from one side of the container to the other a couple of times when Aria stood and came around to his side of the table. She pulled the fork out of his hand and set it down. When she made a move to sit on his lap, he shoved back to make room for her. His arms automatically wound around her hips. When he looked into her face, she was gazing tenderly at him.

"I know you're having a rough time with this, but there's something else you need to keep in mind as we dig into your family tree."

"What's that?"

"Isabel. From what we've found in our records, she was strong and good and smart." She paused to let him digest that.

"Evan told me a little about her," Seth shared, "but it wasn't much, and I was only listening as an outsider then. Now that I know I might be related to her, I need to hear it again. What else do you know about her?"

Aria nodded. "Even though Noor beat her and, from all accounts, made her life a living hell, she had enough strength of character and love for her children to refuse to bring any more babies into that situation. She went to the Burke witches to get a potion which would prevent her from getting pregnant again. She fought back and took that power away from him.

"We're not certain, but we're guessing he found out. Instead of staying and possibly dying at his hand, she took her boys and ran to the coven. They helped her to vanish."

"Bringing about Noor's obsession to destroy your family," he finished.

"But you know what? I wouldn't change a thing, and I don't think those other Burke witches would either. The number one law that we live by as witches, that is the basis for our entire moral code, is an' it harm none. Because of them, Isabel and her children got away. If they hadn't, you may not even be here."

She kissed his lips. "And that would be unbearable."

Seth sank into the kiss and let it wash his doubts away. When he felt the touch of her hand on his face, he pulled back to look at her.

Her blue eyes were shining bright, and her next words

arrowed straight into his heart.

"I love you."

"Even if it turns out that I descend from evil?" His tone was more teasing than troubled.

She grinned. "What woman wouldn't love a bad boy?"

"That's good. Because I love you too."

~~~

Aria drew in a quick breath when Seth suddenly stood and set her on her feet. He ducked his head down and took possession of her mouth. As the kiss heated, she felt herself being walked backwards until the backs of her legs bumped against the bed.

Placing one knee on it to brace himself, Seth supported her as he laid her back and came down on top of her.

The feel of his weight pressing down on her was incredible as his large, rough hands roamed over her and left her shivering in anticipation. He took his time and learned all the nuances of her body. He discovered that a soft touch along her thigh would cause her to shudder in longing, and that if he took a nipple into his mouth, her breath would catch in her throat.

He showed her things about herself she'd never known. Like how if he ran his fingers up the backs of her knees, she'd squirm and laugh. But if he licked that same spot, she'd be helpless but to writhe underneath him and pant with passion.

When he finally kissed his way back up her body, she was so far gone, she begged to be taken.

"Please, please, Seth. I need you inside me. Now."

He fit himself between her open thighs and aligned the head of his shaft to her wanting core. When he only pushed into her mere inches, she propelled her hips upward demanding more.

She felt him draw back and then with a grunt, he buried himself completely inside of her. Aria threw her head back and
~~~

screamed as she shot straight into ecstasy. He didn't give her a chance to recover from the first before he was taking her up again with long, slow thrusts.

Taking hold of her wrists, he slid her hands up over her head and entwined his fingers with hers.

"Pixie," he whispered. "Open your eyes. Look at me."

Aria slowly raised heavy lids to meet his heated gaze. It was like falling into a pool of the most decadent melted chocolate. His love surrounded her and she gladly gave everything she was to him.

The bond they shared as they moved in unison couldn't be broken. Hands, bodies, souls—every part of them was linked, and Aria was never more content.

When they both finally fell panting and replete onto the sheets, he held her close. Aria reveled in how passionate and full of meaning their love-making had been.

Aria was more than happy to lie in Seth's arms for the rest of her life, but she could feel the heat of their spent bodies where her skin met his.

With just a nudge, Aria brought a soft breeze that swirled around them, cooling their heated bodies.

"Damn, that feels good. You're kind of handy to have around."

She gave a quick tug to the hairs on his chest.

"Ow, okay," he laughed as he rubbed it. "Can I ask you something?"

Aria was drifting in a peaceful and happy place. "Anything."

"What's it like having power like that? Where only a thought can direct the wind?"

She raised her head, laid her hands flat on his chest, and propped her chin on them.

"It's hard to explain." She wanted to share this with him, so she tried to find the right words. "From the first moment I can remember, that connection has been there. One big thing that my parents made sure we understood was that this affinity we have with the elements is not to be taken for granted. We were not to abuse our power. When we have need of them, we ask—we don't demand."

She laid her head back down on his chest. "And in return, our elements embrace us." She was quiet for a moment and then revealed something special. "It'll speak to me sometimes."

"How does it do that?"

She smiled at the amazement she heard in his voice. "Not in words obviously, but with a caress or a gust that musses my hair. And once or twice, a harder push in warning. And, it likes to play."

"Really?" He sounded surprised.

She laughed and nodded. "As I'm building my sculptures, I can actually feel the anticipation. And the more intricate I make them, the better. It loves to weave in and around the metal and other materials to set the paddles spinning."

"I would love to see your art." He kissed the top of her head.

"I would love to show it to you."

She snuggled in closer, and content, they both drifted off to sleep.

~~~

Seth was still asleep when Aria woke. She lay in the comfort of his arms and tried to send him good thoughts. She knew he was having a hard time with the prospect of being descended from Edrick Noor.

And she couldn't really blame him. If it were true, it added a whole new layer to what was happening. How could that affect them all? Would it give them an advantage? This was just another piece of the puzzle. The question was, how and where was it going to fit?

She didn't want to add to Seth's apprehension, but she was a little worried about the link Noor seemed to have with him.
~~~

Could he use it to turn Seth against the rest of them? Did Noor know that Seth could be his relative?

Seth's sleepy voice rumbled near her ear. "I can almost hear you thinking. Stop it. It's too early." He rolled until he was stretched out over her. In a smooth thrust, he was seated inside of her. "Let it go."

And she did.

When her brain finally started functioning again afterward, she got up and went to take a shower. He'd offered to join her, but one look at the tiny cubicle, and that idea was tossed. He was going to have a hard enough time in there by himself.

And sure enough, when she heard periodic thumps followed by ripe curses, she had to laugh.

When he emerged a few minutes later, she was still giggling.

"Oh, you think that's funny, do you? You're lucky you're pixie-sized. That shower wasn't made for a normal person."

"Normal?" she scoffed. "Have you looked at the width of your shoulders? You're as wide as I am tall. I'm surprised we didn't need to bring in the Jaws of Life to get you out of there."

He approached her with a glint in his eye. "Don't let my size fool you." When they were body to body, he wrapped her in his arms. "I've fit into tighter places before."

His mouth came down on hers for a brief but hot kiss.

When he ended it with a smack, he looked deep into her eyes. "As much as I'd love to take you back to bed, we'll have to come back to this later."

"Promise?" Aria grinned up at him.

Ten minutes later, they were out the door. And after a quick stop at a fast-food place, they went on to the storage facility. Aria noticed that the closer they got, the quieter Seth became. The light mood of the morning had fallen away, and she couldn't help but wonder what was going through his mind. Even she couldn't decide if finding proof positive would be good or bad. The only thing she was absolutely certain of was that it wouldn't change a single them between them either way. She reached across the seat to take his hand in hers.

He squeezed her hand and entwined his fingers with hers.

Seth pulled in and drove right to a large garage-style door. They got out, and she watched as he pulled a set of keys out of his pocket. After he selected the one he needed, the lock came off with ease. He reached down to grasp the handle and with little effort, raised the door.

The first thing that caught Aria's attention was the old muscle car that sat off to one side of the space. It was orange with white accent stripes.

"Is that your car?"

Seth looked at it, and she could see him remembering. "Yeah, I guess it is. It was my grandfather's. He'd had it since the day it rolled off the line."

"What is it?"

"A 1970 Dodge Challenger."

"Does it still run?"

"It did when I pulled it in here. It'll need some work after sitting for so long, but someday, I'd like to get her back on the road."

"I can tell it means a lot to you."

"Yeah. One of the few things he and I did together was work on this car. But that's for another day." He turned away and motioned to the back and opposite side. "As you can see, there isn't a lot here."

"Let's just hope one of those boxes contain something we can use."

Together, they carried all of them out of the unit and brought the whole mess into the light. There were seven in total, and they all varied in shape and size. Aria chose one at random and started going through each item inside. Seth did the same.

It was a little strange for Aria to be searching through someone else's life. For a man who had lived over seventy years, there wasn't much to document his life. Some old photos, a few ancient receipts she could barely read the print on, and books with dust still coating them. She went over each and every scrap of paper, looking for any clue.

When she'd finished the third container with nothing to show, she looked over at Seth, ready to ask him if he'd found anything. The words halted in her throat when she saw him sitting on the ground, clutching something in his hands, pain etched across his sharp features.

Setting her box aside, she slowly rose to go to him. She lowered down next to him and looked to see what had brought him to a stop.

It was a picture of a young couple. There was a small, dark-haired boy—perhaps two—sitting on the man's shoulders. Hints of the grown Seth were stamped in the toddler's face. This was the family he had lost so many years ago. These were the parents who had been ripped from his life by violence.

They were a pretty couple. Aria could see now where Seth had gotten his size. Other than the brown hair which clearly came from his mother, Seth was his father all over again.

"Are you okay?" she asked gently.

"Yeah. I'd forgotten what they looked like."

"What were their names?"

"Kelly and Thomas."

Aria noted the house in the background. "Is that the house you lived in?"

He nodded. "It's not too far from here."

"I'd like to see it if we have time."

Seth set the picture of his parents back in the box and rose to open another one. "Yeah, maybe."

When he'd turned his back to her, Aria reached in and lifted the photo back out. Without a second thought, she slid it into her pocket and then went back to her own pile of records.

She was going through a stack of papers when her heart

took a solid thump in her chest. She'd found a couple of old birth certificates. Studying the names, she found one was Seth's grandfather's. The other was years older. The ink was faded, but Aria was just able to make out the name of the child.

Aria realized she'd just seen that name. Picking up the first document again, she looked it over. The older certificate belonged to Seth's great-grandfather. And though the letters were barely legible, it also listed his parents' names.

This was just what they needed. It would give them somewhere to start. She called Seth to come check it out.

He looked them over with an air of surprise. "I honestly didn't think we'd find anything here. Yet, here are the names of my ancestors." He read over them again. "I should be glad I don't see the name Noor on any of this, but I know Isabel probably gave them all new names when she ran."

"Even without that, I think we've found enough to get a search going."

With only one box remaining, they set the documents aside and poured over the last of it on the off-chance that something else might turn up.

It didn't.

Aria picked up the birth-certificates. "All we have to do is find a genealogist and give them your great-great-grandparents' names and pertinent details. Hopefully, they'll be able to discover if anything questionable turns up. It's going to be a pain-staking process, but we'll find the answers."

Seth only nodded. He remained quiet as they restored all the boxes and left the storage facility. She let it go until they stopped for lunch. Once they were seated, she turned to him.

"Talk to me. Please."

He never took his eyes from his clasped hands on the table top. "I didn't even remember what they looked like until I saw that picture. I've forgotten them completely. I have no idea how my mother's laugh sounded. What did my father smell like?"

She was surprised to see anger in his gaze when it finally met hers. "I've been racking my brain trying to find that, but there's nothing. Not one damned thing."

"Your grandfather never showed you that picture?" Aria stroked his arm in comfort.

"No. I didn't know he had it. But then again, I never asked. Why wouldn't I have asked about my parents?"

She slid closer to him in the booth and rested her hand on his thigh. "I don't know, and I'm so sorry you don't have any memories of them. There isn't anyone you can talk to who knew them?"

He dropped one of his hands to cover hers. "I left here when I was four. I wouldn't know who their friends were, or even if they had any."

She gazed up at him. "Then I suggest, after we eat, we go back to where you lived. We'll knock on doors and talk to people. There's bound to be someone there who remembers them."

"It's been over twenty years, Pixie. It's not likely."

"We'll just have to wait and see."

~~~

Seth didn't want to get his hopes up that any of the old neighbors would still be around. He'd been searching his mind since he'd found that photo, trying to find a memory of the people in it.

At four years old, there should be some recollection. A sound, a smell, something. But no matter how hard he tried to dig some out, they just weren't there.

After leaving the restaurant, he drove into the middle of downtown Genesee. At the golden arches, he turned right. About midway down the dead-end road, he slowed and came to a stop in the middle of the street.

He stared at the blue house that sat back off the road.
~~~

"Is that it?"

He didn't trust his voice so he simply nodded.

"It's a nice house. Do you want to go up and see if they'll let you walk around?"

Seth's heart was pounding in his chest. He'd not been back here since the day his parents had died. He only knew where it was because he'd had a buddy do some research and find the address. When he'd needed a place to hide his old self, this had felt like the right choice.

As he turned up the driveway, a middle-aged woman came out onto the front porch. Seth pulled to a stop and shut the car off.

He couldn't take his eyes off the house as he exited the car. Aria appeared next to him at the same time the woman did.

"Hi, can I help you?"

Seth didn't know what he was going to say until it came out of his mouth.

"I, uh, used to live here with my parents. A long time ago," he qualified. "I was wondering if it would be all right to maybe take a look around?"

"Certainly. We've only been here for about a year. Come on in."

When Seth stepped into the house, he was in the living room. Straight in front of him was the dining room, and beyond that was the kitchen.

The woman swept her arm out. "I'm sure it's changed a lot since you were here."

"I wouldn't know. I only lived here until I was four."

"Oh, then you must be the Lawson boy. Tragic what happened, I'm sorry."

Seth's breathing backed up in his lungs. "How would you know that?"

"When we bought this place, the neighbor two houses down filled us in on what happened. I felt so bad, and I didn't even know any of you."

"That neighbor," Aria spoke up for the first time. "Are they still here?"

"Oh, yeah. Mr. Dort has lived in the same house for over forty years."

"Do you think he'd mind if we stopped by?" Aria pushed.

"Not at all. He'll probably be out on his porch. And knowing him, he's already seen that you're here. He likes to keep an eye on the comings and goings in the area," she laughed.

"Perfect, thank you." Aria smiled at her.

The woman showed them through the house, but Seth didn't get any twinges of familiarity. Had he blocked out his first four years? Why couldn't he remember?

They walked out into the sunroom on the back of the house. Seth was pulled to the sliding glass door that looked out over the back yard. Without a word, he slid it open and stepped out onto the deck. Straight ahead, probably a hundred yards away, was an enormous tree.

On one of the lower branches was an old tire swing.

The memory hit him like a baseball bat to the head. It slammed into him with such sudden force, he had to grasp the railing in front of him.

In his mind he could see the world passing back and forth around him. The wind was in his hair and the heat of the sun on his face. On the backward arc, he felt hands push against his back, sending him higher and higher.

He heard his own childish laughter and another that was deeper, more masculine. His father.

Then he heard a woman's voice. "I think that's high enough, Thomas. He's just a baby."

"He's no baby," his father called back. "He's a big boy now, aren't you, Seth?"

He staggered under the weight of the memory. Aria was right there to lend him support.

"Did you remember something?" she whispered.

"Yeah, being pushed on that swing. I heard my dad laugh and my mother calling out to him."

Aria's hand rubbed up and down his back, offering comfort. When he looked down at her, she gave him a soft smile.

He hadn't been optimistic that this trip down memory lane would work, but it had. And now he had a snippet of time to recall when they'd been happy. When they'd still been a family.

"Thank you so much for your time," Aria told the woman. "And for showing us around the house."

"Any time. I'll walk you out."

When they got to the driveway, she pointed to the left. "The yellow house there, that's Mr. Dort's."

"Thank you again," Seth told her. "You don't know what this has meant for me."

"I'm glad I could help."

Seth reversed out of the driveway and then stopped at the road. He picked up Aria's hand and brought it to his lips, kissing it.

"Thank you for that. It gave me something priceless."

"You're more than welcome." She held his gaze. "I love you."

"I love you too."

"Now, let's go talk to Mr. Dort. I think he's going to be a well of information. He sounds like the type who doesn't let anything happen around here without his notice."

Before they even pulled into Mr. Dort's drive, they saw him sitting on the covered porch, watching them. He followed their progress onto his property. When Seth opened the door and unfolded his large frame from the car, Mr. Dort rose from his seat.

"You're Tommy's boy," the elderly gentleman said from the top step.

Seth glanced at Aria and then stepped forward until he stood at the bottom of the stairs. "Yes sir, I am. I was wondering if I could ask you some questions about my parents. I don't know if you knew what happened to them—"

"Oh, we knew. The whole neighborhood was in shock when they were killed. Your mom was still pregnant when they moved in." He turned and sent a momentary look at the blue house down the street. "Nice young couple. And when you came along, they were so proud. They'd walk you up and down the street in your stroller. Everyone would go out to take a peek at you."

"That's kind of what I wanted to talk to you about," Seth told him. "They died when I was so young that I don't have any memories of them. We stopped by the house, and the woman there said you'd lived here a long time. I was hoping you'd be willing to talk with me about them."

"Sure, come on up." He led them back to where he was sitting. "Have a seat. I'll go get us some tea." Seth and Aria took a seat on the old porch swing while he went inside.

He returned a few minutes later with three tall glasses of iced tea. As he stepped through the doorway, a little blonde dog, about ankle high, followed him out. Its whole body wriggled with excitement when it saw they had guests. It immediately jumped up into Seth's lap and checked him out.

"That's my Abby," Mr. Dort told them as he handed them their tea. "Just put her down if she bothers you."

Seth looked down into the big, round, happy brown eyes. "No, she's fine."

Mr. Dort took his seat. "So, what would you like to know?"

"Anything you can tell me." Seth unconsciously petted the dog.

Over the next couple of hours, Mr. Dort regaled Seth and Aria with stories of Thomas and Kelly Lawson. It was tradition in the close-knit neighborhood to have a block party in late summer. Everyone got together and had a good time. The Lawsons fit right in, and all the women oohed and ahhed over

Seth when he'd been born.

Mr. Dort didn't have a bad word to say about Seth's parents. And some of the tales had them all laughing out loud. Seth learned his father wasn't very handy when it came to home improvements, but he'd tried. Usually his mother would end up calling Mr. Dort or one of the other men to come fix whatever Tommy had messed up.

He was overwhelmed with what he'd learned and hated to go, but he could see the older man was tiring. Seth looked down at the little dog sleeping in his lap and smiled. Gently he roused her and set her down.

They were getting ready to take their leave when Mr. Dort offered, "If you're not busy come August, stop back by. That's when our cookout is, and I know everyone would be happy to see you. We like to think of each other as family around here. And you'll always be welcome."

Seth shook his hand. "Thank you very much, sir. I may just do that."

Driving away, Seth had a better picture of who his parents had been. And he had Aria to thank for that. If she hadn't suggested going back to his old house, he'd still be wondering who they'd been and where he'd come from.

"He seemed really nice." Aria's features softened when she spoke of Mr. Dort. "Living there sounds like it would have been great."

"Yeah." Seth thought of the picture of his parents he'd left at the storage facility. "I need to stop back by the rental unit real quick. There's something I forgot."

Aria shifted slightly in the passenger seat, and then her hand reached across the interior of the car. When he looked down, she was holding that very same picture out to him.

Surprised, his gaze shot to hers. Understanding shone in her eyes. "I knew, at some point, you'd regret leaving this behind. I wanted to make sure I had it when that time came."

He couldn't have loved her more than in this moment. She'd known, even when he hadn't, that he would need this piece of his family. "Thank you."

There was love reflected in the pale blue depths of her eyes when she looked at him. "You're welcome."

17

When they got back to Anna's place on Sunday afternoon, they immediately got in touch with a local genealogist they'd found online. Aria gave her what they had and explained they were looking for any connection to the name Noor. Aria thought it best to warn her that it wouldn't be easy, as names may have been changed at some point for protection.

With that done, all they could do was sit back and wait to see what the genealogist found.

Early Monday morning, they were awakened by Seth's phone ringing. Aria knew it was Evan by Seth's responses. And the news wasn't good.

"I'll meet you there." He hung up and started reaching for his clothes.

"What is it?" Aria slowly rose to a seated position. His silence told her he really didn't want to tell her.

"Seth?"

"The body of a young girl was found."

Aria gasped. She knew exactly who'd been responsible. "JD."

What were the chances of multiple predators in the area that had a preference for young women? She sat quietly on the bed as he disappeared into the bathroom to shower.

Had this happened because she'd gone out of town? Had JD seen her leave with Seth and taken his frustrations out on this girl? Had Noor been involved too? They'd assumed he'd have to slink away after his stunt with the fire, but maybe he was gaining strength and didn't need as long in between to recuperate.

The idea of that made her feel sick.

Once Seth left, Aria got up and went to Anna's room. When she opened the door, her twin was awake and looking at her.

"Is it bad?" Anna asked.

Aria nodded and sat on the foot of her sister's bed. "A girl died. We have to do something, Anna. We can't let this continue."

Anna pushed herself up and sat against the headboard. "What do you suggest?"

"I'm not sure yet, but I won't rest until we end this sick partnership Noor has with JD."

Aria left Anna to get dressed. She wanted to go talk with their mother. If anyone knew what kind of spell they needed, it would be her.

Aria had just pulled on her jeans when she heard Anna screaming. She took off down the hall and found that the sounds were coming from the bathroom. She burst through the door, tore the curtain aside, and there was Anna, huddled on the floor of the tub. Her hands clutched her head tightly as she cried out. Her whimpers of agony ripped at Aria's heart.

Aria turned the water off and stepped into the shower with her.

"Anna, what is it? What's wrong?"

At first she didn't answer. She just rocked back and forth on her knees.

"The pain," she whispered, as if the sound of her own voice was too much. "I can't push it away. She's screaming."

Aria didn't know why, but Anna's shields had failed. The torment was able to break through, and she was lost as to how to help her.

"What can I do?"

Anna continued to sway.

Aria was terrified. She'd never seen Anna in so much pain. Whatever had gotten through must have been some extremely strong emotions. Aria had seen firsthand how durable Anna's mental armor was. With nothing left to do, she made the decision to call their mother.

"I'm going to call Mom." Aria started to stand.

"Wait." Anna reached out and grasped her wrist. "Just give me a minute. I'm trying to rebuild. I think I've got it."

Aria waited, standing guard over her sister while she tried to restore the barriers she used to protect herself from the horror and misery of the world. When Anna's tear-stained face tilted up to look at her, she attempted a reassuring smile, but it fell well short.

"What the hell happened? How did it get through?"

Anna stood on shaky legs. "I don't know. It was like a bombardment. All of a sudden, the pain and fear blasted me out of nowhere."

Aria helped her out of the shower and wrapped her in an oversized towel.

"It was Noor," Anna shared. "I recognized the evilness of his touch."

"Son of a bitch," Aria muttered. "And he cut right through your shields."

Anna nodded.

Aria studied her sister for a moment. "He's getting stronger."

"You're telling me." Anna lowered onto the toilet seat and sat down while Aria grabbed another towel to gently dry her hair.

Aria thought the timing just too coincidental. She had a feeling that the emotions Anna had just experienced belonged to the girl who had been murdered sometime during the night. Noor had somehow broadcasted what had been done to her, attacking Anna with it.

"Could you please not think so much right now? My walls

are still a little shaky, and your proximity is making it hard for me to block you."

"Sorry." Aria winced and made an effort to wipe everything from her mind.

"I'm taking you to Mom's," Aria announced. "You can hang out there today while we look for a way to stop JD."

"No," Anna argued as she stood. "I'm going to lay down for a bit, but then I'm going to work. It's too late to call in a sub."

Aria couldn't believe what she'd heard. "What do you mean, *no*? You can't spend that much time surrounded by a school full of children and all their over-the-top angst, while your barriers are still so unstable."

"I will because that's my job." Anna held her ground. "I just need a few hours of quiet to shore up my defenses and I'll be good."

Aria's inclination was to push it further, but she'd learned recently that she didn't always know better where her sister was concerned.

"All right," she gave in. "If you're sure you can handle it."

"I am."

She helped Anna to her bedroom and left her there to quietly recover from Noor's onslaught.

Aria finished getting dressed and drove straight to her parents' house. When she rushed in, her mom was there to greet her.

"What is it?"

"Seth got a call from Evan this morning." Aria recounted the call, and then went on to describe the attack on Anna.

"Is she okay? Why didn't she come with you?"

"She refused," Aria admitted. "Dug her heels in. Said she'd lay down for a bit, but then she was going to work."

Aria saw the worry in her mother's eyes.

"She's fine. Or she will be." Aria needed to divert her mom's attention, or she'd race out the door and drag her daughter back here.

"I need your help," Aria told her. "We have to find JD before he strikes again."

"Have you heard from Seth or your brother? Do we know for sure this is JD's work?"

"No, I haven't heard from them, but who else could it have been? We know his preferences. I've seen them work together, and I think the screams Anna heard were, somehow, from the girl they found this morning. Plus, Anna said she could feel that it was Noor."

Aria looked at her mom and finally voiced what she'd come here for. "Do you know of any spell we can use to discover where JD's hiding?"

"I might," Mary said after some thought. "But it's been a while since I looked at it. Let me go see if I have everything we need."

Mary took off down the hall.

Aria was about to follow when her father approached her. "How is she, really?"

"I think she's all right, Daddy. She's stronger than we thought."

"Oh, I've known that for a long time." Pride filled his eyes. "She just needed to believe it of herself. That's why I made sure to leave that flier for the self-defense class where she would see it."

"You know she's been going to that gym?"

He nodded. "Joe and I actually met some time ago." Paul grinned at her. "I like him. The more I got to know him, the more I thought he'd be perfect for your sister. And not just as a trainer."

"So the whole thing was a set-up?" She raised an eyebrow and crossed her arms over her chest. Her dad had a sneaky streak.

He just stood there and smiled.

It was too much. "I can't believe you," she laughed. "I went with her the other day, you know," she told him. "She'd told me a little about him, but I wanted to see this guy for myself."

"And...?" he trailed off.

"I think you're right. I saw the way he looked at her. He could be good for her." Aria chuckled at the memory of her sister's reaction. "She was completely oblivious to him though, until I said something. She admitted that she's all nervous around him now, and she's not sure how to act anymore. But I think she's close to figuring it out."

The conversation was cut short as Mary came back. "I know what we need. But we may have a problem."

Aria didn't like the sound of that. "What?"

"We could be missing one crucial element."

"What do you mean 'could be'?" Aria's stomach threatened to plummet at the thought of not being able to catch JD.

"This particular spell requires something of the person you're trying to track," Mary told her. "Blood."

"We have that," Aria reminded her. "The limb that impaled him is at Anna's house."

"I know." Mary's eyes clouded. "But it's weeks old now. It may be too degraded or tainted to work."

"We still have to try." If there was any possible chance it could stop JD, then she had to see it through.

"I agree, but you need to know it may not work the way we'd hoped," Mary cautioned.

Aria nodded.

Mary started giving out orders. "Okay, Aria. You go back to the house and cut off the branch. Make sure not to disturb whatever blood is still there. While you're doing that, I'll go out and pick up what I need. It might take me a few hours to gather everything, so let's meet back here this evening. Then the five of us will cast the spell."

~~~

Seth stood in an overgrown field looking at the body of a petite blonde woman who could have easily passed for Aria or her sister. He glanced over at Evan and saw that he too had noted the resemblance.

If not for the fact that he knew them both to be safe, this scene might have driven him to the edge of sanity.

As it was, he was sick to his stomach at what had been done to this innocent life. The ones responsible had taken great pleasure in tormenting their victim before killing her and throwing her out as if she were trash.

Her long pale hair was matted and saturated with blood, the gaping wound on the back of her head the obvious cause of death. Ligature marks were evident on her wrists and ankles, as were the clear signs of torture over the rest of her naked form. She'd also suffered a brutal rape as indicated by the bruising and blood on her inner thighs.

Seth noticed darker gashes high up on her thighs and squatted to take a better look. They were the crescent-moon shape of bite wounds. Seth swore under his breath and stood.

He, as Aria had, knew this was most likely the work of JD and Noor. He'd refrained from passing judgment until he'd seen what had been done to her. He was sure now. He'd seen this handy work before. JD didn't stray too far from his chosen MO.

Seth was also confident the choice of victim had been deliberate. It was a sign to him and the Burkes. A taunt. The message was clear: it could be Aria or Anna next time.

Over Seth's dead body would that ever happen.

He turned to his partner. "We need to catch this sick bastard."

Evan nodded in agreement as they got started on processing the scene.
~~~

Once they'd completed their investigation and collected what little evidence there was, they returned to the PD, letting the coroner and the crime scene analysts finish up.

Seth was typing up a report when both his and Evan's phones alerted to a text. They picked them up at the same time, and Seth saw it was a group message from Aria.

"Working on a plan. Meet up at Mom's later."

"What kind of plan?" Seth looked at Evan across their desks.

Evan had already turned back to his computer and resumed inputting the data from the scene.

"A magical one would be my guess." The tone of Evan's words indicated he wasn't too happy about the prospect.

Seth stared at his partner, his brows coming together in confusion at his reticence. "You don't think that's a good idea? Shouldn't we use whatever tools we have to find this scumbag?"

"I just wish they'd let me do my goddamned job," Evan snapped back and continued to type.

"We've been *doing* our jobs, and *still* a girl is dead at their hands," Seth reminded him starkly. "I know I'm new to all this," he lowered his voice, "witch stuff, but shouldn't we be exploring all the possibilities? I'm kind of surprised you haven't gone that route before now."

"Look." Evan pushed the keyboard away from him and focused on Seth. "When it comes to Noor, I'll do my duty to my family." Evan's dark eyes were hard and his features set. "But JD is a flesh and blood man. His crimes are here and now, and human. That means it's for the police to handle. And I'm a cop, damn it. It's my *job*."

Evan stood swiftly, the force sending his chair rolling back across the floor to bump against another desk. He paid it no heed as he stalked off.

Seth was left sitting there, stunned. *What the hell was that about?* There was definitely something brewing under the surface. He understood about being a cop and putting the bad guys away, but as Aria had reminded him, this was no ordinary adversary. Regular police work wasn't going to cut it. He was amazed Evan hadn't realized that yet.

Seth's thoughts were interrupted when another detective delivered a note to his desk. "This was called in a few minutes ago."

Seth read it over and jumped to his feet. "Thanks."

He dialed Evan's cell as he raced out the door. It went straight to voicemail. "Hey, Evan. Just got a call that someone matching JD's description was spotted out by the house the MC rented. I'm headed out there now. Meet me there."

He dropped the phone into his pocket at the same time he reached the parking lot. Pulling out his keys, he hit the fob to unlock his personal vehicle, leaving the unmarked squad car for Evan for whenever he got his message. He slid in behind the wheel and hit the button to start it up. Within seconds, he was out of the lot and speeding away.

As Seth drove, he thought about what he was walking into. He wasn't stupid, nor did he believe this was as simple as it seemed. For weeks, there had been no sign of JD. He'd completely hidden himself away from all detection. Whether or not he had Noor's help with that still remained a mystery, but he'd been able to stay off their radar. So why was he getting sloppy now?

The fact was—he wasn't. Which meant this was most likely a trap.

Seth knew he should wait for Evan. Strolling straight into a set-up alone wasn't the smartest way to handle it. But if he could finish this now and put an end to JD, he had to try. And who knew when Evan would get his message, given how pissed off he'd been when he left?

He drove on, and fifteen minutes later pulled to a stop at the end of the drive. He'd go the rest of the way on foot. No sense in alerting anyone to his presence just yet.

Seth shut the car down and pulled his weapon. A push of a button had the magazine dropping into his hand. A quick glance told him it was full and ready. He shot the mag back into place and racked the slide.

Eyes scanning the area, he opened the door and got out. After softly closing the door, he took hold of his gun in a two-handed grip, muzzle angled at the ground, ready to raise and fire in a split second.

Seth slowly eased his way up the long drive. On high alert, he used all of his senses to warn him if someone was there. As he neared the open area in front of the house, he stopped and waited. Hidden in the trees, he searched for any sign of movement.

He held his position for a full five minutes. In a waiting game like this, the first to move was usually the first to die.

When enough time had passed without incident, Seth crouched low and darted across the open field. He approached the house, but instead of gaining the front porch, he skirted around the side of it and pressed his back up against the side of the building.

He paused and listened.

Not a sound.

Haltingly, he began to circle the structure, keeping a wary eye on the tree line off in the distance. When he came to a window, he peered around the frame to see inside.

It looked empty, but to be safe, he ducked below the sill and continued on. At the corner, he chanced a peek around the side to get a quick look. Clear.

Ears alert and eyes wide and searching, Seth encircled the house but saw no sign of anyone. Back where he'd started, he took the two steps onto the covered porch and moved toward the door.

From his time here, he remembered the screen door squeaked as it opened. Moving it an inch at a time, Seth was able to open it silently. Retaining his grip on the gun with his right hand, he dropped his left to grasp the door knob.

It gave way easily, and he pushed it in. He was hyper-aware of his surroundings, ready for whatever JD or Noor had planned for him.

What he wasn't ready for was the ripe smell of death and decay that greeted him upon entry into the house.

A sound from behind had him spinning on his heel, weapon raised and aimed center mass.

Evan stood with his own gun drawn, but neither man said a word. As if they'd done it a thousand times, they split off and searched the house.

The farther into the interior Seth went, the stronger the odor became. As he made his way down the hall, a sick feeling began to settle in his stomach. The room he'd stayed in was just ahead on the left. The door was closed where all the others were open.

He hated to see what was behind that wooden panel, but he knew he had to go in. He started for it when Evan eased into the hall.

"The rest of the house is clear," Evan whispered tonelessly.

Seth nodded and then returned his gaze to the closed door, waiting for his partner to catch up. In a hushed voice, he said back, "I think whatever was left for me to find is in this room."

"Why this one?" Evan questioned.

Seth met his eyes. "Because this one was mine."

Understanding dawned in Evan's black eyes. He moved into position to enter when Seth did.

Seth reached out with his left hand, grabbed the knob, and turned it. He gave Evan one last look before he swung it open.

They both covered their mouths and noses with their arms in an attempt to block out the overwhelming stench of decomp that assailed them.

JD and Noor had not been idle as they'd thought. What

they'd done was torture, rape, and murder eight other young women. And every single one of them was petite and fair and blonde.

"Fuck!" Bile rose in Seth's throat. He swallowed it back and rounded on Evan. Seth was barely holding on to his anger. "You still think regular fucking police work is going to catch these bastards?"

Leaving Evan there in the hall, Seth stormed out the way he'd come until he was outside and sucking fresh air into his lungs. He didn't think he'd ever get that smell out of his system.

When he could finally think past the rage, he put a call in to the PD to report what they'd found.

Evan joined him just as he was putting his phone back into his pocket.

"You're right," Evan began. "I don't know why I've been so opposed to using what I am on this case." He paused for a second as they both stared out over the yard. Seth heard him take a breath. "That's a lie. I do know. The first twenty years of my life were consumed with our destiny. It was a situation I had no control over. The police force was a chance for me to take charge of my life, and I found out I was pretty damned good at being a cop."

Evan slid his hands into his pockets. "I've done more good in the last six years on the force than I've done in twenty-four years of being a witch. This prophecy crap was dropped on my head—on *our* heads. We didn't ask for it, but we've dealt with it the best we can. Being a cop, though…I know you know what I'm talking about. That feeling you get every time you slam a cell door on the scum we get off the streets."

Seth knew exactly what he was referring to. It was that same drive that had put him on the task force.

"I do understand," Seth told him. "And ordinarily I would be right there with you. But this situation is anything but ordinary. JD may be a flesh and blood man, but this partnership he has with Noor is giving him a huge advantage. We can't afford to ignore that any longer."

"You're right," Evan repeated. "When we're done here, we'll go see what my family's come up with."

18

They didn't get back to the department until sometime in the afternoon. With so many bodies, the scene had taken hours to catalog. Even though the coroner's office had taken all the victims to be processed, the tech guys were still there, tagging and logging everything into evidence.

The first thing Seth and Evan did when they got back was grab extra clothes out of their lockers and scrub that smell off their bodies in the showers. Seth's clothes were ruined. The blood and stench would never come out, so on his way out of the bathroom he chucked it all in the trash bin.

Captain Reynolds was waiting for them when they got back to their desks.

"What have you found out?"

Evan began. "The coroner's preliminary findings estimate that the first victim was killed approximately six weeks ago. The last just a few days. Prior to the one that was found this morning," he added to establish a timeline.

"He did say," Seth picked up, "the evidence supports that the bodies had been recently dumped there, and that it wasn't the original kill site. He also mentioned that some seemed to have sustained more severe wounds than others, indicating times of extreme rage or psychosis. But until he takes a closer look at all of them, he won't know the extent."

"Any ID on them?" Reynolds folded his arms over his chest.

"No," Seth told him. "We're going to check with Missing Persons. Someone must have reported these girls."

Reynolds grunted, and Seth knew he was considering what a monumental task that would be, since they all bore such a striking resemblance.

"Well, get to it." The captain turned and walked back to his office.

"What do you want to bet," Evan said as he rounded his desk, "that they took turns—JD and Noor. I think Noor would have a lot more pent-up aggression, having been denied for so long. Plus, if it holds true that he has to recoup after expending energy, I'm thinking while he was down, JD carried on without him. When they're together, it gets that much worse."

It made sense, Seth thought. But either way, this reign of terror had to end.

By seven o'clock, they'd only identified three of the girls. Seth and Evan decided to call it a night and start fresh in the morning. Neither had called to tell the rest of the Burkes what had happened—only that they'd be late. They owed it to them to break this gruesome news in person.

Seth was dragging ass when he pulled into the driveway of Aria's parents' house. Evan parked right behind him and together they walked in.

The first thing that greeted them when they stepped into the living room was the enticing smell of food. A far cry from the last house they'd visited. After the morning he'd had, Seth hadn't thought he'd ever be able to eat again, but the aromas coming from the kitchen changed his mind.

Evan stepped around him, crossed to the couch, and sat next to his brother. Before Seth could make a move, Aria came out of the hall and walked into his arms. As he wrapped them around her waist, he hoped he'd gotten all of the day's muck off. He didn't want that vileness touching her.

He leaned his head down and kissed her upturned face,

absorbing the goodness that was Aria Burke. After all he'd done is his life, and some of that was pretty questionable after living with the dregs of society for so long, he knew he didn't deserve someone like her. But he'd be damned if he could give her up now.

Seth reluctantly ended the kiss when he remembered where they were.

"Long day for you," she soothed.

"You have no idea." Seth knew they couldn't put it off any longer. "Can you call the others in here, please?"

Aria gave him a curious look but did as she'd been asked. As soon as everyone was assembled, he and Evan explained what they'd found.

Shock and dismay was written on every face in the room. Most sat with horrified expressions at the extensive loss of life at the hands of Noor and JD. Anna was silently crying, and Aria just looked pissed off.

"Your text earlier said you were working on a plan." Seth looked at her. "I hope to God it's one that'll stop these monsters."

"I hope so," she told him. "We've been working on it all day. We were missing a few ingredients, but we were able to get them. I think it's ready now."

"What exactly is it?" Seth was completely out of his depth when it came to anything witchy.

"A tracking spell," Aria supplied.

That sounded fairly self-explanatory.

"How does it work?" Seth saw a look pass between Aria and her mother and wondered what it meant.

"It may not," Aria said on a sigh.

Seth waited for her to explain.

"It tracks through blood," she spelled out. "We have JD's from that day he came to Anna's, but it may not be fresh enough to activate the spell."

"Is there another way to find him?" Seth asked.

"This is our best shot," Mary filled in. "Blood is a direct link. He can't hide from that. Even if Noor is shielding him, this tracker spell would find him."

Seth took that in. "How will we know whether or not it worked?"

"When the blood is added to the rest of the ingredients, it should cause a reaction," Mary simplified. "If we see that, we move on to the second step, which is casting the actual tracking spell. But if the first part doesn't work..."

"We're SOL," Aria supplied.

Seth had no clue of what he was getting into, but at this point he'd try anything. "Okay then, let's do this."

The seven of them moved into the library. The four, plus Mary, took up positions around a large metal bowl that sat atop a tall pedestal table. Arranged close to the vessel were small bottles and drawstrings bags. Also on the table was the stick containing JD's blood. It was no longer bright red, but had faded to a sickening black.

Seth followed Paul to stand off to the side where they could observe. When everyone was ready, they began.

"We're going to call to our ancestors first," Mary said for his benefit. "We'll use the magic from the entire Burke line to help us build this spell."

Mary looked at each of her children and gave them the sign to begin. Their five voices blended into one.

Burke to Burke, back through time
We call to you, our family line.
To guide our hearts and steady our hands
As we strive to wipe evil from our lands
We send our love and honor thee
As we will, so mote it be."

Seth was shocked to actually feel the air come alive around

him. It was like the whole room had gained an electrical charge, and the hairs on his arms and neck stood on end.

Just as suddenly as it had come, it was gone, and all was normal again.

His gaze shot to the left to where Aria's dad, the only other non-witch, was standing. He looked as if nothing at all odd had just occurred. Paul stood, relaxed, with his hands resting in his pants pockets. *Maybe he hadn't felt it.* But that theory was blown when Paul turned to him and gave Seth a knowing smile.

This show of magic was obviously old news to him. Seth, on the other hand, was awed at the level of power he'd felt. He had a lot to learn about this side of Aria's life.

Mary spoke and drew his focus back. "Now we'll move on to what we're here for."

She picked up a vial of herbs of some kind, uncapped it, and then reached in with her thumb and index finger. She grasped a pinch of the dark green leaves and dropped them into the bowl.

Seth watched, mesmerized, as she mixed and sprinkled and stirred all the ingredients—some dried herbs, some powder, and some liquid—except the last. When she picked up the branch, Seth held his breath.

She reached for the knife she'd laid out for this purpose. Taking both in hand, she scraped some of the dried blood off the limb and into the bowl.

As the particles drifted downward, every eye in the room watched their descent. When Mary set down the blade, the five around the bowl leaned in to see if the addition of the blood had caused any kind of reaction with the ingredients.

Seth could feel the tension in the air as everyone waited. From where he and Paul were standing, nothing could be seen.

But judging by the disappointed faces of the others, he could guess what the outcome was.

"It didn't work." Mary's shoulders slumped.

"Maybe if we give it more time?" Aria protested.

"That's not how it works, Ari." Her mother sighed ruefully. "We'll have to try something else."

"If we could get some fresh blood," Seth said into the tense silence, "could you try it again?"

"Of course," Mary confirmed with optimism. "But how are we going to get it?"

He looked at Evan. "We need to check with the lab techs—see if any of those girls got a piece of JD. There could be samples under their nails."

"You want to tamper with evidence?" Evan stared at him, shocked.

It wouldn't be the first time Seth had bent the rules in order to get the job done. He was trying to put his outlaw ways behind him, but in this instance, those tactics might come in handy.

"Not if I don't have to," Seth stressed. "But we may not have any other choice. Let's see if there's anything there first before we decide what action to take."

~~~

Aria was still upset that the spell hadn't worked when they fell into bed later that night. She let Seth pull her back into the curve of his body, and they lay for a while, neither saying a word.

When he finally did speak, the sound was startling in the quiet. "I'm sorry that didn't go the way we wanted."

"I knew there was a chance," she sighed. "But I honestly thought it would lead us to him."

"It will," he promised. "It'll take a little more time, but we will stop him."

Aria took that promise with her as she dropped into sleep, but at some point she started to dream. In it, she was running through an enormous field. As far as the eye could see, bodies
~~~

littered the ground. What made Aria's blood run cold was the fact that each and every one looked the same.

Was one of them Anna? Had Noor or JD fulfilled the vision she'd seen? Was Anna lying in this meadow somewhere? Alone, hurt…dead?

Aria raced from one, to the next, to the next. The longer she searched, the more frantic she became. Each girl here was someone's loved one, but not the one she sought. She stumbled to a stop and slowly turned around and around, the bodies becoming blurred as tears filled her eyes and obstructed her vision. There were so many…too many. She'd never find her. A scream bubbled up her throat, and when it erupted, it was a long, agonized wail.

"Annnnnnaaaa!" Her voice shook with terror at the thought of never seeing her sister again.

Suddenly, strong arms broke the hold of the dream as they grasped her tight. The low, murmuring voice in her ear pulled her the rest of the way out.

"Shhh. It's all right," Seth soothed her. "I've got you. Come back to me now, Pixie."

"I'm sorry," Aria said when she could speak past the knot in her throat. "I didn't mean to wake you. It was just a nightmare."

"I don't think that was *just* anything. You were whimpering and crying, and you're still trembling." He tightened his hold as if his strength alone could stop her shaking.

"Tell me," he pleaded.

In the shadows of night, Aria told him about the dream. When she was done, she turned in the circle of his arms until she lay facing him. She could just barely make out his face, but she needed to be looking at him when she asked her next question.

"Am I going to lose my sister?" Tears clogged her words.

"No." His answer was quick and firm and left no room for doubt. "I will not let anything happen to either of you. You have my promise."

The confidence she heard in his voice allayed some of her fears. She was able to relax into his warmth and doze off. When she opened her eyes again, the room was brightening.

As the sun returned, so did her fight. And with it, a plan.

19

She felt the change in Seth's breathing and knew he was waking. She tipped her head back far enough to look up into his face. When his brown eyes fluttered open, she smiled at him.

"Good morning."

"Hi." His voice was gruff with sleep. "You okay?"

"Yeah, I'm good," she assured him. "I have an idea."

He studied her for a moment before speaking. "I don't think I'm going to like this, am I?"

"Probably not." She softened her words with a grin.

He huffed out an exaggerated breath. "Okay, hit me."

"I want to see the bodies of those girls."

Seth slid his arm out from under her, propped himself up on his elbow, and stared down at her. "Absolutely not."

She sat up next to him. "I think I can help."

"How?"

"If I can get a vision from them, it may give us the clues we need."

Seth left the bed, grabbed his pants, and pulled them on with jerky movements. "I already told you I was going to look for a new sample of his blood. You don't need to subject yourself to that."

She had to do something. She couldn't sit back and wait. Aria rose up to her knees. "How many of them have you identified?"

His dark eyebrows came together over his wary eyes. "What difference does that make?"

"How many?" She held her ground and waited.

"Three," he answered grudgingly.

Because she knew he wouldn't let her anywhere near the victims if he knew what it would cost her, she purposely made it sound like it would be no trouble to touch a dead body. Or to see what had been done to them.

"What if, simply by touching them, I could put names to faces and possibly find where JD is hiding?"

Aria could see the thoughts racing in his mind. He wanted to fight her on it, but she could tell he was reluctantly entertaining the idea. She knew it could take him and Evan days to identify all the girls, and even then, they'd be no closer to finding JD.

She didn't push. She'd planted the suggestion; now she'd let him come to it himself. Stepping off the bed, she went to the closet to grab her robe.

"I'm going to go make us some breakfast," she reached up on her toes to kiss him, "and let you think about it."

Aria walked past him and into the hall. At the same time, Anna came out of her bedroom dressed in her workout clothes and her hair pulled up into a messy knot.

They walked arm-in-arm to the kitchen.

"Do you want something to eat before you leave?" Aria asked as she got bacon and eggs out of the fridge.

"No thanks, just coffee." Anna went straight to the counter and poured a cup from the carafe.

"So…how's Joe?" Aria asked over her shoulder.

Anna was taking a sip of her coffee but threw Aria a dirty look over the rim of her cup. Aria laughed as Anna went to sit down.

"Have you at least talked to him?" Aria asked her.

"Kind of."

Aria turned to face her. "And?"

"I told him I know how he feels about me. And now he's avoiding me. Probably out of embarrassment." Anna stared sullenly down into her mug.

"Oh, boy," Aria muttered. She gave the bacon a stir in the pan, set the tongs aside, and went to join Anna at the table.

When she sat, she took her sister's hands in hers. "You two need to stop dancing around and just sit down and talk. You both obviously have feelings for each other. Get on the same page and see where it goes."

Anna dropped her gaze to their clasped hands. "What if I'm too scared to see where it goes? What if my walls slip and I sense something in him I shouldn't? And what happens when he finds out about all the rest? What if he can't handle who I am and turns on me?"

"Oh, Anna." Aria's heart tore at the fear in her sister's words. As tough as she tried to be now, the sheltered empath was still under the surface. "You can't live your life on 'what-ifs.' And even if any of that were to happen, you'd get through it. Don't forget—you're a kick-ass bitch now." Aria took a breath. "Look, if you give it a try and it doesn't work, or he's not the guy you thought he was, then he didn't deserve you anyway."

Aria wanted to make her smile. "And if he hurts you, you have two Goliath-sized brothers who would gladly stomp him into the ground."

Anna's face split into an easy grin as she'd hoped.

"Don't let your fear hold you back, sweetie," Aria told her. "You've fought too hard to get to where you are. And I, for one, am so proud of you."

Aria watched a change gradually come over Anna. She sat up straight, and her delicate features firmed and became set as she regained control.

"You're right." Anna nodded. "That weak, insecure girl was the old me. The new Anna is strong, confident, and tough. If I decide I want Joe Conrad, then by damn, I'm going to have him."

She stood and bent down to kiss Aria on the cheek. "Thank you."

"You're more than welcome. Now go get him."

Anna turned and left, and a few seconds later Seth stepped through the doorway.

"I didn't want to interrupt." He pulled her up and into his arms. "But can I just say, whoever this Joe Conrad is, he doesn't stand a chance."

Aria smiled. "No, he doesn't."

He studied her face for a moment. "Neither did I." He gave her a quick kiss. "If you think you can handle what you have planned, I won't stand in your way."

"It's not going to be easy, but I really think this might work."

He held her gaze. "I'll trust you to know how much you can deal with. But there's one aspect of this plan that I won't be swayed on. You will *not* go in there alone. I'll be with you every step of the way."

"I have no problem with that." She leaned up and pressed her lips to his, losing herself in the kiss until she caught a whiff of burning bacon. She pulled away. "Oh, crap."

"Not quite the reaction I was going for there," Seth teased as she darted out of his arms.

"The bacon is burning, you idiot," she laughed as she flipped the pieces over. "Get your coffee and sit down. This'll be done in a minute."

After breakfast, Aria showered and dressed so she could leave with Seth.

A short time later, they pulled into the parking lot of the county building. They were quiet and thoughtful as they traversed the long white halls. Finally she saw a set of double doors labeled "Morgue."

Seth held one open for her to enter. The attendant looked up from the notes he was taking.

"Hey, Seth. Didn't expect you this morning."

"Hey, Scott. I was hoping we could have the room for a little while."

Scott looked from Seth to Aria, and she saw his eyes widen just a bit. She knew he was seeing her resemblance to all the women lying in the room beyond.

"Is this for identification?" Scott asked.

Seth nodded but didn't elaborate.

"Yeah, sure. Take as much time as you need." Scott gathered his paperwork and quietly left.

"He thinks I've come to find a family member." Aria stared at the second set of doors.

"That'll work to our benefit," Seth said. "He won't disturb us."

Aria nodded. Now that she was here, about to go into the same room with nine dead women, she was having second thoughts. But then she remembered the conversation she'd had with Anna just a little while ago about not letting her fear hold her back.

So she did as Anna had. She squared her shoulders and pulled on her big girl panties. She would walk in there and not only find JD, but she would give these girls back their identities. They all had families that needed closure.

Seth caught her attention. "You ready?"

"Yes."

As before, he pushed the door inward for her to pass through. She had a moment where the smell of the place nearly stopped her, but she blocked it out and proceeded. The first sheet-draped figure was to her right.

She moved to stand next to the metal gurney. When she reached out to lift the cover, Seth stayed her hand.

"Do you really need to see them? What if I expose a hand? Would that be enough for you to work from?"

Aria nodded, grateful for Seth's quick thinking. "Yeah. That should work."

Soon a pale, slender hand lay in front of her. Aria took a breath and laid hers over the top.

She had a moment to register the coldness of it before she was pulled into the last horrific scene of this girl's life. She tried to stay detached and not get swamped in the pain and fear she was seeing. It was an almost-impossible task, but she did it.

When it was over, Aria stepped back and braced her hands on her knees, taking deep breaths to fight off the nausea.

"Mandy. Her name was Mandy," she told him when she could stand without her head spinning.

Seth stepped to her. "Are you okay?"

Aria smiled up at him. "No. But I have to do this." She reached up and cupped his cheek. "I love you."

He placed his hand over hers, turned his head, and kissed her palm. "Love you."

On and on it went, each one's ordeal harder to block out than the last. Over and over Aria witnessed what these girls had gone through. Some she found names for, some she didn't.

Aria's head was pounding, making the urge to vomit a constant battle. She knew she was pushing too much, but she had to keep going. Each one she touched gave them a few more clues. She hadn't found the big one that would finally reveal JD's location, but the longer she worked, the more they'd get.

She was down to the last two, and her head was one huge unrelenting ache now. She could barely see through the pain. When her legs gave out as she walked to the next table, Seth was there to catch her.

"That's enough. You're done," he demanded.

"I'm fine," Aria lied.

"No, you're not." Seth grasped her by both shoulders. "You're whiter than these dead bodies, and your eyes are glassy with pain. This stops now, damn it."

"We don't have enough yet," she protested. "There's only two more. I can do this."

She pushed out of Seth's grip and spun around to continue despite his concern. But the movement was too much for her overworked and traumatized brain. Before she completed the turn, she crumpled to the floor.

20

When the darkness finally released her, she found herself in her bed at Anna's. She made a move to sit up and ended up flat on her back again as her head swam and throbbed. She clutched it with both hands to keep it from bursting into a million pieces.

She was still breathing away the pain when someone came into the room. Aria peeked out through barely-open eyes to see her mom with a cup of something in her hands.

"Please tell me that's your miracle fix-anything tea." She kept her voice low in consideration to her head.

Mary looked down at the mug in her hand and then back to her daughter. "Yes, it is. And I should pour it over your stubborn head instead of letting you drink it."

Uh-oh. Aria closed her eyes again and waited for a wave of nausea to pass.

"I had to, Momma." Tears gathered behind her lids and slipped out of the corners. "I couldn't let him just get away with it. The blood spell didn't work. I had to do something."

The mattress shifted as Mary sat down on the edge. She took one of Aria's hands away from her head and placed the warm cup into it. Aria opened her eyes and slowly adjusted her position enough to take a drink of the hot brew.

"I know." Mary smoothed the hair back away from Aria's face. "I would have done the same thing if I'd been able. But..."

Mary dropped her hands into her lap. "You should have gone about it in a different way. You made yourself sick by pushing so hard. Do you honestly think that was smart? That man of yours was frantic when he called me."

"Seth called you?" Aria hadn't given any thought to how her mom had come to be there.

"He said you'd collapsed, so he brought you home. But when you didn't wake up, he got concerned and called me. He was ready to tear something, or someone, apart when I got here."

"I told him it wasn't going to be easy," Aria defended herself as she sipped more of the tea.

When her mother didn't respond, she looked up. Mary was drilling her with a look that said 'Really? That's how you want to play this?'

Aria ducked her head a little. "He wouldn't have let me do it if I'd told him how bad it might get."

"You still should have given him the truth. He can't do what he needs to do without knowing all the information."

Aria rested her head back against the headboard. "I know." She glanced at the bedroom door. "Where is he?"

"Probably still out there, ready to wreak havoc on something." She paused a beat before continuing. "I know he put his old life behind him to come back to you, but there's something you have to remember, Aria. That edge, that danger, is still a big part of him. And right now, he's fighting that by sheer will alone."

"I need to talk to him." Aria made a move to get up.

Mary stopped her. "Finish your tea first."

Once it was gone, she slowly got to her feet. Her mom's concoction had worked its wonders once again. Her head wasn't threatening to fall off her shoulders, and her stomach was settled and calm.

Until she left the safety of the bedroom. Butterflies took wing and beat against the inside of her belly at the thought of facing Seth. She reached the doorway into the living room just as he turned to face her.

The banked rage in his eyes and the clenched fists at his sides told her that her mother had been right. He was waging a battle within himself not to lose control.

Gradually as they stood facing each other, he was able to push the outlaw back. As the anger receded, worry, fear, and finally relief took its place. Aria felt awful for having put him through so much distress. As she approached him, he tucked his hands in his pockets. She figured it was either that or throttle her. She didn't blame him.

Out of the corner of her eye, she saw her mom smoothly exit out through the kitchen. The back door closed with a soft thump.

"I'm sorry," Aria whispered.

He didn't say anything.

She held his gaze unflinchingly. "I should have warned you. It was wrong to downplay the effect it would have on me. I was wrong."

He blinked. And that small movement was the breaking of the shackles that held him. His voice was strained as he gritted out, "I thought you were dead."

Those five words, said with such emotion, stole the breath from her lungs.

"I couldn't function," he went on, the floodgates falling open. "The world closed in on me at the thought of living without you. I was afraid to touch you. Afraid of what I'd find. Or wouldn't find. I've never been more scared as when I reached out to lay my fingers on your neck. When I felt your heart beating and I knew you were still here, mine started again. But then you wouldn't wake up."

Aria's insides clenched as she realized just how much her selfishness had hurt him.

"Then I was pissed off." The rugged features of his face went hard as stone and just as cold. The brown of his eyes became icy chips. "After the talk we'd had this morning about trust, I didn't want to believe you'd lied to me. Or purposely withheld something that could have cost you your life."

She stood and took his anger and recriminations. She was in the wrong; she deserved every bit of it.

"I know I'm new to this whole magic thing. Did you think I couldn't handle it? Did you think I wouldn't understand?"

Aria was already shaking her head. How could he doubt her faith in him? "No. No, that wasn't it at all." She took a steadying breath and went on. "The harsh truth is, I was afraid you wouldn't let me try if you knew."

"Wouldn't let you?" He plowed his hands through his hair in frustration and then turned and walked a few paces away. She jumped when he abruptly swung back around. "Of course I didn't like it, but you're the witch here. I thought after twenty-four years that you would know what you the hell you were doing."

"I *do* know what I'm doing."

He gave her an incredulous look.

Aria's frustrations were building too, because he didn't seem to understand. "I was desperate," her voice rose a little. "I had to do it."

Seth just watched her as if he couldn't believe what he'd just heard. "You think you're the only one who feels that way?" He advanced on her until he towered over her. "Do you know what it does to me every time we discover another fucking body of a woman who looks just like you? It fucking kills me every goddamned time, because for a split second," he held up one hand with a fraction of space between his thumb and finger, "I think it could be you lying there, bloody and broken."

Seth turned and stormed into the kitchen. She heard the refrigerator open and slam closed as she followed. He was twisting the cap off a beer when she reached the doorway. She waited until he lowered the bottle after drinking half of it down.

She walked up to him and after a brief tug-of-war, took the beer from him and set it aside. When his hands were empty, she stepped into his arms and wrapped them around her waist.

With both hands, she reached up and cupped his face. She slowly pulled his head down until it rested on her shoulder. Aria slid her own arms around his neck and hugged him tight. She held him that way until she felt his grip tighten on her.

"I am so so so sorry," she murmured in his ear. "I completely messed this up. Can you ever forgive me?"

He held her against him so close she could barely breathe, but she didn't dare loosen her hold. They both needed the reconnection. Slowly, she felt some of the tension drain out of him until he finally raised his head. He gazed down into her face for a long, deliberate moment. His eyes gradually lost the coldness and became warm pools of chocolate once again. A hint of fear lingered around the edges, and she regretted having put it there.

"Pixie, my heart forgave you as soon as you woke up." A small smile curved his perfect lips before becoming serious again. "My head though—that's going to take a little longer."

"I can't promise to never screw up again," Aria told him. "But I will promise to be more open and honest with you from now on."

He rested his forehead against hers. "You really scared the shit out of me."

"I know, and I'm sorry."

They stayed face to face, just breathing for several minutes.

Aria eventually raised her head. "Do you have to go back to work?"

"I should, but I don't want to leave you alone."

"I'm fine," she assured him with a smile. "That tea my mom makes can heal anything from a hangnail to the plague."

"Are you sure?" He still sounded worried.

"I'm fine." She caressed his cheek and kissed his lips. "Really."

She hated to do it, but she broached the still-touchy subject. "Do you think any of the information I got will help?"

"The names will definitely help to cut down on the time it takes to search for their families, but there's a couple left we still need to identify. As far as JD," he paused. "I don't know. It was all pretty vague, but we'll add it to the rest and hope something shakes loose."

When Seth released her and stepped out of her arms, she asked, "Do you want me to make you some coffee before you go?"

"Why?" He gave her a quizzical look.

"You downed half that beer in one gulp," she reminded him. "You're on duty."

He grinned at her. "I'll be fine. Half a brew is like a sip of water."

She thought back to how he'd lived the last few years of his life and shook her head. "Yeah, I guess it would be."

Aria followed him to the door. "Will you let me know what you find out?"

"Yeah." Seth leaned down and kissed her. "I'll see you tonight. I don't know how late I'll be."

"Okay. Love you."

"Love you, too."

Aria locked the door and then went to pour the rest of the tea her mom had left warming on the stove. She brought it with her to the living room where, after collecting a pad and pen, she sat on the couch. She wanted to go over everything she'd seen and make sure she hadn't missed any last detail.

When Anna arrived home later that afternoon, Aria had pages of notes. A few snippets of information concerned JD, but most of it had been about the girls themselves. She was glad she'd been able to identify four out of the seven she'd read.

Mandy, Patricia, Molly, and Brianna would soon be returned to their families for final goodbyes.

Anna dropped her bag on the floor in front of the couch and, tucking one leg underneath her, sat down facing her. "I heard through the grapevine you were a bad girl today."

"I just pushed my power too far. I didn't listen to my body's warnings to stop."

"Seth had to call Mom?"

"Yeah. It really scared him when I went down."

"I imagine it would. He's never seen the extent of what we can do or what it takes out of us sometimes. As we get closer to our next birthday, I'm sure there'll be plenty more that shocks him. And us."

"I wish I could have gotten more about where JD is hiding. There's still two I didn't get a chance to read."

"If you didn't get anything from the others, what makes you think the last two would be any different?"

"I have to try. Maybe one of them saw or heard something that'll give us the break we need."

Anna looked at the empty cup on the table. "Was that Mom's fix-anything tea?"

"Oh, yeah." Aria smiled. "Still works the same. I don't know what she puts in it, but it works every time. Hopefully when I have kids, she'll give me the recipe."

"Kids, huh?" Anna grinned. "Planning the future already?"

"Yeah. I can't wait for our children to grow up together like we did."

A playful glint lit Anna's blue eyes. "Oh, and now you're planning my future too?"

Aria laughed. "I've missed you so much."

Anna reached over and hugged her. "I've missed you too."

~~~
~~~

When Seth sat down heavily at his desk, Evan looked up. "Where have you been?"

Seth was still trying to wipe the image of Aria lying motionless on the floor of the morgue out of his mind. He didn't like having to recount it with his partner, but Evan needed to know.

"I spent the morning at the morgue. With your sister."

That had Evan's full attention. "Why?"

"She got the bright idea to visit the victims. See what she could...get from them."

"Not a bad plan." Evan leaned forward on his desktop. "Did she see anything?"

"Before or after she collapsed?" Seth ground out.

Evan's face registered shock. "She passed out?"

Seth nodded grimly.

"That shouldn't have happened just from connecting with a dead body."

"*A* body? Try *seven*."

"Seven?" Evan almost shouted. "She relived all of their last moments. Saw what they'd seen, and felt their pain and fear. It was input overload. No wonder she passed out. Is she nuts?"

"Apparently." Seth drew in a deep breath and let it out. "As much as what she did pisses me off, I can't really blame her. We're all a little desperate. We're nowhere even close to finding this fucker, much less putting him down for good. He's playing with us."

"I take it she didn't see anything?"

"A few flashes—tall grass, a fence, an outbuilding of some kind, and lots of sky and treetops. The sick bastards raped and killed some of them right out in the open." Seth shook his head. "Others he must have done inside, because Aria also described a room of a house."

"You're sure what she saw wasn't where we found them? Some other room maybe?" Evan questioned.

"By the way she described it, it wasn't the house we stayed in," Seth confirmed. "I would have recognized it."

"And the outbuilding? I'm guessing that's not familiar to you either."

"Nope."

"So that means," Evan laid it out, "the kill site is near a fence and has a storage structure on the property. It's most likely set back in the woods for maximum privacy, and it's abandoned, if the tall grass is any indication."

Evan thought it through further. "You said she saw trees. Were they palm, pine, or what? Maybe that would give us a clue to its location."

Seth could see now why his partner had risen through the ranks so quickly. His mind sorted through information like puzzle pieces, fitting ones together that Seth hadn't even given a thought to yet.

"I couldn't tell you."

"Okay. I'll get that from my sister." Evan made some notes. "We're closing in on him. In the meantime, we still have IDs to make."

"I *can* help with that," Seth informed him. "Aria was able to pull four names out of the seven she touched. Now instead of just a description, we have their first names to narrow down the possibilities."

Seth relayed the information to Evan, and over the next hour, they were able to positively ID all four of the girls Aria had given them. The next order of business was to make the calls no cop ever wanted to make.

Once the disheartening job of notifying the families was done, Seth got down to searching the Missing Person's reports for the rest. While he did that, Evan took a minute to call Aria and pump her for more information.

By the time he hung up, Seth had made one more ID. The victim they'd found in the field was Sarah Henderson, formerly of Kentucky. She was twenty-two and a college sophomore. Her parents had reported her missing a month ago when they hadn't heard back from her after a trip to Florida for spring break.

And now Seth had to call and inform them that she was never coming home. At least, not in the way they would have wanted.

After hours of delivering such tragic news, Seth couldn't take it anymore. He needed to get out. Breathe some fresh air, wash the heaviness away. He still wasn't used to being behind a desk all day. In his whole law enforcement career, he'd never had to deal with being confined like this.

He'd thought being removed from the dangers of his previous assignment would be nice. But now the walls of the precinct were starting to close in on him. He wasn't accustomed to the sedentary lifestyle or the heart-wrenching aspects of the job.

"I've got to get out of here for a while," he told Evan. "Let's go grab some food." He wasn't really hungry, but as long as he was away from here, he didn't care where they went or what they did.

Evan glanced up and without a word, rose and followed him out.

They were in the car when Evan spoke. "It'll take a while to get used to."

Seth looked over at him and then back at the road. "What will?"

"The grunt work. The time sitting on your ass. Not being in the middle of the fray."

He shouldn't have been surprised that Evan understood. This man was one hell of a cop, and Seth was glad to not only call him his partner, but also his friend.

"I know," he breathed out. "And I expected a time of adjustment. But it just got to me today. Hours staring at the computer and shuffling through all the random details. Then to top it off, having to make all those damned phone calls..."

"Yeah, that's one part of the job that always sucks," Evan agreed with a grimace.

Seth lapsed into brooding silence, but he should have known his friend wouldn't let him wallow for long.

"The paperwork sucks too."

Seth looked over at his partner. His eyes were on the road, but his voice sounded despondent.

Evan sighed. "You could get buried alive in all that shit. Not to mention, those painful little cuts. Man, those are the worst."

Seth wasn't sure how to take his partner's admission. His expression was serious, but when Evan glanced over at him, there was something brewing in his dark eyes.

"And don't *even* get me started on the way your ass starts to mold to your chair after sitting for so long. If you're not careful, it'll be as wide as your seat before you know it."

Evan looked over at him again, deadpan.

Seth couldn't hold it in any longer. A laugh burst out from between his lips. "Man, you are such a dumbass."

Evan lost the battle he'd waged to keep a straight face and laughed too. "I know."

"Just for that," Seth chuckled, "*you* can pay for lunch."

The levity felt good, and it alleviated some of the weight that had been pressing down on his shoulders all day.

All humor gone, Seth looked over at Evan after he'd parked. "Thanks for that. This day has been shit from the get-go."

"Hey, I understand. We're all feeling the strain on this one."

They exited the car and Evan spoke over the roof to his partner. "But we'll get him. One way or another."

Seth nodded and together, they walked into the restaurant.

21

The much-needed break had put Seth back on track. For the rest of the afternoon and into early evening, they poured over aerial maps of Daytona and the surrounding areas. They were looking for any place that fit all of the elements Aria had gotten from JD's victims.

So far they had nothing. The area was just too vast.

Evan was standing next to him at the board where the map was pinned up, trying in vain to pick out where the monster could be hunting.

"We just don't have enough information," Evan grumbled.

"Fuck." Seth sighed and scrubbed his hands back through his hair, knowing what he had to do.

Looking at him curiously, Evan turned to him. "What?"

Seth glanced at him. After what had happened, he couldn't believe he was even going to suggest it. "There were two girls Aria didn't get to read. She was hell-bent on finishing, but she passed out before she could."

He saw a spark in his partner's black eyes, but there were a few things Seth needed to know before he moved forward with his idea. "If we do this, is there any way to protect her from overloading like this morning?"

Evan nodded. "Oh, yeah, that's easy."

Seth was a little taken aback. "Then why the hell didn't she protect herself?"

"Because she was working alone," Evan clarified. "If we'd all been there, it wouldn't have hit her so hard."

Seth thought it over. He hated to see Aria go back into that room, especially so soon after the morning she'd had. But if that fix-anything tea really worked the way she'd said, and if she could be shielded from the worst of it, wouldn't it be worth trying? Evan sounded convinced that it wouldn't affect her so much this time.

"All right. So how do we get five people in there without a fuss?"

"You let me take care of that." Evan slid his cell from his pocket. "I'll put out the call."

Seth returned to his desk to finish up some paperwork, while Evan disappeared into an empty conference room to coordinate the plan with his siblings.

When Seth walked through the doors of the morgue exactly thirty minutes later, he saw the quads gathered at the far side of the room.

It still gave him pause when he saw all of them together. Two sets of identical twins as opposite in looks and stature as they could possibly get. Yet, because of destiny, they were each a part of a whole that would fight in the coming war.

He watched them talk and interact, and as he did, he noticed Ethan was slightly separated from the others. Seth didn't know too much about Aria's other brother—only that he kept to himself a lot of the time. He came when his family needed him, but otherwise he stayed away.

As close as Aria and Anna were, Seth would have expected the same to hold true for Evan and Ethan. But oddly, that didn't seem to be the case. Aria had mentioned that she was worried about this quiet brother. She'd explained about Ethan's lost love and how he couldn't seem to recover from the loss.

But Seth had a feeling there was more to it than that. His gut told him that Ethan was hiding something. Something he didn't want the others to know about.

Before he could give it further thought, Aria spotted him. He moved forward as she approached, and when they met midway, she flowed right into his arms.

"This was your idea?" Her pale blue eyes were serious.

"Yeah," Seth admitted as his arms automatically encircled her.

She studied his face. "I didn't think you'd ever agree to let me in here again."

"I didn't want to," he confessed, gazing down into her perfect face. "My worst fear is that the next time, you won't wake up."

Guilt clouded the blue and she opened her mouth to speak, but he talked over her. "Evan assured me that with the rest of them here, you'll be safe."

"Thank you." She went up on her toes, laid her palms on his cheeks, and kissed him. "For trusting in me again. In what I can do. What *we* can do."

He rested his forehead against hers. "Just don't make me regret this more than I already do."

"Prepare to be amazed," she teased as she backed out of his embrace and started back towards her family.

Seth followed, and soon they were all standing next to a gurney. Five sets of eyes stared down at the body concealed beneath a plain white drape.

He backed a couple of paces away to let the four of them do their thing. He kept a watchful eye on Aria. If it looked, in any way, like she was in distress, he'd put a stop to it instantly.

Aria took her position in front, and her siblings arranged themselves around her. Anna stood to her right, Ethan on the left, and Evan behind her. They each touched her in some way, and Seth had to assume it formed some kind of connection between them.

He studied her closely as Aria reached out and lifted the cover away to expose a long, pale arm. His breath caught in his chest when she laid her hand over it. And released when nothing seemed to happen.

Slowly, he made his way around the group so as to have an unobstructed view of the woman who'd come to mean so much to him.

Her eyes were closed as she witnessed the last images of the woman's life. She appeared steady and solid to him. The assist from her family seemed to be working, but then again, this was only the first.

Seth took a moment to check in on each of the others. They, like Aria, had their eyes closed in concentration. Evan and Ethan both stood tall and calm as they lent their assistance, but when his gaze landed on Anna, his heart took a dive. She was crying.

Could she see what Aria was seeing? Could she feel the pain of the last tragic moments of this poor girl's life?

He knew all of the Burkes were extremely cautious with Anna. Was this hurting her? He hadn't considered how this would affect the others. His worry had all been for Aria.

Should he step in and stop them? Anna was clearly distressed.

Just as he was ready to call a halt, Aria opened her eyes. The others followed suit as she tucked the bare hand back under the sheet.

"She didn't see any more than what we already had," Aria shared before turning to the last body.

"Hold up a minute." Seth felt he needed to say something. They all stopped and looked at him. He slid his focus over to Anna, who was wiping away her tears. "Are you okay?

"I'm an empath. I'm as okay as I can be." She smiled at him. "Don't worry. I didn't get the full hit. When we link up, we each take a little of the...*excess* away, so the one dealing with the worst of it doesn't get overwhelmed."

Seth nodded. He still didn't like it, but they seemed to be sure. He watched as they moved to the opposite side of the room and took up the same positions.

This one didn't go as smoothly as the first. Seth saw Aria's eyebrows dip together as whatever she was seeing obviously troubled her. Beside her, Anna also had an adverse reaction. Her breathing became short pants as her grip on Aria's arm tightened.

Aria's head was thrown back and then jerked about on her neck as if she was frantically looking around. Only her eyes were still closed.

Ethan grunted like he'd been hit in the gut. And when Evan's knuckles turned white from clenching Aria's shoulders, Seth knew something bad was happening in there.

The next ten minutes were unbearable. All he could do was stand back and watch as each of them suffered in silence, experiencing something horrific.

Finally, they came out of it. All four of them stared down at the woman lying on the slab with what appeared to be admiration.

"Rest easy now." Aria gently covered her back up and then touched where her face would be under the drape. "You did all you could. Now leave it to us. We'll make him pay."

Seth waited until they were all out in the hall before he questioned them.

"What happened? She seemed different from the rest."

"Oh, she was." Aria's smile was sad but yet a little proud. "She'll be JD's downfall."

Deep down, he hadn't really held out hope that this would work. He should have never doubted the power of this family. And the power of this woman.

"What did you see?"

"She fought him," Aria recounted. "She fought with everything she had. She got away at one point and ran. I saw the house, I saw the surrounding area. He chased her down and tackled her to the ground again." Her mood dimmed. "She wasn't able to escape him again, but she continued to fight." Aria's gaze turned fierce and held his. "She punched and hit him. His face will be riddled with bruises, but he was just too much for her."

"You said you saw the house?" he prompted.

"I did. But that doesn't mean I know where it is."

"Describe it," Evan interrupted. "It may strike something with one of us."

Seth's gaze swung around. His focus had been so completely on Aria, he'd all but forgotten the others were there.

"Before we get into all the specifics, can we please get out of here first?" Anna suggested. "I don't think I can stand being here any longer."

The rest of the discussion was delayed until they'd all met up at Anna's house. Evan was the last to arrive. By the load he carried in, he'd evidently made a couple of stops. His arms were laden with the aerial map of the county from the precinct and a bunch of pizzas.

Anna jumped up to take the food from him and laid it out on her dining room table. The map was spread over the coffee table.

As they ate and studied the map, Aria recounted as much as she could remember about the property.

"There's an old dirt road that runs close to the house. If I read the sunlight right, it would be on the east side."

"Where was the shed in relation to the house?" Evan asked.

Before she could answer, there was a knock on the door.

They all stared at one another for a second before Anna got up. "Wonder who that could be this late?"

Seth and Evan exchanged a look, nodded, and followed. They stood off to the side but close enough to intervene if it were needed. Seth caught movement and saw that Ethan had followed their lead and had taken up a defensive position as well.

Anna glanced to Evan, and he gave her the go-ahead to open the door.

"Joe?" Surprise was evident in Anna's voice. "What are you doing here?"

Joe Conrad stepped into the entryway. When he took in the three men standing guard over Anna, he paused. His body language underwent a subtle yet dangerous shift. He was now on full alert, ready for whatever came his way.

Seth saw a man who could, and would, beat the shit out of anyone. About his own height, Joe was solid. Muscled but lean, the shadows deepening his dark skin and emphasizing the definition in his arms.

"What's going on?" Joe's light brown eyes sparked fire as he glanced around the room.

"Nothing," Anna hurriedly explained. "These are my brothers, Evan and Ethan, and this is Seth, my sister's boyfriend."

Joe eyed each man. "If nothing is going on, then why were they ready to jump me?"

"They weren't going to jump you." Anna sent them all a look that said to stand down and turned back to Joe. She grasped his arm. "Come outside. We'll talk."

When Seth heard that, he felt the need to caution her. "Anna—"

"I'll just be on the porch. I'll be fine." She held firm and closed the door behind her as they went out.

Seth returned to his seat, but the brothers remained standing.

Evan pinned Aria with a foul look. "Is there something you need to tell me?"

~~~

Uh-oh. That cat had just jumped right out of the damned bag. And right in front of two pit bulls.
~~~

"He's a friend of Anna's," Aria hedged.

"Who shows up at her door in the middle of the night?" Ethan demanded, sounding more like their father than their brother.

"It's not the middle of the night, you idiot. It's barely dark."

"Late enough," Evan scowled at her. "Who is he?"

When she didn't elaborate, Evan growled, "Aria," dragging her name out with an expectant tone.

"Evan," she mimicked him. "If you want answers, you'll have to ask Anna."

"You know who he is, don't you?" Ethan probed, backing his twin.

"Yes, I do." Aria eyed them both and crossed her arms over her chest in defiance. "But it's not my place to tell you."

"It's mine," Anna agreed as she entered, unnoticed, through the door. "And I'll thank you not to interrogate our sister."

The two black-haired guard-dogs turned as one, but neither uttered a word because, behind Anna, was the man in question.

"Or ask me." Joe's deep voice rumbled as he took a half-step that placed him partially in front of Anna. "Better yet, why don't you explain what the hell is going on here?"

Aria threw a questioning look at Anna.

"He refused to leave," Anna responded out loud.

"And I won't, until I know Anna isn't in any danger."

At his words, Anna's blue eyes sparkled and a soft smile lit her face. Aria could almost see the hearts twirling around her head as his protectiveness settled over her.

Aria had to wonder what Joe's reason for coming here was. Had he and Anna worked it out and gotten on the same page finally?

Her thoughts were pulled back when Evan spoke next to her.

"And just who the hell do you think you are to walk in here demanding answers? I don't even know who the fuck—"

"Whoa, whoa," Seth interrupted, holding up a hand. Turning to face Joe, he asked, "What makes you think she's in danger?"

"Because I'm not stupid. She came to me for self-defense training, but she's far surpassed that. Now she only seems interested in how to kick ass. That, along with the show of force at the door, tells me there's a reason behind all of this. And it isn't good."

"She came to you for self-defense?" Evan's anger seemed to evaporate as he looked at the stranger disbelievingly.

"Yeah, almost a year ago. I own Knight's Place."

"That's an MMA training facility." Ethan's dark eyes went hard. "That's no place for her."

Joe straightened to his full height and faced off with her brother. He was a good four inches shorter, but that didn't appear to sway him. By the stern look on Joe's face, Aria knew Ethan was about to get the same dressing-down that she'd gotten for underestimating their sister.

"And why is that?" Joe taunted and stepped in closer. "And don't you dare say it's because she's fragile or weak, because she is the strongest person I know." Joe eased up enough to send Ethan a pride-filled grin as he threw his arms out. "Take her on. She'll wipe this floor with you without even breaking a sweat."

Ethan shot a look at Anna and then to Aria. She shrugged and nodded. "She can. I've watched her throw *him* around."

"Now," Joe broke in, "if we're done with all the bullshit, someone needs to fill me in."

All eyes turned to Anna. It would be her decision on how much to tell him.

"We're trying to track a serial killer," she said after a moment's hesitation.

"Why the hell would you do that?" Joe shot a glance to Evan and then Ethan, and then turned to look at Anna. "Isn't one of these guys a cop?" Turning back to her still-hulking brothers, he addressed them both. "That's a job for the police. Anna's a teacher, for Christ's sake."

"His targets of choice are fair-skinned, petite women with long blonde hair," Anna added.

The meaning of her words sunk in, and Joe flashed a stunned look between Anna and Aria.

"Now you understand our caution," Seth added as he rose to extend a hand to Joe. "I'm Seth Lawson, by the way—Evan's partner at the Daytona Beach Police Department."

Joe accepted the handshake. "Joe Conrad." His gaze slid to Anna, and he held it for several heartbeats before returning to Seth.

"You think they're on his list."

Seth nodded.

"Then how do we protect them?"

Aria recognized in Joe something she'd seen in Seth. A need to defend the one he considered his. And no matter what their official status was at this moment, Joe had laid claim to Anna.

Before Seth could answer, Anna interrupted. "Why don't we all sit down?" She turned to Joe. "Are you hungry? We have plenty of pizza. Do you want a beer?"

He refused and Aria watched the interaction with interest. Her sister's nerves had just notched up, and Aria thought she understood why. This would be a telling time for Joe. As he was dragged into the world of magic, he'd have to make a choice. To stand by Anna, and everything she brought with her. Or walk away.

Anna had to be wondering how Joe would handle learning about that side of her. Aria watched as her sister fidgeted around. She grabbed a chair from the dining room table and brought it to where Joe was standing. Even though he'd declined her offer of food, Anna got him a plate of pizza anyway.

He took it from her and sat, but his attention was still on Seth.

"What are you doing to catch him?"

This would be another test for Joe. Right now, he knew only

of one aspect of their killer—the human depravity. What would he do when he learned the rest of the story?

There was no way to keep that separate. JD and Noor were too closely tied. And everything they'd done to find them contained an element of magic.

"We have a few avenues we're pursuing," Seth answered. "But so far he's eluded us. When you arrived, we were trying to locate where his base is."

Joe looked around the room. "Wait a minute. You're doing that here? Why? Shouldn't you be at the police station?"

"The DBPD is on it," Seth assured him. "But we came into some new information late this evening and felt it was important for the girls to know."

Aria didn't like how quiet Evan was being. He'd not said anything since the moment Seth had taken the lead in the discussion. What was going on in his mind?

"There's something still bothering me." Joe leaned forward and rested his elbows on his knees. "I could understand putting Anna and Aria in protective custody since they match the description of the victims. But you seem to have brought them into the middle of the investigation. Why would you do that? Anna's not a cop."

When Seth turned and looked at her, Aria knew what he was about to reveal and nodded.

"It's not just that they resemble his preference. We believe that Aria will be his final kill. And because Aria and Anna are identical, he may well take Anna by mistake."

"How could you possibly know all of this?" Joe sat up straight.

"Because I'm the one who brought this monster into their midst."

Seth's words hung in the silence for a moment.

"How?" Joe studied Seth carefully, the untouched plate of food forgotten in his hands.

"I worked undercover for a long time, in a special unit that brings down corrupt motorcycle gangs from the inside. When the smoke cleared on my last assignment, we discovered one club member hadn't been brought in and jailed with the rest.

"This particular asshole has a penchant for young girls. I'd caught him at it before and did what I could to stop him without breaking my cover. Ever since then, he's had a score to settle with me."

Seth caught her eye. "I met Aria while I was still working. When he…learned of her, he turned his attention to exacting his revenge on me by hurting her."

Aria knew why he'd so carefully chosen his words. He was telling him just enough to give him the gist.

Anna picked up the explanation. "He's tried for her a couple of times already but missed. Now he's killing every woman he can find who looks like us. There have been nine so far."

"*Nine*? Son of a bitch," Joe muttered in disbelief. "And you know who he is." It wasn't a question he fired at Seth.

"Yes," Seth confirmed.

Joe's gaze tracked around the room to everyone there. It lingered on the woman seated beside him before returning to

Seth.

"Count me in."

"You should probably hear the rest before you make up your mind," Aria advised.

"I don't think that'll be necessary. He knows enough."

Aria looked over at Evan when he spoke. He stood with his shoulder propped against the wall and his arms folded over his chest. His expression was decidedly grim, and it was aimed directly at Joe.

She finally put two and two together and figured out why her brother—the warrior, the protector—had held silent for so long. He was *pissed*. Joe had slipped right past his notice and gotten too close to Anna without his knowledge. And now, to make matters worse, he was about to be let into family business.

"And why is that?" When Aria saw the look in Anna's eyes, she knew she'd figured it out too. Their sister wasn't brainless by any means.

"We have all the people we need on this." His tone was decisive, as if his word was final.

"Oh, really?" Anna came up out of her chair with a purpose. She crossed the room to stand in front of their brother. "Or is it more that you don't trust him to know?"

Evan glared back at her but remained mute.

Suddenly, he pushed away from the wall and his features hardened. He snapped out one word.

"Don't."

Aria blinked at the implication. Anna must have attempted to read him, to get to the root of his unease. That action alone told Aria how upset Anna truly was. Anna always respected their privacy, and never would have attempted that without prior consent.

"Fine," Anna said. "But answer me this. Do you trust *me*?"

"In most things," he qualified. "But I don't want you hurt."

"So, what? You think you can tell the future now?"

"No," Evan ground out. "But then neither can you."

Aria harbored the same fears Evan did…that once Joe found out about the more unusual side of things, he'd bolt. Leaving Anna broken and alone.

But as much as they all wanted to protect her, Aria knew that wasn't their job anymore. Their sister was strong and confident and knew the risks. And she could take care of herself.

Only, her dense-ass brother refused to see that.

She was about to tell Evan as much when Joe came to his feet behind the arguing pair.

"Look, I get it," Joe began. "You don't like me or the fact that I know your sister, but there's nothing you can tell me that would make me turn my back on Anna."

"Really?" Evan taunted dangerously.

Aria sent a pleading look at Seth to get Evan out of there before he and Joe came to blows.

After a quick nod, Seth rose and went to Evan. "Come on. Let's get some air."

Evan fought him at first but then relented and followed Seth outside.

The three siblings stared at each other in disbelief. Evan had always taken it upon himself to act as guardian, but this was pushing it too far.

"Is someone going to tell me what's going on and what all the cryptic comments were about?" Joe asked of the three who remained.

Anna slowly came around to face Joe. "There's something I haven't told you about myself—about my family."

Joe waited for her to continue.

Aria watched him carefully as Anna laid it all out.

"I'm a witch. We're all witches, except for Seth."

Joe didn't look anywhere but at Anna. Aria couldn't tell what he was thinking; his face was impassive and gave nothing away.

"The reason we're all involved in hunting this killer is that he's not an ordinary criminal. He has a partner. Someone who isn't…human."

"Not human." Joe looked around at each of them. Aria wasn't sure if he were searching for evidence that she'd been kidding, but when none of them smiled, he turned his attention back to Anna.

"You can't possibly expect me to believe any of this. That you all are witches and you're hunting what…a warlock?"

"There's no such thing as warlocks." Anna stayed strong in the face of his skepticism. "But witches do exist, and so does this evil force that wants to destroy us."

"Evil…" Joe shook his head. "Do you hear yourself?"

"Yes, I hear just fine. Are you hearing *me*?" Anna stood her ground. "There is an other-worldly bastard out there that wants to completely wipe out my family. He's hated the Burke witches for centuries. Now it's up to the four of us to end him."

"Witches," Joe muttered. And then louder, "Prove it."

"Watch it, Conrad." Ethan's words were spoken through clenched jaws. "Piss off a witch, and you might not like what happens."

Joe's amber eyes narrowed.

If she and the others were going to bring Joe around and avoid a brawl, a drastic step would need to be taken.

Deciding it would be up to her, she stepped directly in front of Joe and looked him square in the eyes.

"Aria," Anna started to scold her.

Aria ignored her. "Remember when you said that no matter what we told you, you'd not turn your back on Anna?" She waited for Joe to acknowledge his own admission and pushed on. "Then let's see if your word carries any weight."

She held both hands out in front of her, palms up, and called to her old friend. In the next breath, in the center of each hand, air started to spin and dance until they formed funnels about twelve inches tall.

Ethan muttered something along the lines of 'trained monkeys,' but he also called to his element and had fire coiling in his hands.

Anna was the last. A quick glance told Aria she was edgy. What would Joe do when he saw the unequivocal proof of her claims? She gave her a quick nod. Anna took a deep breath and pulled water from a glass that had been forgotten on the table. It flowed to her to form swirling spouts on her palms.

Joe's eyes darted between them. Before he could utter a word though, Evan pushed through the door as if he'd been summoned. Seth was right on his heels.

Aria swung around to ward off Evan, but before she could do that, intuition like she'd never felt before urged her to form their circle. It evidently guided the others as well because without a word, they took up their positions. Evan raised his hand and conjured dirt and rocks into it. It had no sooner settled in his palm than lifted and floated about.

Suddenly, Aria's birthmark was like a white-hot brand on her back. Only this time, it didn't subside as it had before. Instinctively, she knew each of her siblings was experiencing the same sensation.

Without knowing the reason, they each pooled their power into one hand and raised the element they wielded to the center of their circle. When their hands touched, her mark, *their* marks, evolved again.

Through their shirts, in the area where each carried the symbol of their birth, a soft light glowed. The left sleeve of Evan's shirt shone brownish-gold for earth. Red lit the right side of Ethan's chest, and low on Anna's belly, a blue illumination could be seen.

Aria knew if she could have seen it, her own back would be alight with color.

They remained that way for several beats, and when the pull

subsided, they extinguished their powers and lowered their arms.

They all wore looks of wonderment and shock.

"Okay, I'll be the first to ask." Seth broke the silence, his curiosity mirroring theirs. "What the hell was that?"

"The next step in our fight against Noor would be my guess," Evan intoned. He turned his gaze to Aria and the rest. "I felt it when you called your powers. It drew me. I *had* to join the circle."

"Four into one," Anna quoted from the prophecy. "Do you think that's what it means? To join all of our powers?"

"After what just happened," Aria smiled, "I'd say yes."

Anna suddenly gasped and swung around. Aria was about to ask what was wrong when she noticed Joe still standing behind them.

She'd forgotten he was there. They all had. As she watched him, he looked a little shell-shocked.

"Joe?" Anna approached him.

"There's the door," Evan sneered. "Don't let it hit you on your way out."

Anna spun on him. "You're being an ass. Knock it off."

When Aria's gaze returned to Joe, he was glaring at Evan over her head. "I have no intention of going anywhere." To prove his point, Joe sat down, leaned back against the cushions, and crossed his arms over his chest, staring up at them.

"All right, then." Anna swept her hands toward the door. "Evan and Ethan. Out."

"No." Evan stayed rooted to the spot, his thumbs hooked into his pockets. "We need to talk about what just happened."

"We will. Tomorrow. Mom and Dad will want to know anyway. No sense in going over it multiple times. We'll meet up there for lunch and discuss what it all might mean."

"Anna—" Evan tried again.

She sighed. "Evan. Go."

Aria knew her brothers didn't like leaving Joe there, but one look at Anna's face told them they had no choice. Evan caught Seth's eye and some kind of silent communication passed between them. After that, her brothers left.

Anna and Joe had a lot to talk about, so Aria pulled Seth with her to her bedroom to give them some privacy.

As soon as the door shut behind them, she asked, "That look Evan gave you—he was telling you to keep an eye on Joe, wasn't he?"

Seth sat on the edge of the bed and took his shoes off. "Yeah. He's not happy that Anna is so close to him."

Aria nodded. "I figured as much."

He glanced at the closed door and back at her. "Do you think he'll stick around?"

"I do." She leaned against the dresser in front of him. "I had the same attitude as Evan when I first heard about him and what she was doing. I didn't like him and wanted him away from her. I even went with her to work out one day to tell him that. But then I saw the way he looks at her. And how she's changed since she's met him."

Aria stepped forward. Placing a knee on either side of his body, she straddled his lap and sat down. As she'd known they would, his strong arms wrapped around her hips. "And I listened to the way they talk about each other." She rested her arms on the tops of his shoulders and toyed with the hair at the back of his neck. "They've been dancing around each other for weeks, each afraid to initiate anything. His showing up here tonight has given that a giant push. He may not completely believe yet, but he'll stick it out to be near her."

"I know the feeling." He leaned forward and kissed her. "Maybe I can talk to him. Non-witch to non-witch."

She grinned. "Tomorrow."

His brown eyes flared with heat. "Yeah. Tomorrow."

~~~

Hours later, Aria lay on her stomach naked, arms tucked under her pillow. She was drifting in that velvety place between sleep and wakefulness. Vaguely aware that Seth traced the swirling lines of the mark on her shoulder, she enjoyed the peacefulness of the moment.

"Looking at this now," he spoke softly, "it's hard to believe what happened earlier when the four of you connected."

Curious now, Aria roused herself enough to roll onto her back. He was on his side with his head propped up on his hand. "I saw all the others glow in different colors. What was mine?"

"Green." He swept the long silvery strands of hair away from her face. "Like the new leaves and fresh shoots of grass in the spring."

He pulled her deeper into his embrace and lowered his head to the pillow next to her. "Noor's not going to know what hit him when all of you take him down."

Aria reveled in his confidence but didn't let herself forget that they still had a lot to learn. The time for the final battle would be upon them before they knew it, and they would need every minute to prepare. But before that, they had something else that needed taking care of.

JD.

~~~

The next morning when Aria made her way into the kitchen, Anna was already at the table.

"Morning," she greeted as she crossed to the coffee pot and poured.

"I sent him home last night," Anna announced unprompted.

"I didn't say anything." Aria kept her face free of emotion as she leaned her hips back against the counter and sipped from her steaming mug.

"You were wondering."

"*That* is none of my business. But I do have to ask... How'd he take it all?"

"Pretty good, actually," Anna considered. "But what other choice did he have, when what we can do smacked him full-on in the face? He had a lot of questions, naturally. About us, about what all we can do. Then that turned into a discussion about Noor and our history."

"How on earth did you get him to leave? I thought for sure your knight in shining armor was here for the duration by the way he was talking last night."

"He didn't want to, but he finally gave in when I promised to call him as soon as I woke up. He just wants to know I'm okay."

"Are you going to the gym this morn—"

Aria gasped and grabbed her head as pain shot through her skull.

Her coffee cup dropped to the floor and shattered.

"Ari, what is it?" Anna was there instantly. "What do you see?"

Her legs threatened to give out, but suddenly Seth was there, supporting her weight. She sank into him as her mind was pulled away.

She was being chased. The sound of her breath heaving in and out as she fled filled her ears. A stabbing cramp tore into her side as she ran for her life.

"He's hunting," she was able to relay.

Tree limbs and leaves snatched at her hair, ripping it out as she raced through the tangle of trees.

"Can you search his mind?" Seth guided. "Find where they're at?"

Aria shook her head. "In...her."

Anna sucked in a swift breath. "She's connected with their

next victim."

"Running through woods," Aria told them haltingly. "Can hear him behind me. Getting closer."

"You have to pull out before he catches her," Anna warned. "You can't be in there when he—"

"No," Aria sharply protested. "Not another one. Have to help."

"But how?" Anna cried.

"Find a way," Aria growled back.

As Aria watched this woman fight for her life, voices spoke around her.

"Hurry," Aria panted. "Coming."

"Can you make the connection stronger?" Anna asked. "Maybe communicate with her?"

"Don't know." Aria understood what Anna was going for. If she could get in deep enough, she might be able to help this woman before it was too late.

Aria blocked out the pain in her head and concentrated on building a bridge that would link her into the other's mind. She'd never tried anything like this before. Her visions usually just played out like a movie.

But then again, nothing had been normal since Noor had gained enough strength to push through into this world. They were all evolving in different ways. Ways, they hoped, would aid them in defeating Noor.

Aria just prayed she had enough to save this one person.

She searched for a pathway that would allow her to commune with this woman. Slowly, she began to hear scattered thoughts of fear and horror.

Oh God, he's coming.

He's going to kill me.

Why is he doing this? Why me?

Have to get away. Have to get away. But where?

Aria tried to speak to her. "*Can you hear me?*" When the

woman stumbled and slowed, Aria shouted, "*No! Don't stop! Keep running! We're going to try and help you. But you have to keep moving, keep fighting.*"

"*I can't.*"

"*Yes, you can.*"

"*Who are you?*"

"*I'm Aria. I'm here to help. What's your name?*"

"*Christine.*"

"*Christine, I need you to do something for me. Don't stop, but look around you. We're trying to find out where you are, so we can get help to you.*"

Aria pulled back enough that she could speak to her sister and Seth. She found it easier to manage now. The pain was still there, but separated enough that she could function through it. "Call Evan. As soon as I know where they are, he needs to be there."

She slipped back into the woman's mind. She was doing as Aria had asked. She was darting glances around her. In one of the brief flashes, Aria thought she saw something.

"*To the left. Go to the left.*"

Without hesitation, Christine veered left and kept running.

To the others in the room with her, Aria said quickly, "Tell Evan to get to the water tower. Now!"

Aria didn't spare them another thought as she dove back into the victim's mind.

"*Do you see the water tower? Head there. Someone will be there to get you. He'll be very tall with black hair. You run straight for him and don't stop.*"

"*I'm tired. He's getting closer.*"

"*I know,*" Aria soothed. "*He's going to catch you, Christine, but don't panic. I have a plan. You're going to make it out of this.*"

"*He's going to kill me.*"

"*I won't let him.*"

Aria hoped to God this worked. "Anna." Eyes still closed to maintain the connection, she reached out her hand until she felt her sister grasp it. "I need your help."

"What can I do?"

"He's going to be on her before she can get to Evan. I need you to guide her through how to defend herself. Something that will immobilize him just long enough for her to get away."

"How? My power doesn't work that way."

"I'm linking you in."

"What?" Anna exclaimed and then asked, "You can do that?"

"I have to or she'll die, and I refuse to let that happen." To the woman, she sent, *"Christine. I'm bringing someone else in. Her name is Anna. She's going to help you get through this. When that man catches you, Anna is going to tell you what to do, okay? You have to do exactly what she says, because it's your only hope to make it out of this alive. Can you do that?"*

"I don't want to die," Christine cried.

"I know, sweetie, and I'm going to do everything I can to make sure that doesn't happen."

"Here we go," Aria warned Anna. "All you have to do is send your thoughts out and I'll get them to her."

"Okay," Anna's grip tightened on her hand.

Aria expanded her mind in search of Anna's. This was so out of her realm, she had no idea of what she was doing. But she couldn't fail. She couldn't let JD take another life.

Her desperation and the closeness of her sister gave her the boost she needed to accomplish her task. She felt the stirring of Anna's mind and pulled her in.

Together they returned to the frightened woman fighting for her life.

"Christine, Anna's here."

"Oh, God. Help me. Help me!"

Aria felt Anna's quick shock of torment, but she quickly pushed it away.

"Christine," Anna's voice filled their minds, *"the first thing you need to know is this is going to hurt. But don't let the pain make you freeze up. One of the first things I learned was that fighting hurts. Whether you're taking punches or giving them. You have to accept the pain and keep thinking through it. I'll guide you."*

"I can't. He's so much bigger."

"That won't matter. We'll use his size against him. I'm about your same build, and I take down guys bigger than him every day."

Anna paused, and Aria knew she felt the presence of JD behind them. Suddenly, Christine screamed as she was tackled from behind. It took precious moments for Anna to get her attention again, but eventually Christine worked through her panic and started hearing Anna again.

Aria stayed silent as she listened to her sister take Christine through movements meant to injure and incapacitate.

The first strike surprised JD enough that Christine was able to get the upper hand. She faltered when JD's fist connected with her ribs in a punishing blow. Anna talked her through the pain and back into the war she was waging.

"Drive the heel of your hand up and into his nose. While he's distracted with that, bring your knee up and ram it into his crotch as hard as you can," Anna guided. *"Send those nuts right into his throat."*

The series of blows worked, and Christine got to her feet and ran.

"Don't look back," Aria encouraged. *"You're almost there. Run to the water tower. Help is there waiting. You can do it."*

Christine took off in a limping run, holding her ribs tightly. When she broke free of the tree line and spotted Evan, she ran right into his arms.

"Thank you," Christine sobbed to Aria and Evan both.

Aria, with Anna, backed out of the other woman's mind. Aria

collapsed in Seth's arms. He immediately swept her up and walked back into the living room to sit down with her in his lap.

She raised her head enough to look up at her sister. Her eyes looked a little glassy but clear as she moved to take a seat.

No one spoke or moved until the phone rang. Anna rose to pick it up. "Hello?...Okay. I'll let them know. Did you catch the bastard?...Shit...Yeah, I'll tell everyone."

Once she'd hung up, she turned to Aria. "That was Evan. He took her to the hospital to get checked out, and then she'll be going into protective custody."

Aria nodded. "That's good. I take it they didn't get JD."

"No. Evan said he came busting out of the trees right behind her, but as soon as he saw she had help, he slipped back into the forest and disappeared. Evan wants to make sure we stay alert. Thwarting JD never ends well."

Aria was starting to feel the strain of the last hour. Expending that much energy had drained her, but she was slowly recovering from the encounter. As much as she'd like to sit right where she was, she knew they had a lot of work to do.

23

Seth and Evan, through Christine, were able to finally locate JD's lair. They put together a strike force and descended on the property.

Seth knew, in all likelihood, JD had already cleared out. But on the off chance he was arrogant enough to stick around, they had to check it out.

He knew as soon as he stepped foot in the house that it was as he'd thought. The place was empty. Their quarry had found another hole to dig into.

"You think you're safe," Seth said to the deserted house, "but we'll find you. Those women you killed will help to bring you down. And when that happens, I'll be there, you sick son of a bitch."

When Seth left the house, he covered the ground with purpose. He zeroed in on where Evan was talking with one of the tech guys and moved in to intercept him. Evan had just caught sight of him when Seth's cell phone rang.

Still on the move, he fished it out of his pocket. Seeing Aria's name, he accepted the call.

"Hey, Pixie," he greeted with a smile.

"Pixie. Isn't that just *too cute*."

The voice that scraped like fingernails on a chalkboard wasn't Aria's. But it was one he recognized. The smile slid from his face as he froze mid-stride.

"JD." The name ripped from his lungs as if he'd been punched in the gut. Seth had to suck more oxygen in just to choke out his next words. "What have you done with Aria?"

His expression must have clued Evan in, because his partner started towards him at a fast clip. He'd been too far away to overhear what was said, but Evan's instincts were always on point.

In his ear, JD continued the torment as a muffled whimper came through the line. "She's here with me, and she's..." Evil laughter rang out. "Well, I was going to say she's fine, but that's not quite the case."

Seth took another crippling blow. This time it triggered something dark and primal inside him. It caused his vision to focus and narrow as a frigid rage began to settle over his body. His voice, instead of rising, quieted to a sharp and deadly edge. His grip tightened on the phone as he stood stock-still in the middle of the yard.

Through clenched teeth, Seth spoke slowly and deliberately. "Touch her, and I *will* kill you."

"Oh, really?" JD mocked. "Then I guess I probably shouldn't do this."

Seth's knees threatened to buckle as a guttural scream of anguish nearly deafened him. It dragged on for what seemed like ages, scraping along Seth's spine before abruptly, unnaturally, going silent.

"Oh, dear." Mirth and satisfaction rang in JD's voice. "That really gets the heart pumping, doesn't it?" He was still snickering when the line went dead.

"Goddamn it!" Seth roared. His whole body was shaking with fear and fury and hate. He needed to rage, to fight against that sadistic, twisted motherfucker for taking the woman he loved. But he knew he had to pull it in. He couldn't lose control now. Aria needed him to hold it together. She was counting on him to come.

Seth turned everything he was feeling inward. He took it all in and shaped it into a lethal blade. One he'd use to slowly, and painfully, make JD pay.

"What happened? Who was that?"

"He's got her." Seth turned cold eyes on Evan. "JD has Aria."

Evan's face convulsed in shock and horror. "What? How?"

"I don't know. It doesn't matter how." Seth forced the words out. "He's hurting her. I could hear her screaming. Then…then there was nothing."

Panic was swimming in Evan's eyes. "Are you absolutely sure it was her?"

"The call came from her fucking phone, Evan. Who else could it have been?" Seth snapped out.

His phone rang again. Thinking it would be JD calling to torture him further, he didn't bother to look at the display before swiping the accept button.

"Where the hell is she, you son of a bitch?"

"Seth?" The sweetest voice he'd ever heard came to him over the connection.

"Aria?" He started thinking frantically. "Where are you? Are you okay? I promise I'll come find you, just hold on."

"Seth, I'm fine. I'm at home."

"What do you mean you're at home?" Something wasn't making sense. "Did you get away from him?"

"JD? He never had me. He tried, but Anna stopped him."

"But…he just called me. From your phone."

"He must have taken it when he ran off. That's why I'm using Anna's. I just wanted you to know what happened and not to worry if you couldn't get a hold of me."

"We're on our way." Seth nodded to Evan, and they took off towards the car. "You both stay in and lock the doors."

"Seth, you don't need to do that. We're okay."

"I'm coming." He hung up and slid his cell back into his pocket as he and Evan pealed out of the driveway and onto the road.

"So, what the hell just happened?" Evan asked, keeping an eye on the road.

"Apparently JD was at the house and tried to attack Aria. She got away, but not before he'd stolen her phone."

"That lying sack of shit," Evan growled, shaking his head. His partner was silent for a moment before he finally spoke again. "You know what that means though, right?"

"Yeah." Seth scrubbed his hands over his face in frustration. "He has someone else. Someone he's torturing this very minute."

They let that knowledge hang between them, knowing there wasn't anything they could do to save her.

Seth was racking his brain for answers when Evan interrupted his thoughts.

"You know, there's something about this whole thing that just doesn't add up."

"What's that?"

"The timing of everything. There's a pattern lurking in there somewhere. I think we all need to sit down and work out a definitive timeline. We're missing something big, and my gut is telling me once we've done that, we'll have a better picture of what's really going on here."

Evan called his brother and told him to meet them at Anna's. Twenty minutes later when they pulled in, he was already there.

Seth was the first out of the car and into the house. He needed to see Aria, to make sure she was okay.

She and Anna were on the couch, but he only had eyes for his Pixie. Seth crossed the distance and pulled her up and into his arms. She wrapped around him like a vine. It took his tortured mind several moments to believe she was here. That she really was safe.

Slowly, the lock on his mind and body loosened. When he

could finally breathe again, he pulled back to look down into her beautiful face. "What happened?"

"Anna saved me," she answered simply.

He couldn't bear to let her go, but the adrenaline surge was abating, and Seth was starting to feel the drain. He sat and pulled her down next to him.

"Tell us."

"Anna and I were headed out for lunch, but since she still had to put her shoes on, I told her I'd wait for her in the car. I was distracted, reading an email I'd just gotten on my phone from the genealogist, and I was just about to get in when JD came out of nowhere and grabbed me from behind. That's when Anna came out, saw what was happening, and shouted. I guess he chickened out when he realized I wasn't alone, because he took off before we could beat the holy hell out of him."

Seth sent a look of gratitude to Anna before turning back to Aria. "How did he get your phone then? He called me just to gloat, to make me listen while he hurt you."

"I dropped everything when he jumped me. When I went back to pick it all up, my phone was missing. He must have taken it with him."

"Could you tell if Noor was present too?" Evan asked.

Aria shook her head. "I don't think so. Why?"

"I'm working on a theory." Evan told them what he wanted to do, and Anna went to her desk. She came back with a leather-bound book, one that resembled the journals the Burkes had used for centuries to document their lives in.

Anna sat down, clutching it close. "I've been holding on to this, waiting for the right moment for us to contribute to the family library. I think this is it."

Each of her siblings smiled and nodded.

"Okay," Evan began. "We'll start with our birthday when we initially felt Noor."

Anna opened to the first page and set pen to paper.

Evan continued. "His first foray into our world was when he possessed that guy to stab me."

"That was on a Saturday," Anna jotted down.

"Right," Evan agreed. "What was next?"

"It was that same night that I had the dream where he possessed Seth and killed him," Aria added.

"And the next night, Sunday," Seth said, "was when he took over JD and tried to gut me." He vividly remembered what had happened after that. "On Monday, JD went for Aria at the library, and I know for a fact he was acting alone that day."

"So, if we go with the assumption that he wore JD again for the shooting at the MC bust, that puts Noor back on the scene on Thursday." Anna continued making notes and drawing lines from one event to another as Evan spoke. "So, between the guy sent to attack me Saturday, showing up in Aria's dream, and then jumping into JD Sunday night, Noor depleted his store of energy and was out of commission on Monday, Tuesday, and Wednesday."

Ethan spoke up for the first time. "And while he's down, that's when JD goes for Aria."

Evan nodded. "Did anyone have an encounter with either of them after Seth was shot on Thursday night?"

Aria picked up the timeline. "They were together on Tuesday when I had the vision of the girl who got away."

"And then JD was alone again when he came for you here that afternoon," Anna said.

Seth was already starting to see the pattern Evan had mentioned, but he wanted more information before he brought it up.

"After JD was impaled," Anna supplied, "they both went into hiding."

Aria nodded. "For a while, but then JD started stalking me at the beginning of April." She sent a sideways glance at Seth and huffed out a breath. "And that's also when Noor started showing up in my dreams again."

When Seth looked like he was about to blast her, Aria hurried to continue. "Just to taunt and harass. It wasn't every night, but often enough."

"And you thought not telling anyone was a good idea?" Seth admonished.

Evan waylaid the argument. "We can discuss that another time. What happened next?"

"I think that was about the time I came back, which would have been on a Tuesday," Seth offered.

"And that leads us to the wall of fire Noor conjured on Wednesday," Evan continued.

"Two days later," Seth said, "Aria and I left for Michigan."

"Any sign of Noor while you were there?" Evan asked.

Seth and Aria looked at each other. "No."

"So the fire set him back a few days," Evan concluded. "And being out of state, you were safe from JD."

"Monday, all hell breaks loose." That was a day Seth wished he could forget. "That's the day we found all the bodies."

"And Anna got hit by Noor's replay of the girl who'd been found that morning," Aria added and then went on. "I connected with Christine yesterday, which was Wednesday. Noor may have been involved with that hunt, but I can't know for sure. But if he were, I'm guessing it took him out of the picture again, because when JD tried to grab me today, it was just him," Aria finished.

It was all falling into place for Seth. They already knew Noor wanted to keep Aria for himself, and that his obsession with having her was what had prompted him to try and kill Seth. So, why then, was he letting JD do this?

He wasn't. It was the only conclusion Seth could come to.

Which would mean JD was going after Aria without Noor's knowledge, waiting until his boss was in one of his recharge cycles to further his own agenda.

Seth shared his thoughts with the others.

"That's the pattern I thought I saw too," Evan nodded. "The back and forth of events just didn't make sense."

"But how is JD hiding his intentions from Noor?" Ethan wondered aloud.

"I don't know," Seth said. "But I think we can use this to our advantage."

"How?" Anna asked, closing the journal and setting it aside.

"What do you think Noor would do," Seth speculated, "if he found out his partner in crime is trying to kill his one and only?"

"Oh, I see where you're going," Aria grinned slyly. "He may take care of our problem for us."

Evan's phone rang, putting a halt on the discussion. He stepped into the kitchen for some privacy.

He returned a few minutes later. "That was the coroner. He has his own timeline finished."

"What did he say?" Seth had a feeling this would shed more light on this mess.

"He's documented the times of death for each victim, and which order the girls died in, along with the extent of their injuries. He's emailing me his findings." Evan checked his phone. When he started tapping on different things, Seth figured it had come through already.

They all waited while Evan read through it once. When he started back at the top, he spoke aloud.

"Victims one and two seem to have died within a day of each other. Victim number three, one who had sustained more severe wounds, was killed shortly after. Four, five, and six over roughly two weeks' time. Numbers seven and eight within three days of each other, and they both suffered more significant injuries again. Then nine—which was found first— showed a lesser amount of trauma than the two before her."

"If we compare this," Seth caught Evan's eye, "with our sequence of events, I'll bet three, seven, and eight will coincide with when Noor was active. The rest, JD did on his own."

"So what do we do with all this information?" Ethan asked.

"We know that JD is working behind Noor's back every time he makes a move on me. I say the next time Noor shows himself to one of us," Aria answered, "we tell him what his puppet's been up to. Maybe he'll dispose of him for us."

Seth suddenly remembered something Aria had said a while ago before they'd gotten into the whole JD-Noor discussion.

"Did you say you'd gotten an email from the lady searching my family history?"

"Yeah," Aria nodded, "I did. It slipped my mind with everything else going on."

"Did she say what she'd found?" Seth wasn't sure he wanted to know.

"No. Just that we needed to go see her," Aria told him.

"Why don't you two go do that?" Evan suggested. "The rest of us will refine what we have. After you're done there, meet us at Mom and Dad's, so we can fill them in on everything."

"I'll let her know we're coming." Aria rose and turned to her sister. "Anna, do you mind if I use your phone again?"

Within a few minutes, Seth and Aria were in the car, headed off to get the news that could change his life. He didn't know what the ramifications would be if it turned out he was descended from Noor. Would it allow them some kind of advantage against him? Or would it only put the people he was coming to love in more danger?

Before he was ready, they pulled into the driveway of a modest little house. He sat and stared at it until Aria reached over and grasped his hand.

"It won't make any difference."

He sent her what he hoped was a reassuring smile. "I know."

As they approached the door, an older woman met them. "Seth Lawson?" she asked through the screen door.

"Yes."

"Come on in." She pushed it open and gestured to the seating area. "Please, make yourselves comfortable."

Once they were seated, Seth began. "Aria said you'd found something."

"I did," she confirmed. "Let me say first, that I didn't see any mention of the name Noor in your ancestry. But since you said names may have been changed, it allowed me to focus on people who didn't have much of a past. The Lawson men were easy enough to trace back. Birth to death, it was all there. Until I got to one Joshua Lawson. He seemingly just popped into existence when he was three years old. What I did then was concentrate on his mother."

"You found Isabel?" Aria asked.

"I think so," she qualified. "You'd given me the date when she and her children disappeared, and the woman I found in Seth's line showed up within a year of that time. She too just appears to have come out of nowhere. I couldn't track her surname past her. That in itself isn't a guarantee, but she did have two small children who were legally recognized by one Tobias Lawson."

"What does that mean?" Aria leaned forward.

"Tobias gave them his name, presumably when he married their mother."

Seth looked at Aria and then back to the genealogist. "What was the woman's name, according to your records?"

"Beatrice Atterberry Lawson. She had two sons, Joshua and Adam." She looked at Seth. "You descend from Joshua, the oldest."

She handed over the documents she'd found and soon after that, Seth and Aria gave their thanks and were back in the car.

"Are you okay?" Aria rested her hand on his thigh.

"Yeah, I am, actually." It had taken him a while to get here, but knowing he came from an evil bastard like Noor had no bearing on who he was as a man. "His wickedness has no effect on me. There are hundreds of years of good men like my grandfather and my father between us."

He grasped her hand and brought it up to his lips to kiss the back of it.

"And I'm okay with that."

24

The rest of the family was already there when they arrived at her parents'. Aria and Seth followed the sound of voices and walked through and into the kitchen.

Mary noticed their entrance. Her eyes asked the question.

All the others fell silent when they too took note of their presence.

"It would seem I *am* a direct descendant of Edrick Noor," Seth told them. "Isabel apparently changed her name to Beatrice Atterberry and married Tobias Lawson, my however-many great grandfather."

"So what does this mean?" Anna asked no one in particular.

"I would hope," Seth answered, "that whatever connection exists between us, we can use it to help your fight."

"It will," Paul declared. "Like Mary said—you were put into our lives for a purpose. I, for one, believe it was to keep my girl here," he smiled and gestured to Aria, "safe and happy."

Just then, an explosive clap of thunder and strike of lightning split the late afternoon sky. Several more bolts cracked very near the house, brightening up the back yard and leaving the smell of ozone hanging in the air.

Understanding spread throughout the room. Everyone in the house knew this wasn't the average Florida storm.

"Noor," voices whispered.

Evan and Ethan were the first to make it to the sliding glass door.

"Boys, be careful," Mary warned.

"Something's out there," Evan announced. He looked back briefly and then slid the door open. He and Ethan stepped out onto the patio.

Aria and Anna followed. As soon as the four of them crossed over the threshold, the door slammed shut behind them with Seth and their parents still inside.

Aria turned back and saw Seth tugging on the handle and beating on the glass. The look in his eyes was one of destruction as he fought to get out, to be by her side. He pounded until blood started to smear across the surface where his fists had struck.

Aria sent her mom a silent plea, and Mary laid her hand on Seth's arm, stopping his assault. But the agony on his face didn't change. He laid the flat of his hand on the glass as if he could touch her.

Her father suddenly appeared behind them, and when Seth swung around to face him, Paul gestured towards the other windows and doors with a shake of his head. Aria could only take that to mean that all the exits in the house were sealed. She and her siblings were on their own against whatever Noor had waiting for them.

After a brief pause, she and the others started across the yard. As they drew further out into the open, Aria saw a monstrous beast standing on the sand a few feet in front of the waves lapping at the shore.

"What the hell is that?" Ethan asked in a low voice.

It looked like some kind of bear mutation, and it was huge. Even on four legs, it stood at least seven feet tall. The hind quarters were shorter than the front, making for a long, sloping back. The entire thing was free of fur, leaving mottled black skin that bulged grotesquely with immense muscles.

The head was wide and round like a bear, but the muzzle was

pushed in. The nostrils of its fleshy nose were open and flaring as it took in all of their scents. Large, pointed ears speared straight up, and they twitched and swiveled as they took in all the sounds around it. Just inward of those bat-like appendages were horns that grew upward and then curved back over its large head. Its eyes were two colorless orbs, glowing white in the lessening light.

The snarling and snapping jaws drew her attention to teeth longer than her fingers. They were jagged and sharp, and they came together with such power, it was like a metal trap slamming shut. If it were to get a hold of any of them, they'd be torn to shreds in seconds.

There was no other word to describe this creature. It was a beast. Evil and deadly.

"Careful," she warned them all.

It paced up and down the beach, prowling and snorting out its impatience. The four gave each other a quick glance and then spread out, forming a semi-circle around it, trapping it between them and the cold waters of the ocean.

Aria reached out for her siblings. Since the day she'd connected with Anna inside her mind, she'd been toying with the idea that the same could be done with the boys. They were not only quads—they were the four meant to fulfill the prophecy.

She found Anna first, her twin's mind already familiar after having linked with her the last time. The boys took precious seconds longer, but finally she saw them.

When they felt her inside their heads, she sensed their shock.

"Don't fight it," she soothed them.

"When did you learn how to do this?" Aria could actually feel the frown on Evan's face.

"Since Christine," Aria sent. *"Oh shit, he stopped moving. I think something's—"*

She didn't get to finish as bolts of lightning shot down all around them. The four of them dove and dodged out of the way, getting back to their feet as soon as they could.

Aria pulled on her power and had a gale-force wind slamming at the animal. Anna brought the water and tried to suck it out to sea, only to have the thing leap up and out of the grasp of the waves.

It roared out its rage and landed closer to them.

Aria didn't know whether Evan had brought the gun with him or conjured it, but it now rested in his hands. He took aim and fired into the beast until the slide locked open to show the weapon was empty.

But it had no effect on him. They passed right through, and Aria would swear the damned thing laughed. It's drooling, snarling mouth pulled back, and what sounded like a cackle spilled out.

"He's enjoying this," Aria told her family. *"We need something that'll wipe that grin off its nasty face."*

"Let's hit it with our elemental power all at once," Evan suggested through their link.

It must have known they were rallying against it, because it struck first. The next arc of electricity came out of the sky and struck Ethan square in the chest.

"Ethan!" Aria screamed as her brother flew back and landed with a lifeless thud on the ground.

She took off running towards him, but the beast flew up and into the air. When it came down, it was standing over Ethan, its ghostly eyes tracking over him as it hovered.

"Stop," Ethan sent feebly to their minds. *"Stay back."*

"It's going to kill you," Anna cried as the monster straddled Ethan until he was fully towering over his prone figure.

Ethan lay still, feigning unconsciousness. What the monster couldn't see was that in Ethan's fisted hand, he'd brought forth his fire. The glow of red warned them of his intentions.

"Same plan applies," Ethan said. *"All at once."*

"Ethan, no," Anna protested. *"You'll be caught in the middle of all that energy. We don't know what will happen when all of our elements come together."*

"No choice. This is our best shot at this fucker."

"He's right, Anna," Evan agreed, but the regret in his thoughts said he didn't like it either.

"Let's do this!" Ethan shouted. *"Get ready!"*

They each gathered their power, banked it, and waited for Ethan's command.

"Now!"

All four of them sent everything they had at the beast. Ethan's fire raged against its unguarded belly, as the forces of air, water and earth beat at them both.

Aria was suddenly afraid this was what her visions had shown her all those weeks ago. Her brother burnt and broken and dead. Had the combination of their magic been what killed Ethan and caused him to succumb to his own fire?

She cried as she continued to pummel the creature with her magic. Even through her heartache, she knew they couldn't stop.

A shocking roar rent the air, and the monster launched itself into the sky. When it came down back on the beach, it panted and shook.

They had obviously injured it, but not badly enough. Aria desperately wanted to go to her brother, but not knowing what it would do now, no one dared take their eyes from it. Wounded animals were extremely unpredictable.

Suddenly, the beast howled once, loud and long. As the eerie sound faded away, it began to shift and change.

Aria couldn't believe her eyes when it slowly morphed into something else.

Nobody moved as it rose from four legs up to two, its body undulating and writhing until it stood fully erect.

As a man.

He extended out his arms and arched his back as his new shape settled over him.

The person standing before them now was a stranger, but somehow Aria knew.

"Noor."

He stumbled and fell to one knee. And then disappeared completely.

Aria immediately turned and ran for Ethan. And that's when she noticed her parents were also racing across the lawn. Noor's departure had released whatever hold he'd had on the house. She barely had time to think his name before Seth's arms swept her up.

"Are you okay?" He held her tight. "I couldn't get out. We couldn't get to you."

"I know. It was Noor. The beast was Noor. We saw him at the end."

"How was he here?"

"I don't know." She pushed out of his arms. "Ethan. I need to see Ethan."

They both turned to see her brother sitting up on the ground. His clothes were scorched and tattered, and his body was a muddy mess of dirt and debris, but he was alive.

"Thank God." The relief Aria felt nearly took her to her knees.

Seth, still holding onto her hand, walked her over to her family.

They too, were wondering how Noor had been able to materialize into this reality.

"Projection would be the next logical progression of his strengthening power," Mary theorized. "And besides the fact that his physical form wasn't really here, I think the reason Evan's bullets had no effect on him was because they're not of the magical world. As long as he is still imprisoned, the four of you and your magic are the only way to counter him."

"Let's take this inside," Paul ordered. "Before anything else shows up."

"It won't be Noor," Evan said. "If the pattern holds, a display of this proportion will take him out for quite a while."

"Yeah, but now we have to worry about JD," Seth reminded them. "He likes to strike when his boss is down."

25

Only, JD didn't come for her. And as April gave way to May, there was still nothing. They lived on-edge, waiting for him to make a move. And as time passed, the possibility of Noor reemerging became a threat once again.

When would they strike?

Aria's dreams had been blessedly silent. But she knew not to grow too comfortable with that. Either he was still too drained to bother with her, or he was hoarding and storing up energy for another big push to kill one of them.

He'd already come too damned close for comfort. First with Evan, and then Ethan.

She worried about Anna all the time. Even though she was spending more and more time with Joe, Aria still hated it when she was out of sight. Joe was turning out to be great for her, but he was just an ordinary guy.

The telepathic lines of communication were still open. Aria and her siblings usually made a point to check in with each other throughout the day. This new progression of their power was one Aria planned to hone and use. She never wanted to be out of reach of any of them.

Her vision of Anna still plagued her in all too much detail. The sight of her laying on the ground, dead, her head covered in blood. Much like the women JD and Noor had killed.

If they were still collecting victims, there'd been no sign of it. Seth and Evan had everyone on the force watching for new listings within Missing Persons, and listening for any mention of dead women having been found.

But again, all was quiet.

Aria was alone for the first time since the night the beast attacked. Usually, if Seth couldn't be with her, someone in her family was in attendance. But somehow, today, something had been missed.

She knew she should check in with one of her siblings, but she was enjoying the peace of not having anyone else around. Besides, all she had planned for the day was sketching some new ideas for her wind sculptures.

The doors and windows were all closed and locked. A few hours on her own wouldn't hurt. With that in mind, she took her pad and pencils and settled into the corner of the couch.

She didn't know how much time had passed when she sensed she was no longer alone. Now she did call out with her mind.

"Hang on," Ethan came back instantly. *"I'm ten minutes away."*

"Seth is with me," Evan told her. *"We're coming. Fight him as long as you can."*

And Anna was in the middle of her class.

None of them would reach her in time.

Aria looked up, and there stood JD in the doorway between the kitchen and the living room.

She could tell by the look in his eyes that he wasn't alone. Noor had come for her. Setting her drawings aside, she calmly rose and stood facing him. She refused to show him any fear, and just to prove she wouldn't cower to him, she struck out with the air. And landed a blow across his face like a slap.

His head snapped back, and he took a step to catch his balance. But when he recovered and brought his head back around, he was sneering at her.

He swung his hand out, and the next thing she knew, she was

off her feet and flying backward. The shock of slamming into the wall knocked all of the air out of her lungs. She crumpled to the floor, and as stars flashed in front of her eyes, she fought to remain conscious.

But Noor-JD wasn't done with her yet.

Before she could catch her breath, he was advancing towards her. She tried to back away, but he reached down, grabbed a fistful of her hair, and hauled her up.

She screamed at the tearing pain it caused in her scalp and grasped his hands with hers. She tried to fight against him, but he kept her off balance, never allowing her to push up from the floor or gain a foothold.

"You will learn your place, bitch," Noor threatened. "I thought my Isabel had, but she deceived me. I will not make that same mistake again. I will enjoy finally having a chance to break you."

He yanked her head around and her body rolled, following his lead. Leaning down into her face, he growled, "First, you must always do as I say." As if to drive his point home, he drew back his foot and hurled it into her ribs.

Aria's breath whooshed out again through a groan as her body instinctively curled upon itself against the pain, trying to deflect another blow.

Noor laughed before tightening his hold on her hair with another edict. "Second, you will not fight me." Spreading his stance and bracing his weight, he jerked her hair again as he sent another hard kick into her stomach.

Aria still couldn't breathe from the last hit, and wheezed as his boot made contact with her unguarded belly. Tears rained down her face in agony as her hands desperately clawed at the fingers still clutched tightly to her roots.

She wasn't sure if it were Noor enjoying her torment so much, or if JD were joining in too, but when she finally had a chance to look up into his face, it was alight with glee and satisfaction.

Catching her gaze, his expression sobered. He bent and angled into her until they were almost nose to nose. His vile stench caused bile to rise up in her throat, and when he spoke, the smell of death blew into her face.

"You know what the final rule is, slut?" He grinned maniacally then, his voice deepening into a vicious snarl. "Never, *ever*, run from me."

And with that, he threw her head back and spun her around, exposing the soft flesh of her middle. He reared back and landed a blow to her center like a kicker on a football team.

Spots burst behind her eyes, and she fought against the darkness that threatened to take her under. Unable to defend herself any further, he pulled her along behind him as he made his way into the kitchen and out the back.

Aria's hips and legs took a beating as he dragged her down the steps leading off of the porch. Her whole body hurt so badly she couldn't think. But then she remembered Anna's words. *'Fighting hurts. Whether you're taking punches or giving them, you have to accept the pain and never stop thinking.'*

She couldn't let him take her. She had to fight back. She had to survive.

Pulling the throbbing pain into her, Aria pushed it down until her brain was able to function again and her breathing had returned. She got a firmer hold on the hands twisted in her hair, pulled her legs up, and spun around on her butt.

Planting her feet into the dirt, Aria locked her legs. The sudden jerk pulled Noor off balance and gave her enough time to stand. Without hesitating, she flew at him with swift kicks and punches.

She remembered some of what Jay had shown her during her one and only visit to the gym. Aria braced her legs and swung from the hip. Every move tore at her battered ribs, but the right hook to his side landed with enough force to make him grunt.

Through it all though, his grip never loosened, and her feeble attempts were nothing compared to Noor's savagery. Using JD's size and strength, Noor overpowered her and took her to the ground again.

"Hold on, Ari." Anna's sweet voice flowed into her mind. *"We're almost there."*

This time he sat astride her waist and rained blows down on her face and head. Aria was dazed. She tried to call to her element for help, but she just couldn't make the connection. She didn't even have enough fight left in her to struggle when her shirt was ripped down the middle.

She felt him shift, and his big hands grasped the waistband of her jeans and jerked. She was trying to dislodge him, when she heard a sharp and deadly shout.

"JD!"

Bared to the waist, Aria rolled to her side when the weight of him released her. Through her one good eye, she saw Noor turn and face off against the man she loved. Seth had his gun aimed steadily, but she had to find a way to tell him that this wasn't JD. He wouldn't be prepared for the magic that Noor now wielded. The gun wouldn't do much good.

She reached deep and gathered enough strength to yell out, but Seth's next words stopped her.

"Or should I say, *Noor.*" He still kept the muzzle pointed straight at him.

Noor only grinned. "That weapon is no match for me."

"If not you, then the fucker you currently inhabit. A bullet to his skull would end your little field trips. And I have no problem taking his sorry ass down."

Seth's brown eyes were as cold and hard as granite.

Trying to breathe through a flood of pain, Aria stood and pulled the tattered edges of her shirt closed. She brushed her hair away from her face and tried to stay ready, so she could aid Seth in whatever way he needed.

Noor looked down at the body he was using. "It would be a shame to lose such a loyal and fun friend."

"Loyal?" Seth snickered right in Noor's face, though his eyes never changed. "Friend? Oh, you stupid son of a bitch. You really *don't* have any clue what JD has been up to every time you slink back into your hole." He paused to make sure he had Noor's full attention.

Aria felt the rest of her family move into position around the yard.

"Someone want to fill me in on the plan?" Aria sent to them.

"Seth's hoping Noor will take JD out," Evan answered back. *"If that happens, and Noor makes an appearance like he did on the beach, we nail him with our power just like before. Drive him back underground."*

Seth's taunts drew her attention back. "You think you're using him, but he's using you. What you want means nothing to him. Take your obsession with Aria, for instance. If he were such a good and loyal friend, why then, does he try to kill her as soon as your back is turned?"

Noor threw his head back and laughed. "He wouldn't dare." He sounded so sure and confident.

"Really?" Seth tilted his head just a bit but said nothing more. He let the seed he'd planted settle in and start to take root.

Noor watched Seth for several moments. When he spun to look back at Aria, she could tell he wasn't quite so sure anymore.

She added to the weight of his doubt. "It's true. And if you don't believe us, take a look for yourself. I'm sure you have a way of getting into JD's thoughts and memories."

Every inch of her body rebelled against her slightest movement, but she'd remain strong. She would not give in— she had to stay ready.

As Noor stood silently, Aria assumed he was scanning JD's

mind, looking for the proof of his betrayal.

She was startled when he suddenly bellowed, "No! You liar! I will not suffer another Judas! No one shall cross me and live!"

Whatever Noor was doing to JD, it was obviously causing him tremendous agony. JD grabbed his head in both hands and screamed. The cry was cut off when he started choking and clawing at his own throat. He dropped to his knees, still gasping for breath. As he'd done with Seth in her dream, JD's chest bloomed bright red with thick, sticky blood. It spread and saturated the cotton of his shirt, spilling lower to drip viscous red tendrils down his jeans.

Noor was killing him from the inside out. And when he toppled over and lay motionless, she knew it was over. JD was dead.

Noor's disembodied form shimmered, standing over the man he'd just murdered. He looked back at Aria.

"This is not over. I *will* have you."

"Over my dead body," she growled.

Aria felt the surge of power as her siblings stepped out into the open, already spaced around Anna's back yard, surrounding Noor. They called to their elements, and she heard their chant in her mind as her own voice joined in.

"We call to our elements for protection and grace
Gather now in this blessed place
Grant us your strength and your power
On this day and in this hour."

As before, air, water, earth, and fire swept them up and filled them to bursting. Aria's pain and weariness faded away in the wake of the energy flowing into her.

Noor spun in a circle, his eyes darting from one whirling force of nature to the next.

"He's going to run," Anna warned.

"Then let's do this," Evan urged.

They all turned their concentration to Noor and let loose the power and magic they wielded.

It slammed into him, wrenching a scream of agony from deep within him. Aria knew they couldn't destroy him yet, but maybe this would set him back for a few weeks.

On another scream, Noor withered away into nothing.

As Aria thanked her element and let it slide away, the residual high remained. She knew it would eventually fade and the pain from her injuries would creep back in. But now was the time for the people she loved.

Seth ran to her and gingerly folded her into his arms as the tears she'd fought for so long fell unchecked onto his chest.

The rest of the family swarmed around them as Seth carried her back into the house.

~~~

Late that night, battered and bruised, Aria lay in the safety of Seth's arms.

One adversary may be gone, but Aria knew this was only the beginning. Their twenty-fifth birthdays were still nine months away, and there would be bigger battles to come. Noor was still out there, and he was growing stronger. He'd continue his vendetta against the Burkes while harboring an unholy obsession with her.

Aria wondered what was in store for them next. There were still so many questions that needed to be answered. And as she had since her visions had turned dark, she worried about Evan, Ethan, and Anna—

A vision slammed into Aria. She clenched her eyes tightly closed, trying to make sense of what she was seeing. Images assailed her, and she fought to focus on the blur flickering past. And as the premonition abruptly cut off, her eyes flew open and
~~~

she gasped.

Dear readers –

I hope you enjoyed Aria and Seth's adventure (though I do have to admit I'll always think of him as Law. There's just something about a tattooed bad-boy on a Harley, lol.) My wish is that you laughed with them, cried with them, and cheered them on.

The next book in the series will be Anna's Knight due out in April. Look for updates on my website: www.mishamckenzie.com. There you can also find links to my twitter account and my Facebook Author page. I would dearly love to hear from you.

And whatever you happen to be reading, whether it's me or someone else, please take a moment and post a review on your favorite online blog or retailer.

Thank you and Happy Reading!

MISHA MCKENZIE

Misha McKenzie has been an avid reader since learning how at four years old. Countless books later, she still loves to immerse herself into the lives of the people within those pages. After graduating high school, she went on to earn a degree in Business Administration, married her high school sweetheart, and had two beautiful boys. At thirty years old, while working as an office manager for a construction company, a family of witches began to brew, and The Magic of the Heart Series was born.